I0738683

Northern Seas
Ice Mountains
Ice Palace
Lagoon
Glacier
Waterfall
Waterfall
Sunken City
Old Ones
Glacier Cave
Swamp
Kepyr Sanctuary
Western Seas
Kepyr Village
Waterfall
Hidden Valley
Kepyr Village
Eastern Seas
Home Cavern
Desert
Kepyr Village
Southern Seas
W
E

Enchantress Sacrifice

Copyright © 2017 Denice Hughes Lewis

For information: Prism Arts LLC, 60020 Stirling Drive, Bend, OR 97702
ISBN: 978-0-9984547-1-9

Enchantress Sacrifice

Denice Hughes Lewis

To Julia and Violet

Readers and Writers Extraordinaire

Acknowledgements

My gratitude is unending for the inspiration and love I've received in bringing this story into manifestation.

Thank you to my husband, Bill, for his unfailing belief in my writing and for working while I played with words.

And thanks also to my daughter, son, daughter-in-law and granddaughters for their enthusiasm.

I want to especially thank my son-in-law, Peter Chadwell--cover designer extraordinaire--for his unfailing grace in providing me with fantastic covers for my books.

This story might never have been written but for the push by my best friend, exceptional writer and artist Suzan Noyes. Her insistence that I join her at a writer's conference sparked the idea of the story. I needed something to read aloud and wrote the first few chapters. It was so well received that I was encouraged to finish it. She is also the artist for my map!

Many, many thanks go to my editor, Linda Sterling, for her excitement and invaluable help. She was the first person outside of family and friends to read the story and inspire me make that leap of faith in myself.

Thank you to other members of various critique groups for their valuable input: Suzan, Tom, Skip, Nicole, Mike, Patricia, Cricket, Maralyn, Nickole, Tammy, Wendy, Tim, Robert, Kara, and Roxy. The book is better because of you.

Thank you readers. Without you, stories would remain in the minds of their writers. You make the hard work so worthwhile.

They call me Aru. Deep within this island, I absorb the petty struggle of native and invader. After millennia, my end is near. Bloated in misery, twisted by their hatred and prejudice, I will destroy everything and all will be consumed as easily as a drop of rain. Unless . . . unless the unborn child survives her birth and lives to inherit gifts that could destroy me. She cannot hide. I am the Beast and hear the heartbeat of her soul even now.

One: A Beginning

I slip into the arms of a wrinkled woman, newly born, uniquely aware. Shadows blur sight. I cannot breathe. Gasp. Kick.

"This one, she is strong," an old woman says, "though she comes early. You wise to seek my help."

"Thank you, Laruna," my mother says.

I struggle against shadows.

The old woman gapes at me. "She has violet eyes. God Aru, I beg you, forgive me." She shoves me into my mother's arms and backs away in horror. "You created Enchantress."

Rays of sunshine beam through the trees overhead. I suck in half-strangled gulps of light. Sunlight streaks into the strands of my hair. I cry. Breathe more light. I have no use for air.

The old woman shrieks. "Kepyr is forbidden to mate with Ice Lord. You and child die." She spits at my mother and flees.

I lock onto my mother's deep brown eyes. Her feelings ripple through me in warmth. I later learn this is love. And that love can be soft and sweet, fierce and fiery, proud and possessive, or as pure as an unblemished soul. Being minutes old does not limit the knowledge within me, it only restricts my use.

"You will save us all, Elandra," my mother says. "Of that I am certain. Your father saw this in a vision."

Native drums pound the air with fear. They will lodge forever in my heart. I feel and remember everything around me, a curse.

Mother drags herself up from the ground of my birthing place and sways in weakness. She wraps me in soft fur.

"We must reach your father in the Ice Mountains. Our plan did not include your early birth."

She stumbles toward a dense forest. Her feet plod to the endless beat, beat, beat of the drums.

Towering slabs of ice loom in the distance. Something shadowed and sinister awakes within their depths. My soul shudders. I know this darkness waits for me.

Two: An Ending

My mother reaches the edge of the dense forest. The woods hang in silence. Lush undergrowth and thick trees hamper her progress. Branches tear her skin. Her racing heart beats close to my cheek. She stops to catch her breath and sinks to the moist ground.

A profusion of pink flowers hangs overhead. Colors tickle me and I giggle.

"Shh. My people will send their bravest warrior to hunt us. We must reach your father before we are discovered."

She pulls herself up and pushes deeper into the forest. I inhale the sweetness of her skin.

Hidden life electrifies the trees around us. It hums through my senses. Unseen creatures rustle through bushes, shrieking, warning of danger.

My skin pricks and I tremble, knowing something else has entered the forest. Stealth, arrogance and hatred try to steal into me. Strong heartbeats bang next to my faster ones. I squirm against the uninvited feelings.

"Pray for the coming darkness to hide us, Elandra," my mother says.

A muscled warrior crouches in silent shadow. Dark hair hangs over his fierce, painted face.

I cry out to warn my mother. Too late.

An arrow swishes through the air. It rips through her back and deep into her heart.

I screech, feeling as if the arrow tears into mine.

My mother falls to her knees and stares into my eyes with endless and unconditional love. "Forgive me, my child. I have failed us both." She hunches over me in final protection.

Staring into her face, I long to help her. My tears blur her beauty. Emotions war inside me. . . my mother's agonizing pain, anger at my inability to do anything, the warrior's pleasure. Helpless, I feel her life seep away.

Triumph overwhelms all senses as the warrior swaggers toward us. Pride in his ability to kill my defenseless mother pours into me. He kicks her aside.

I recoil and roll away from the warmth and safety of her arms.

He glares down with a satisfied smile and unsheathes a knife.

I shriek.

Wind whips through the trees, echoing my fear. Air shimmers and expands from my hair in a small bright circle.

The warrior steps back in surprise, then laughs. "You are too weak to fight me, Enchantress." He hovers over me, the strange symbols on his knife glinting in the dying light. "I sacrifice you to Aru. For my prosperity and health."

A roar of rage shakes the ground around us. A tall monster streaks through the woods on two legs as large as tree trunks. The creature mows through plants, all speed, power and grace.

The warrior yells a battle cry and backs away.

The monster rushes past me, its body covered in white fur. Leathery feet with sharp talons dig into the ground next to my head. Ridges of bone protrude from its back.

The warrior hides behind a tree and fumbles for an arrow.

The monster's arms rip away branches with clawed fingers. Scales of icy purple cover a leathery head. Smoke furls over the long snout and pointed horn on the forehead. The creature is upon him.

I close my eyes, shuddering against the rage and terror of their feelings.

The warrior's spine snaps in a crunch of bone and searing torment.

My cry echoes his. I writhe in agony, gasping for breath. Light seeps into my hair and the pain lessens.

The monster hurls the warrior's body into a tree. He dies and I feel nothing. Not even remorse. He murdered my only link to life.

The forest relaxes, serene once again.

The monster lurches forward. Blue eyes stare at me in awe. I am surprised to touch the intelligence of a female soul, not a monster.

She raises her scaly head to the sky. Her screech shakes the very air. It is a cry so mournful that I feel her heart might break. Silver tears fall from her eyes and down her leathery cheeks. Emotions tumble so erratically through her and in such waves of despair that I whimper.

She kneels. Her eyes meet mine and shine in a kind of acceptance—of what I know not.

I have no fear of her when she lifts me like a precious gift. Sheltering me in her furry arms, my gentle savior carries me into the darkening forest.

Three: Another Beginning

My monster tramps deeper into the trees. I fall asleep in her arms to the music of her humming and only awake when she stops.

The sun slants out of sight. I do not fear its disappearance for I know my hair stores enough light for breath.

Aching memories of my mother's love crawl through my mind. Never truly knowing her is a loss I will always carry.

Why did she and my father bring me into a world that could only mean my death? Who am I? What is an Enchantress?

We stop before a great slab hidden in tangled, emerald vines. My monster shoves its rough surface. The stone pivots, quiet as the night. She hunches low and hurries inside. The rock swings shut behind us.

Firelight shines on the walls. Our shadows waver as we travel down a long staircase that winds through a maze of metal: walls, floors and sculptured arches.

She turns into a large cavern, pauses and bows in respect.

A man sits at a wooden table scribbling in a huge book. His head is wrapped in twisted cloth. Black eyes glint over a straight nose in a pale face. He looks into her eyes.

A powerful feeling of love sweeps through the room and shimmers between man and monster.

"Bryntar, my dear, never hesitate to interrupt me," he says. "What did you bring us now? Yet another wounded animal to heal?"

His voice is tender. Yet steel resolve and great guilt hide beneath the surface and shudder through me.

Her voice rasps, deep and low. "Much more, Taroc."

The pain it takes for her to speak burns my throat.

Her tone makes Taroc rise and stride toward me.

I smile up at him and gurgle, feet kicking into the soft violet robe that covers his tall body. Shock fills his handsome face for a second, then is gone. He looks into Bryntar's eyes. A great sadness spreads through the cavern.

In a quiet voice, he says, "The prophecy is accurate, even so."

Bryntar says nothing.

My heart tightens with her grief. I cry and pat her furry chest.

Taroc stares at me with curiosity. "I do believe she feels your pain. That will make it even more difficult for her. Was she abandoned?"

Scales ripple as Bryntar shakes her great head. "Kepyr mother, warrior, dead."

"I see," he says. "They will not cease their search without evidence." Taroc returns to the table and picks up a sharp knife that flashes gold in the candlelight.

Smoke furls from Bryntar's nostrils.

His voice becomes gentle. "This is necessary if she is to remain safe."

A moan escapes from Bryntar. "Another way. Please."

"There is none." He walks calmly toward us and reaches up to caress her rough cheek with long graceful fingers. "Hold her tight."

Bryntar clasps me to her chest. Her love engulfs my growing fear like a blazing pink flame. I coo and smile at her.

Taroc grasps a tuft of hair at the nape of my neck and quickly slices through it. He yelps when white-hot sparks leap from my hair and sizzle into his hand.

I scream. Thrash against the sting and fight for breath.

He quickly squeezes the wound closed. A cool tingle from his fingers ends my pain. I sob and suck my fist.

Bryntar shoves me at Taroc, her expression a conflicting mask of anger and acceptance.

I shake and gasp for more light. A melody rises deep inside my heart. Quiet at first. It grows in tenderness and beauty and sings of strength, of purpose, of service. And of forgiving.

The severed strands of hair glow in his hand. He passes them to Bryntar. "I know you hate the Kepyrs. It is necessary that they find her hair with the bodies. Please go with extreme care, my dear."

Bryntar hisses and thumps out of the cavern without a backward glance.

Taroc places me on the table and covers his burn with his other hand.

When he removes it, the burn is healed. He sighs. "Well, it is done. If you are to survive, that will be the least of your pain, little one."

Four: The Growing

I grow quickly and walk early. Because of my smallness, it is easy to disappear when I explore my home. Bryntar always finds me, but she is too loving for reprimand. Taroc has no trouble with the task. His black eyes and furrowed brow sear my nerves with disapproval. I am doubly punished because his feelings combine with my guilt.

"It would be wise to learn obedience," he says, "or take the consequences."

Bryntar hisses. "Cannot punish baby."

"The knowledge of eons, of those who have gone before, courses through her. Even if she cannot access all of it yet."

He turns to me. "Will you behave, Tufts?"

Taroc knows I hate that name. My hair is the only thing that does not grow as fast as my mind or my body. It is barely longer than when I was born. Perhaps that is as it should be, since it can never be cut without draining light and causing my death.

Instead of throwing my usual tantrum, I lift my chin and stare into his eyes. "Call me Elandra."

He chuckles and pats my head. "See my dear Bryntar? This child has more ability than any one of her kind ever born. The first to converse at such a young age."

I glow in the praise and behave—until after my first season when Taroc can no longer outrun me. The underground caverns become my playground.

I explore with abandon. Several caves spread in a half-circle around the main one. Every wall is hard, covered with a glittery metal surface that is cold or warm, depending on the need. I discover a room filled with books, a cave for food preparation, smaller caves for sleeping, another for waste. The locked door barring the entrance to Taroc's private room is the only place I cannot go.

Turning another corner I stop, enchanted at the vast underground gardens that expand before me. Sun beams from high overhead. My head swirls as I inhale the brightness. Bryntar usually takes me to a room with a small hole of sunlight when it is necessary to fill my hair with light. This is so much better. I giggle and twirl around, arms lifting to the light.

Plants grow in masses of red, green, orange, purple. Some as tall as Bryntar. I touch an intricate leaf as soft as breath. It folds around my finger, tingling me with its love. Exotic fragrances tickle my nose. Water tumbles down walls in narrow ribbons and splashes into large ponds of floating plants. I plop down on the grass, inhaling the rich soil. I close my eyes to feel every living thing and soon fall asleep.

Taroc gently lifts me into his arms. For once, his eyes hold no anger. "I, too, love this garden. It represents the beauty of life which provides my only escape from responsibility."

Too sleepy to think or wonder about his responsibility, I snuggle closer in his strong arms, content.

The next day, Bryntar becomes my first teacher. She instructs me about which plants, seeds or flowers are for eating or for medicines, and which are poisonous. I adore her and she feels the same. There could never be a more loving or protective mother than my Bryntar.

My heart has belonged to her from the moment she saved my life. I watch in wonder as the five claws at the end of her fingers sew me garments made from leather and fur. She does not disclose where she finds the bright cloth she sometimes uses. She never answers my questions about her life before I was born. I finally stop asking.

Happiness and peace fill me during these times. The hurtful memories are buried deep inside and keep away the fears of what I am and why I was born.

When I am five seasons of age, I take an interest in Taroc and the scribbles he makes on parchment. "Why do you do that?"

"I am documenting the history of this island."

"How? You never leave the caves."

"I have knowledge from past experience and Bryntar keeps me informed."

"When does she go outside?"

"How do you think the wounded animals arrive for my healing?"

I stamp my foot. "She never lets me near them."

"They are wild and must return to their natural state without interference from you."

"I need someone to play with."

"Not with your behavior."

I laugh when I remember throwing rotten fruit at him.

He frowns. "It is past time to rectify the situation. You will begin your education now."

He leads me into the library. Books rise to the ceiling. Lost in the huge room, I sense emotions hidden in the pages of every volume. The age and density of the books and their knowledge weigh heavily.

Overwhelmed, I ask, "Did you write these?"

He chuckles. "No. I am merely the custodian of knowledge from past civilizations. I believe this island and its people are all that remain of the world."

"Why do you live underground?"

He hides the twinge of fear so fast I wonder if I imagine it.

"I do not care to associate with the people of the island."

"Why not?"

"Their forms of society do not allow for individual thought or true freedom."

I gaze at the tiny lines that cross his forehead and etch his mouth. He has aged. More seasons than my five.

"You are old."

He stares into my eyes and does not hide his resignation. "Too old. That is why you begin your studies today. You will acquire the knowledge that resides in these books."

"All of them?" I gaze around the room. "Impossible."

"Not for you, Enchantress."

I cringe at the remembrance of that hated identity. It is easy to forget who I am in this safe, hidden place. Emotions from the past tumble through me in throbbing waves. In the protection of these metal walls and floors, I never feel the thing that waits for me under the mountains; the thing I keep secret from everyone; the thing that wants my soul. I tremble.

Taroc pats my head. "I am sorry for the burden you must carry."

It is rare to feel any emotion from him and I savor the love, even though it is tinged with sadness.

He gazes at me, his face an enigma. "Never forget who you are. Your life and the life of this island depend upon your powers."

A chill slides into me. "Powers? What do you mean?"

"You will know when the time is right."

"Tell me now."

"You have much to learn before you need concern yourself with your destiny."

"What destiny?"

He shuts his feelings away where I cannot access them. I know he will tell me nothing until he is ready.

Taroc sits me in a chair and pulls four books from the shelves. "I want you to read these today."

I shove the books off the table. They clunk on the metal floor in layers of dust. "I do not know how."

His eyes blaze into mine. "You do and you will. If you have questions pertaining to what is written within, I shall be glad to answer them." He strides out of the library.

"Wait." I chase him to his study.

He locks the door in my face.

I bang on it. The dull, metal clang echoes down the hall. "Let me in."

Thoughts burn in my mind as I pound on the door. What does he write in his books? What healing power does he hold in his hands? What secrets does he keep from me in his study?

I kick the unmoving metal walls and scream all the way to the library.

The books pretend silence, but I feel them. My fingers touch warm leather as I gather them from the floor. I peek inside. Strange marks on yellowed paper turn into words that I understand.

The rest of my childhood is spent reading the books when I am not doing chores or working in the garden or eating with Bryntar and Taroc. Reading provides a relief from the unspoken feelings between them. Books are my only escape from the loneliness and boredom of my underground home.

As the seasons pass, I lose sense of myself and ignore a growing restlessness and concern about my narrow existence. Words unfold my imagination. I am daunted by the chronicles of the world beyond this island—the sciences, languages, religions, wars. Life, love, and death. I do not understand how this knowledge applies to me. As usual, Taroc does not answer my questions about how and why these books are here.

My hands reluctantly close the final book. I have almost reached my sixteenth season. Regret sweeps over me. Complete recall of the knowledge has made the library obsolete. Books have been companions in this solitary place. Reading made it easy to forget who I am—an Enchantress, a fugitive who hides from those who would kill me on sight.

I hurry out of the library, excited to share my accomplishment.

Taroc and Bryntar stride from his study. He locks the door.

I try to keep the pride from my voice. "I am finished with the books. What is next?"

"Now you will learn how to save the island and its people," Taroc says.

I laugh. "From student to savior. You must be kidding."

My mother's words float from a distant memory. *You will save us all Elandra.*

I can still feel her intense love filling my heart. How I wish she were here. A stray thought of my unknown father interrupts, prompting other unanswered questions. Is he still alive? Will we ever meet? I shove the thoughts into the dark places of my mind.

"I am quite serious," Taroc says with a scowl on his face.

"Why me?"

"I doubt even the Kepyr Priestess or the Ice Lord Seer could foresee what is to happen. They are blinded by too much greed and prestige to care about their parts in the descent of the island. Your parents were pure enough to be guided, pure enough to create an Enchantress. Even against their laws."

The strength of his seriousness streaks through me. I shiver. "I did not ask to be a savior. Let someone else do this."

"There is no one else," he says. "You were created for this purpose."

Panic pinches my throat. "It is not fair."

Taroc's eyes flash. "No, it is not. You must live with the consequences."

"Surely, I have a choice?"

"There is always choice," he says.

I hate the finality of his words and take Bryntar's claws in my hands. "I know nothing about the island. I cannot do this."

"It is your destiny," she says.

I glare at her, stunned. Everything fights inside me: Taroc's unflinching resolve, Bryntar's stoicism, my stubborn resistance. I shout at them. "How can I save a whole island?"

"Your full power will come soon," Taroc says.

"Well that is a relief," I say.

Smoke puffs out of Bryntar's scaly nose. "Sarcasm fails you, Elandra."

Heaviness seeps inside my bones. I can barely breathe in the light. I am no match for the strength of their resolve. Resigned, I say, "What is my power?"

"That remains to be seen," Taroc says. "You must learn patience."

"Patience? I have been imprisoned underground my whole life. Suffocated with your rules, your demands. I have done everything you ever asked of me while you kept secrets!"

"Now is not the time to answer them," Taroc says.

Bryntar hisses. "Now is the only time." She stomps down the hall.

Taroc plods after her and I realize how much he has aged. He leans heavily on a cane of twisted wood. Wrinkles tread across his once handsome face.

I swallow my anger and wish I could read his mind instead of his feelings. It is hard to trust with the secrets he keeps and his reserved kind of love. He has never shared anything about himself throughout our seasons of questions and confrontations.

I catch up with them and wonder if our protected lives will ever be the same after this day.

Taroc's hand rests on Bryntar's arm.

She stares down at him. Her sorrow pounds inside my body like a living thing and I tremble. She turns away, knowing I feel her anguish.

To stop her pain and mine, I say, "What am I supposed to do now?"

Taroc sighs. "You must leave here to learn about the island."

Leave the caverns? Chills crash through me.

"She is not ready," Bryntar says. "You prepare mind, not heart."

He shrugs. "She will learn or die."

Shocked, I gape at them.

Bryntar's eyes shine with anger.

Taroc meets them with defiance. "It is the only way. Her emotions weaken her. Do you know what will happen if she cannot control them?"

Bryntar scowls at him. "Too well."

He yells, "It is not something that can be taught."

She roars. "You never tried."

My heart thumps hard against my chest. "I am right here."

They ignore me.

Agony flits across Taroc's face. "Her emotions made it too dangerous."

Bryntar hisses. "For you."

"Soon I will have no time left for apology, my dear Bryntar."

I yell to relieve their horrible guilt and fury that streak through me. "I am not going outside to risk my life!"

"You cannot save an island you know nothing about," Taroc says.

"Who cares?"

His eyes sadden. "You would rather die with all of us when the island destroys itself?"

"You expect me to believe you?"

He winces. "I have lived and studied a long time. Trust me. The destruction will happen unless you help. Go with Bryntar. Do not show yourselves to anyone." His eyes flash a warning to Bryntar. "No one must know about Elandra until she can protect herself."

Tears fill Bryntar's eyes. She screeches and flees down the corridor.

Taroc watches her go.

Conflicted with her grief and his remorse, I hover on the threshold of my uncertain future.

"I wish I had the power instead of subjecting you to this burden, Elandra. You are our only hope. Stay close to Bryntar. There are those who would kill you on sight."

Terror makes a knot in my stomach. "You expect the impossible."

"Then you doom us all." Taroc turns his back on me and slumps away.

My heart fills with his disappointment. A far greater pain than I thought possible. I run and embrace him. "I cannot promise I will succeed, Taroc."

"If you do your best, that is all I can ask. All anyone can expect."

"I will be careful."

He smiles wanly. "I doubt that."

I grin and turn away.

His words filter behind me. "Learn quickly or all will be lost."

The words barely impact the flutters of dread and growing excitement that churn through me. Only in the depths of my heart have I ever imagined what it would be like to be free of the caverns.

I run to meet Bryntar at the top of the massive metal stairs that curve up to my destiny.

"Obey," she says. Her eyes and heart are grave with warning. "Promise on our lives."

"I promise." And try to ignore my quivering nerves.

She pulls fabric from a large bag slung over her shoulder. "Cover hair. Too easy to see."

I take the brown cloth she offers and hide the silver hair that falls past my shoulders.

"Do I need anything else?"

"Summer. Dress will do."

Bryntar presses the panel that opens the stone door.

My heart thumps, trying to escape my chest. I tentatively step outside.

The island slams into me: light, color, sound, movement.

I collapse into it.

Five: The Saving

"Breathe," Bryntar says, hovering over me.

Unable to move, shivers course one after another up and down my spine.

"Elandra. Close your eyes."

I obey and remember the sunlight slanting through deep green trees, the shadows of a thousand branches, the aroma of rich soil. I sense the stillness of the animals now hiding.

"Please. I want to go back."

Bryntar hisses. "Heart feels. Mind controls. Focus on one thing."

Moss is wet and soft beneath my fingers. I thrill to the sensation and open my eyes to dewdrops glistening all around me. I concentrate solely on the moss and its soft white, star-shaped flowers. Stroking one, I hear a tiny tinkle and relax.

A slight breeze ruffles the few strands of my hair that escape their cover. I sit up and absorb the forest, never to forget this first, true communion with nature so unlike the gardens underground. This life feels different. . . free. A gentle peace floats through the burgeoning life.

"Where first?" Bryntar asks.

I shut out intruding thoughts of finding my father. "To see the ocean. I cannot imagine how it feels from reading books."

"We go to Western Seas, away from Kepyrs." She trots through the trees.

Birds chirp overhead, trilling with wondrous melody. I laugh and experience the air ruffling their feathers as they swish above me. Dizzy, I experience their flight and fall over.

"Focus," Bryntar says.

It becomes easier when I concentrate on one sensation at a time: bare feet sinking into soft, damp ground, wind making myriad leaves sing, sweet-smelling flowers.

"It is so beautiful. How can you stand to live underground?"

Bryntar sighs. I am hunted."

"Are there others like you?"

"No."

She says this with such finality I know it is useless to continue my questions.

"Thank you for risking your life."

Bryntar says nothing. We travel a long time. Huge roaring breaks into the silence of the forest. Bryntar stops before a waterfall that bursts from a hole in the mountain. Dazzling in sunlight, silver sprays against wet rocks before splashing deep into a river. We drink deeply of the fresh, cold liquid. The feeling from the water is relaxing, even with the noise. A longing to be free from the caverns pours through me.

"Ooohhh." My leg suddenly thuds in agony and I fall to one knee.

Bryntar feels my leg. "Were you bitten?"

"It is not my pain. Someone is hurt."

Bryntar hisses. "Sshh. Do not move." Her taloned feet make little sound on the forest floor.

I jump up and wince. "Wait." I limp after her.

"Stay in back."

Her fear thumps inside me.

We stop at the edge of a cliff. Spellbound, I can only stare in awe. The vast ocean spreads far below with more shades of blue than I ever thought possible. Giant black rocks pierce the water like teeth. Tides race toward the shore, alive with hidden energy. Waves crash onto the sand in rolls of white and slide back into the surging sea in never-ending thunder. I swell with them, one with the unceasing movement.

A deep-voiced yell breaks the spell. "Help."

Bryntar points. "There."

Splintered wood from a ship slams against the rocks. A male figure rolls in the water, struggling to stand in the surf.

Pain shoots through my leg again. I cry out and slip to the ground as my feelings entwine with the man's. Frigid waves toss me over and over. Salt spray stings my eyes. I choke on mouthfuls of water, stumble up, dragging a twisted leg. The ocean throws me ashore. The man passes out. My pain subsides and I am myself again.

Tears straggle down my face. "Bryntar, help him."

She glares into my eyes. "Better he dies here than from Kepyrs."

I stare at her in shock. "We must save him. Please, Bryntar. You saved me. You save wounded animals."

She hisses. "Control what you let inside." She plunges down the embankment.

How will I learn to separate my emotions from those of others? My heart and body feel everything, regardless of what my mind wants.

Bryntar returns with the unconscious man in her arms. She lays him next to me. "Must destroy remainder of ship."

"We need to get him to Taroc."

"Kepyrs sacrifice gifts from sea. They track, kill him." She leaps away.

The man wears strange clothes that fit his body like skin—a shirt with short sleeves and pants made of heavy blue material with silver fasteners. On one wrist is twisted leather.

The cover slips from my hair when I lean to move the light wavy hair from his face. His fair skin, weathered by the sun, is rough under my fingers.

Shocked, I realize this handsome stranger has the body of a man, but is only a boy, not much older than I am. A boy with a leg so mangled and a face so white that I wonder if even Taroc can save him.

He moans and blinks in confusion. "Emergency room. Now. If I pass out, don't let them cut off my leg." Agony shoots through his body and mine.

I wonder that I understand him and realize he speaks a version of my language.

"What is emergency room?"

Horror flashes into his face.

"You're an angel. Oh, God, I'm dead."

He clutches my hand. Unfamiliar warmth ripples through me, overpowering every sense, even the pain. What magic does this boy have in his hands to make my body react this way? I shiver, but it is not unpleasant.

"Heaven can't hurt this much." He moans and closes his eyes. Blood oozes down his spine and mine, his life slipping away like a whisper.

It would be so easy to let go. To drift into unconsciousness with him. To cease to be. I close my eyes, ready to surrender to the darkness.

The melody I have not heard since I was young sings in my heart again, a melody of strength, purpose, service. It overwhelms all other senses.

I fight against my body and shake him. "Wake up."

"Ow. Lay off."

"You must fight."

He groans. "Go away."

"Do you want to die?"

He twists in my arms and gasps. "Yes! It hurts too much."

"Do not give into pain."

"Give me some peace."

"I cannot bear it if you die."

"Why? We're strangers."

"You cannot throw away life because of pain. Please."

His green eyes captivate mine. He moans. "Only because you asked nice."

I gaze into his soul and am forever changed. Facing a stranger who will sacrifice his desires for those of someone else frightens me.

Bryntar runs up and scoops the boy in her arms. "Kepyrs come. Cover tracks."

Horror fills the boy's face when he sees Bryntar. He starts to scream and Bryntar covers his mouth with her claws. He passes out.

"Hurry." She races away.

I cover my hair and stumble after them. The terror in her mind of what the Kepyrs will do if they find us spurs me on.

The journey is a blur, a fight against fear. Keeping Bryntar in sight takes all my concentration as I cover our tracks.

She veers from the forest, following the coastline between high jagged cliffs and waves smashing into rocks. Although we startle animals and birds, we see no one. Drums pound, but only in my mind.

Finally, the shore disappears as broken boulders from the cliffs parade into the water. Bryntar leads me up through a small, rugged path with sharp rocks that jab into my feet.

I pant from exertion and look at the boy in her arms. His breathing is shallow, but steady. Unconscious, he cannot feel his pain and for that I am grateful.

We reach a stand of trees. Hundreds of gray trunks and green leaves rise to the sky. The image of the white-painted face of my mother's murderer hides behind every tree. I shudder and climb over the rise. The dark forest rests in the distance. Much later we finally reach the stone slab.

"Open the door," Bryntar says.

I do as she orders. She rushes forward with the boy and disappears down the stairs. The door closes quietly. I wobble in exhaustion after her.

Taroc examines the unconscious boy in the main chamber. "Where did he come from? He is not a Kepyr, nor does he bear the sign of the Ice Lords."

Bryntar says, "Half a ship."

Taroc's eyes fill with surprise, then excitement. "A ship broke through the invisible barrier? I thought it impossible. Life still exists beyond this island!"

I scream at him. "The boy is dying. Save him or I will die."

Eyes of black ice meet mine. "Remove her from this chamber."

Bryntar picks me up.

"No." I wiggle in her arms.

Bryntar says. "You learn control to survive."

I tear away from her and stand in defiance before Taroc. "Save his leg. He does not want to live if you cannot."

He glares at me. "The decision does not belong to you. His choice determines his fate."

"He told me how he feels."

Taroc's eyes glitter. "There is only one thing in this world over which you have any control and that is your own mind. Learn to use it. Bryntar, take her away."

With no energy left to fight, I let Bryntar carry me off. "Take me to the gardens."

Surprise fills her face. "You order me?"

"I am no longer a child."

Her love, regret, and pride fill my heart.

When we reach the gardens, I pull away from her. "Please leave me."

She turns and strides out.

Spasms throb in my leg and I crumple under the canopy of plants, barely conscious.

Six: The Exploring

Flowers brush my nose. I do not remember curling up under the pure white bells. *Thank you for watching over me.*

Sun streams through the thick plants. I crawl out, careful not to damage the delicate flowers. I rip off my head-covering and inhale deeply. A dull ache thumps in my leg. My heart skips a beat. The young man is alive and whole.

I stare at my leg, willing away the pain. Without success. My survival depends on learning how to stop feeling everyone. To know how I alone feel. I am not prepared for life outside, regardless of the knowledge I have gained from books.

A screech echoes down the hall from Taroc's private chambers.

I limp to the door, unable to ignore the ache in my leg.

Bryntar pushes out of his room. The door locks behind her. The tray she holds shakes in her claws.

"What happened?"

"Boy saw monster."

I blink. "You are not a monster."

Her eyes hold a sad smile. "You know nothing else, my Elandra."

"I am sorry. He will change when he gets to know you."

"Will he? His world is different." She thumps away.

I knock on Taroc's door.

The mumbled conversation inside continues.

I bang on the door. "Let me in, Taroc!"

He unlocks the door and peeks out. "The patient is not allowed to have visitors. I have little time left."

"Why not? This day is like any other."

He stares into my eyes with great despair and quickly veils his feelings.

I want to scream at him, but whisper. "How long must I live with your secrets?"

He inhales deeply. "You will have your answers soon. I cannot guarantee you will like them. Go away and do not return until I summon you. I need to learn everything I can about the outside world. In the meantime, learn to control your emotions."

Rage and rejection boil in me as he starts to close the door. I push inside. "I am no longer a child you can order around."

The sun beams into the room from high above. Glimpses of ancient volumes of books with strange markings catch my eye. My mind burns with curiosity.

"Why have you kept these books from me?"

Taroc grabs my arm and pulls me forward. "Elandra, meet Daniel."

"My angel."

Taroc releases me. "She is far from that."

Annoyed and distracted, I turn toward the young man on the bed. Warm chills flutter to my toes when his green eyes meet mine.

A weak smile splits his pale face as he holds out his hand. I touch it lightly and step back, overwhelmed with his feelings.

Never talking with anyone my age, I do not know what to say and stammer, "I-I-I am happy to see you. I-I mean, I am glad that you did not lose your leg."

"Or my life," Daniel says. He winks at me. "Must be the power of violet eyes."

An unusual flush of heat rushes to my face.

Taroc laughs at my discomfort.

"Thank you for saving me."

"The monster saved you," I say.

Daniel's face flushes with embarrassment. "You brought me back."

"Taroc is responsible for heal—"

He interrupts me. "You have to forgive her modesty."

I flush with discomfort. "Have you explained—?"

"This man needs rest, not explanation, Elandra."

"Doc here says I will regain full use of my leg, even if it still hurts. How did he save it? Where am I?"

I look at Taroc, who shakes his head. "Please, go to Bryntar." He grabs my elbow and steers me toward the door.

"Come and visit later?" Daniel asks.

I hurry through the door, face flaming.

Taroc starts to close it.

"Why does he still hurt?"

"It is what he expects." Taroc says. "His world does not believe in real magic."

"Are you going to tell him?"

"He has enough to absorb right now."

"I want to know more about him."

"I imagine so."

"Then let me stay."

"It is more urgent that you explore the island. Go to the surface and learn as much as you can. Take Bryntar with you." He shuts the door in my face.

I smolder and do not understand his interest in this stranger. I am the one in danger of losing my life. I stomp away. Indecision floods my thoughts. It is time to take action and decide the course of my life, to accept responsibility. For what? A destiny I do not choose? I search for Bryntar, my life a nagging question. I only know I do not want to be different.

I pass the gardens, lush with fragrant berries. My mouth waters, thinking about their tangy sweetness. Sobbing interrupts the sensation. I rush through an orchard and find Bryntar lying prostrate on the ground. My heart clenches when I feel her overwhelming grief. She may look like a monster, but inside I have no doubt she is a woman.

I cannot stop my tears as I watch hers fall. I throw my arms over her wide neck. "Please stop, dear Bryntar. I cannot bear to see you unhappy. You know you are not a monster."

She sits up and wipes the silver tears from her scaly face. "You know me no other way. How I wish. . ."

Her voice trails away as her mind relives an inner vision. I feel a deep sorrow and loss for something wonderful that is long gone.

I hope that a change of subject can stop her sadness. "Taroc wants me to see more of the island."

Bryntar nods. "Not much time. Your power comes soon."

I stand up. Daniel's pain once again pounds in my leg. I limp up the spiral stairs after her. My anger flares to endure Daniel's pain, to think of him spending time with Taroc. Until I wonder why I did not notice the discomfort sooner. My mind focused on Bryntar, instead.

She pushes on the stone door and we are once again free of the caverns.

I am prepared for life above ground this time. The peace of the forest encloses me—ground damp with heavy, dark soil and fragrant with spicy, sharp pine. I long to remain, to savor the energy surrounding me, but sense Bryntar's urgency.

I look toward the Ice Mountains. "Someday I will find my father."

Smoke rises from her nose. "Ice Lords kill on sight. Their greed makes island of slaves."

"What do you mean?"

Her eyes flare. "Ice Lords rule. Trade meat, fur, jewels Kepyrs use for ceremony. Not allowed to mate with Kepyr. Penalty is death."

"What about my mother and father?"

"I do not know." Bryntar's voice grows to a hoarse whisper.

Knowing how painful it is for her to speak, I ask no more questions.

We slip silently through evergreen trees, heading south. Much later, the forest gives way to wide stretches of grassy meadows that dip and roll far into the distance. My neck tingles and I spot a red tail swishing under thick bushes. Furry, six-legged creatures skitter into holes.

Grasses rise to my waist and tickle my legs with blades as soft as feathers. The wind waves through vibrant shades of green and patches of brilliant flowers.

Bryntar keeps to the large trees, ever alert.

I look back at the Ice Mountains, hovering like huge birds of prey over the island. I shiver. Death awaits me in their depths.

"How large is the island?"

"From center can traverse to each ocean in day. Except through Ice Mountains."

Eventually the meadows slant toward a rise that hides a quiet cove. Below, a calm ocean of aquamarine water licks golden sand. The sea is clear. Brightly colored fish frolic among jade plants that sway on the ocean floor.

I sigh in contentment. "How beautiful. Is it safe to swim?"

She surveys the area, sniffs the air, and nods.

Ignoring my dress, I race down the hill. Again, I notice the pain in my leg has vanished. With no more time to think, I plunge into the sea. Hot skin meets delicious cool water. The currents calm my soul; a memory to cherish, like the melody that lays hidden in my heart.

I want this perfect time to last forever. So much so that I do not want to mar it by the questions Bryntar needs to answer for me. We laugh and swim, free from worry. When we rest, we pick fresh berries and devour their juicy plumpness. Lying in the warm sun, I almost believe there is a chance to escape my fate.

Bryntar sits up, alert. "Get in water. Hurry."

I jump in the sea while she covers our tracks.

She leaps in and drags me far underwater. We stay in the cover of sea plants, the tide sweeping against us.

Will Bryntar's white fur and my silver hair be visible from the surface? Since she breathes air, how long she can hold her breath? What is on the beach that causes her fright?

We cling to thick leaves and fibrous stems, pulling ourselves farther and farther away from the cove. While we inch along, fish dart in swarms of frenzy.

We swim underwater to another edge of the cove. Bryntar sticks her head out of the water, gasping air in huge gulps. We emerge and creep in the shadows cast by the rocks along the shore.

The sun rests on the horizon, layering rainbows of reds, oranges, and purples over the land. Bryntar crawls up a steep hill in silence. I scramble after her. We reach the top and peer down.

Below is an old woman, bent and twisted with age,. kneeling on the sand. When she turns to empty the leather pouch by her side, her bitter face strikes my memory. It is the old woman who helped with my birth, Laruna.

Heartbeats thump hard in my throat. Drums beat in my head. I try to close off the feelings of reliving my mother's death.

Bryntar touches me. It breaks the flood of memory.

I dare to look at Laruna. Slip into her feelings and reel in fright. Hate and vengeance course through our bodies.

Control. Do not let her in. Think of something else.

Staring intently at her headpiece of feathers and bits of jeweled bone, I break free of her feelings.

Laruna kneels in front of a makeshift shrine covered in colorful cloth. From the leather pouch she pulls out a skull. Lovingly she speaks to it, stroking it as if it were alive.

"Before I die, I avenge your death, my son."

Bryntar's claws clench the sand.

The old woman lays a sheath of arrows next to the skull. I hold my breath as she snatches something from her pouch. The sunset hits carved symbols. I recognize the knife she holds in the air. It belonged to the warrior who murdered my mother.

Bryntar's claws cover my mouth to stop me from crying out.

The woman chants and slaps the sand with the knife. Harder, louder. "Mighty Aru. Forgive my sin of birthing Enchantress."

My ribs feel like they will break with the pounding of my heart.

She pulls something shining from the pouch and raises it up to the darkening sky. Screeches. "Hear me, the Kepyr Priestess. Enchantress lives. I see in a sacred dream."

My head swirls. I cannot tear my eyes from the strands of hair she waves in the air. They are the tufts Taroc severed from my head the day I was born.

The old woman swings the hair in a circle over her head. "I live until she dies."

A tremor shakes the ground. Sand and water undulate under the land like a buried snake.

The old woman cackles. "Hah. Aru knows the truth now. Revenge is mine." She screams the words over and over.

Darkness sucks at my soul. Sudden waves of dread crawl up and down my spine when the sinister beast moves underground. It has grown larger. Heavy heartbeats hammer from deep inside the center of the island and throb inside my head. Aru knows I am alive.

My mind screeches. Hide! Hide! Find safety! I stagger up. My traitorous body seems detached and shakes uncontrollably.

Bryntar yanks me down.

Tremors rock the island again. We careen down the hill.

Then I hear it. A hideous roar deep below the ground.

Without thought or control over my body, I leap up. My hair flashes, standing straight out in a halo of sparks. Energy shimmers through me, overpowering everything. Lightning cracks overhead and strikes into me with burning white-hot fire. Uncontrolled power races through my veins with such force I feel ready to shatter.

Bryntar snatches me, throws me to the ground, smothers me in sand.

The burning stops. Horror slams through my mind as the heat smolders.

What happened? Am I a monster? If being an Enchantress means this, how can I ever control the burning?

The old woman screams. "I will be avenged!" Her hate creeps into me.

Hunger and longing flare from the dark thing deep underground.

It is Bryntar's terror that sends me over the edge. My thoughts slide into darkness.

Seven: The Knowing

A cool breeze caresses my face. I open my eyes to the wonder of a night sky overrun with sparkles of light—so close, my fingers can almost reach up and touch them.

I remember the stars that sailed across the hole at the top of my garden cave, but they were too far above for my appreciation.

Now spellbound by this beauty, I recognize constellations from the books in the library. Then, memories of the old woman sneak into my head and I cringe.

"The sleeping child awakes," Bryntar says.

I shiver. "Are we safe?"

Bryntar hisses. "The witch is gone."

I relax slightly. "What happened? I almost exploded."

"You learn control or be lost."

I drag myself up and brush sand from my hair.

"Tell me what happened? I almost died. No more vague warnings. I need to know the truth."

Bryntar stands up and smiles. "Enchantress, light is your power." She bows before me.

"Stop." I pull her up. "Never do that again."

Why did I ever leave the caves?

Overwhelming responsibility digs at me. Taroc flashes into my mind, and his mention of the burden of responsibility.

Bryntar's eyes gleam. "Now there is hope. No other Enchantress had this power."

My insides lurch. "How do you know?"

"We go." She turns away from me.

I catch her arm. "There can be no more secrets between us."

"Some are not mine to tell," Bryntar says. She turns away to avoid looking at me.

I persist. "How do you know about other Enchantresses?"

Steam furls out of her nostrils. "Taroc has ancient book of all who have gone before."

"There were others?" I do not want to control my anger and scream at her. "Why has he kept this information from me?"

Bryntar clasps her clawed fingers over my mouth.

"Quiet. Danger from wild creatures."

My teeth clench. "I welcome my death. Better to die from something I can see than facing the unknown. Does Taroc expect me to save his life and everyone on the island by keeping things from me? Nothing has prepared me for this."

Bryntar says, "What you learn has value."

I stomp away. "Always more mystery."

One stride and she catches up with me. "You have strength of light."

Fear creeps into my mind. "I do not want it."

Shadows cross her face. "Cannot deny who you are."

"Control my feelings and control light? Simple. What happens if I cannot?"

"You learn."

"How?"

She shrugs. "Why did it happen?"

I shudder and let the memory slide into being. "It was automatic when I felt…"

Bryntar finishes my thought. "The beast?"

I gasp. "You know about the beast?"

Her blue eyes bore into mine. "Legends tell of Aru."

"My survival depends on knowing everything."

"I know. Kepyrs sacrifice lives. Feed Aru with darkness. Ice Lords feed darkness with power and greed. Aru absorbs evil."

"Has anyone seen this beast?"

"Not for two thousand years."

Cold and hot chills collide and slither down my spine. "Tell me the fate of those who faced Aru."

Bryntar does not flinch. "Some hide until found. One disappeared. Most killed at birth. Some try to fight and . . ."

"Die? It is awake because of me?"

"Because you live."

"You should have let me die."

Bryntar grabs my arms. "No. You defeat Aru."

I yell in frustration. "A beast that has killed before? I do not know how." My hair rises in the air and flashes light. Stunned with the heat, I fall to the sand.

A claw rests on my shoulder. Bryntar kneels beside me. "You can destroy it."

I sense her hesitation. "The beast can cause the ground to move. It would be easy to take my life. Why did it leave?"

"I do not know."

"What else have you neglected to tell me?"

Her eyes fill with love, but a terrible sadness sweeps through her soul. She sighs. "Taroc spoke truth. Too much darkness now. If you fail, island and all people destroyed."

"Along with Aru?"

"Yes," she says.

"Maybe it is better for everything to sink into the sea."

She hisses. "No."

An ache so deep and a love so pure wraps around my heart. I do not need words to know what would happen to Bryntar if I die. "I did not ask to be born."

I tremble as a deep heaviness slides like a shroud over my mind. My destiny lies before me. There is no choice. Only the acceptance of responsibility, of trying to save those who want me dead. I laugh at the irony. And laugh. And laugh. Until tears start to fall.

Bryntar encloses me in her arms and holds me until I have no tears left.

Eight: The Continuing

My eyes open, swollen with grief. The stars still shimmer. The wind still kisses my cheek. The sand still squishes under me. I have changed. "Please, show me the rest of the island."

Bryntar blows on the sand, erasing our presence. We wade along the shore. The sea washes away our footprints as easily as the choices of my life wash away. I have no hope for a normal life.

We walk until sunrise shoots splashes of brilliant pink in the sky. At the eastern side of the island, the sea gives way to a mass of tumbling black rock. A silent, crippled forest stands encased in instant death from an explosion of lava long ago.

I feel nothing.

We continue north, leaving no trail. Huge boulders of glassy black rock give way to a stream. It flows under a large, bowed tree turned to stone.

"Wait inside," Bryntar says.

She disappears over the lava flow.

I am glad of the rest. Cave life has not prepared me for traversing an island. My legs ache. It is more than that. Fear rides inside my body on knots of tension.

Time crawls, like the shiny iridescent insect poking through grass by the edge of the water. Relief spreads through me when Bryntar appears with roots of wild plants. We eat in silence.

She finally speaks. "Eastern shore does not change."

"There are no villages by the ocean?"

"Keprys fear sea. Live inland."

"That is where I want to go."

Bryntar leaps up. "Too dangerous."

"It is my right to see who I have to risk my life to save."

Her shoulders shrug, heavy with acceptance. "We wait until dark."

I have nothing more to say and sleep until Bryntar wakes me. We move out of the protection of the stone arch. Moonlight silvers the landscape. Bryntar leads the way like a specter in the shadows. Solid rock turns to pebbles under my bare feet and then into soft dirt. Another spectacular sunrise tries to touch my heart. I watch it coldly. Maybe this is the way to control my feelings. By not having any.

A long time later, the sun radiates over the landscape and I breathe deeply. Bryntar crouches behind a barrier of brambles that tower over my head.

I peer through a hole in the thorns. A young girl skips along the edge of planted fields and picks wildflowers. Her pink-tinged, chubby face has big eyes that light up when she discovers another flower. She laughs when she picks it, a sound so pure and sweet that it breaks through my defenses. Warm tingles of energy fill me in response to her unblemished innocence.

A sharp call sends her running. In the distance, her mother stands silhouetted against the thatched huts of the Kepyrs.

I whisper to avoid detection. "How many Kepyr villages are on the island?"

"Three large."

"Do you know how many people?"

"You fail? Enough for biggest sacrifice to Aru."

Though the sun is hot, I am as cold as ice. "Take me home."

"We cross in dark."

Until nightfall, we spy on the Kepyrs. I am amazed at these beautiful people. The sun tans their skin in colors ranging from light to dark. Their blond, red, and brown hair shines over strong, healthy bodies. The love displayed in the family units makes me long to be with them, long for what my mother could have given me. Children happily work in the fields with their families, encouraged and protected.

There is darkness, too. A chief promenades through the fields, causing fear and awe in the people. Prayers and kneeling are forced upon the workers while unintelligible words boom from their religious leaders.

Power and greed are not only attributes of the Ice Lords. They bloom here. This society is no different from the ones I read about in my underground library. Keeping the natives uneducated and in fear is the surest way to maintain control.

Emotion exhausts me as twilight overtakes the day.

Will I ever learn control?

Bryntar rises to lead us home. I take one last look through the thorn thicket and wonder what my life might have been.

The face of a young boy stares back at me. His eyes grow wide with fright. He races back to his village screaming, "Violet eyes. Violet eyes."

Blood slips down my spine and roots me to the ground.

Bryntar lifts me. Races back toward the way we came, leaping over obstacles that stand in her way. She covers ground faster by carrying me. Her heart thumps next to mine. I hope for the same safety as the first time she carried me.

A drum beats through the darkness. More and more join it and pound in time with my banging heart. I tremble uncontrollably and do not understand how my body can work separately from my mind.

"Control," Bryntar hisses.

Concentrate on one thing. Focus. I count her steps. One, two, three. The shaking stops when I reach five hundred and three, a tiny lesson to remember in the days to come. Do not let my mind wander. Change the unwanted thought to something different and repeat it to the exclusion of all else.

"Will they catch us?" I ask.

"No."

I search her feelings to see if she tells the truth. Her confidence gives me mine.

The cloudy night covers our movements. We eventually reach the beginning of the lava flow. Bryntar turns north and anticipates my question.

"Kepyrs not expect this way. Treacherous."

She places me on the ground. We climb down the jagged rocks and stand on a ledge overlooking the ocean.

Eerie fog rolls along the water and muffles the roar of the waves. Rain spews from the crashing storm clouds.

Bryntar turns me to face her. "Much danger in Eastern Seas."

Torches of fire flicker in the distance. I cannot hear the drums, but they thump inside my head.

She says, "We swim deep. Safer from storm."

Ready to do anything to escape the beating of the drums, I plunge into the sea.

Nine: The Swimming

Cold bites into me. Waves toss, twist, tear. Dark water hides the surface. For the first time in my life, I am thankful I do not have to breathe air, for it is impossible to discern up from down.

Something hard brushes my body and snatches my arm. I choke on a mouthful of seawater. My hair lights up to reveal Bryntar. The terror in her eyes fades. She encloses me in her arms and kicks to the surface. Wind and water lash our faces.

"Swim north." She coughs as waves devour us. "Home is west of Ice Mountains."

I do not allow myself to think why she is telling me this.

Wind smashes the water. A huge swell lifts us up. Up. Up. Up. To the top of a huge wave of swirling black water. We drop down, down, down. The undertow drags me deep. My arms rip away from Bryntar's. Ocean currents spit me into the air. Catch me and roll me over the surface. Bryntar roars and then there is nothing but the maddened sea. I strain to feel her. She is gone.

A bolt of lightning slashes across the sky.

I scream, "Come and hit me! I do not want to live without Bryntar!"

Thunder booms overhead. My hair glows. Lightning sizzles through the water and strikes me, jolting, white-hot. And still I live, at one with the light that fills me with energy and shining heat. I do not care.

Giant waves toss me like a twig. I flow up. . . down. . . .up.

Thoughts of Bryntar creep into my mind. She would not want me to give up and I hate the knowing. The lump in my heart grows heavier. My legs weaken. I cling to the idea that she can survive somehow, even in the thrashing of this relentless storm. It is all I have to hope for.

I plead with the sea. "Please bring her back to me."

Waves slap me in the face. I am alone for the first time in my life. I wonder how long the light in my hair can last if I let go and drop to the bottom of the sea, to never take another breath of light. Battered, I go under too many times to count and finally stop struggling. I sink down, a slow descent into deep calm. There I drift in darkness.

Fish dart in this quiet depth. I feel their lightness, but can see nothing.

A beautiful song floats through the water. My soul vibrates with the melody. Warm body after warm body glides next to me and away. My hair shines and I see the creatures.

Several gray bodies swim around me. They are huge, as long as trees, but my senses tell me these creatures mean no harm. I relax. Stare in awe at their grace and know that they breathe air.

Do I want to return to the surface for light? Or die in these depths?

I swim to a smaller creature and straddle its tail, giving myself a later choice. Holding tight, and thankful to touch a gentle soul, I close my eyes and merge with the glory of an animal at home in the water.

My mind floats in and out of consciousness, at total peace. I lose all sense of time, aware only of the cold sea washing over me, the warmth of the body next to me, the rhythm of a strong, slow heartbeat.

Much later, the creature ascends. Faster. Faster. It bursts into air, spraying water from the hole on the top of its body. I wipe my face and look around. The storm has passed, leaving a calm sea.

Where is the island?

Only the expanse of water stretches before me in the still-dark night. My ride starts to submerge. It has been too long since sunlight filled my hair. To stay underwater with my companions and die becomes my next choice.

I whisper, "Thank you," and let go to become a lonely speck in the vast ocean.

Clouds drift away from a shining moon. The dark silhouettes of distant mountains stand stark in the light. Numb in frigid water, I stroke slowly. My legs hang in heaviness. I have little desire to think. Where is the light within when I need it? I know that strong emotion seems to connect me to the energy. I am too tired to feel anything.

Water churns behind me and I twist. A creature slithers through the waves, long and black. Sharp spines ridge a sinuous back. Ancient pictures in the library flash in my mind.

Sea serpent.

I tremble and duck under the water, trying to hide the light that shimmers unbidden around my hair. I know without doubt controlling fear means controlling my power. I remember the spikes protruding from the massive snake-like head, the glowing eyes, the teeth as large as my hand. I refuse to hold the images in my mind and replace them with images of home. The light in my hair fades. I remain motionless, hoping I am too small, too insignificant for consideration.

Hunger overpowers my every sense, drowning me with a desire for the unusual thing in the water ahead—me. I fight to pull out of the serpent's feelings as it surges forward.

I cannot reach land or out-swim the creature. I surface and face it. Can it feel my thoughts? I calm myself, even though heartbeats bang in my throat. My feelings merge with the monster, warning it of danger.

The sea serpent stops. Rears its ugly head out of the water. Red eyes stare into mine as it swings back and forth over me in indecision. It breaks our connection. My feelings snap back, stinging.

The serpent bellows, maw drooling green poison. It plunges toward me.

Raw horror expands the light in my hair. It radiates over the water and blinds the monster. The head crashes into the sea. Misses. Strikes in fury again.

I dive underwater. It thrashes around me. Scales whip over my leg. I scream as it cuts into my flesh. The tide pushes me to the surface.

The serpent hovers over me. Shrieks in fury.

I cannot breathe. Or think. Or move.

The monster lunges.

I dive sideways into the churning waves, terrified. Consumed by fear, I am unable to stop the light from circling my head like a beacon.

The monster attacks again. Exhausted and having no knowledge of how to use my power, I sink underwater. The light around me disappears. I hold as still as possible.

The information about sea serpents does not explain their acute sense of smell. I feel the monster searching, searching. It will find me.

I surface and wait for death. My only hope is that the pain will be quick.

I am sorry, Bryntar. Goodbye.

The water suddenly quiets to shining black. I look around in desperation. The sea serpent snakes toward me. Deadly. Silently.

A roar bellows from deep within the island. Aru?

The ocean floor heaves as the earthquake hits. Waves throw me toward the shore and catch the serpent in a maelstrom. It writhes in the whirlpool, roars, and disappears under the sea.

I stare in shock. It would have been easier to die now, instead of waiting for the time when Aru wants my soul. I am too numb to care or understand why the beast saved me. I close my eyes in exhaustion, propelled by a powerful tide rushing me toward the rocky shore.

Ten: The Searching

A yank on my hair jerks me into awareness. Salt sticks my eyes closed. Rubbing them, I moan and squint in the bright light. Black rocks blur, then clear. My mind adjusts to a feeling that is enclosing, protective. A seabird yanks harder on my hair.

"Get away." I scare the squawking thing and moan.

Damp sand cools my back. There is no memory of landing on the beach. Judging from the daggers of pain knifing through me, it was not a soft landing. Everything aches. I inhale sunshine that touches me in warmth and gasp a smaller breath to ignore protesting muscles. Sunlight means one thing. It is necessary to seek shelter or be discovered.

I wiggle stiff toes, legs, and arms, and sit up to lean against the rocks towering over my head. Bruises cover most of my skin in colors of black, red and yellow. One wound with pus from the sea serpent throbs on my leg. There is little hope of discovering a healing plant here that can rid me of infection.

I wobble to my knees and hold onto a rock. Groaning, I peek out. The beach is empty save for waves washing sand and birds scavenging sea debris. Walking means searing pain. My choices are slim. I need protection and food, and Bryntar.

Gritting my teeth, I limp forward.

"Think of something besides the pain." My voice is barely a croaked whisper. Bryntar seeps into my mind.

"Think of something else."

The caverns of home fill my mind as I hobble next to the cliffs that shelter the beach. It is strange to think of being so far away and on my own, exposed. Home means safety with Taroc, peace in the underground gardens, interest in the boy who fills an unfamiliar place in my thoughts. I push away doubts of finding my way back.

Each step is torture. I hide between boulder, stone, tree snag, and cleft. My bare feet strike sharp pebbles, muscles shriek in weakness, welts thump all the way to my head. My vision swims in and out of focus as my mind wavers between wakefulness and sleep. There is no way to know how much time passes. Clinging to a rock and breathing heavily, I push myself on and miss seeing the driftwood. I trip and sprawl across the sand. Spasms roar through me like a wild beast, making it impossible to breathe. Pain and loss slice into my heart.

Please. Please. Let me die.

I burst into tears and sob out of control.

Birds suddenly shriek, swooping at me with open wings. Tears stream down my face and shudders course through my body. Barely able to see, I peer over a stone. Baby birds with fuzzy heads chirp in a nest. New life. Everything on the island will die if I do not live. I hate the burden and crawl away.

No cave offers protection. I stagger on. The twisted roots of a giant tree open with a wide entrance and offer welcoming darkness. I stumble inside. Knots of dark wood swirl upward, forming black crevices for hiding. The setting sun shines on the sandy floor. Scattered bones of long-dead animals form a kinship with me.

I sway and try to sense life, feel nothing, but hesitate to trust myself. I hobble deep into the back of the root system. Squeezing between rough, dry bark into a small cleft, I sink into instant sleep.

A loud growl wakes me. Something big rips into the tree roots, shaking my hiding place. Crackling bark and debris plunge from above. I cower and cover my head. An arrow whips through the air. An animal roars. I grab my mouth to keep from crying out as instant pain sears through me. The creature crashes to the ground. Relief fills me as it dies quickly.

Footsteps run inside. I squeeze deeper into my hiding place.

"A good chase and a good fight," a deep male voice says. "I am smarter and faster. You were outmatched."

His satisfaction and pride for the kill fills me with sick dread. I dare not move even though my leg burns. Footsteps pad away. When they return, the man, for that is who I think he is, drops several things that thump together. Then stone scratches stone. A flash of red illuminates the area near the front of the tree.

I crawl closer to the edge of my hiding place. A large pile of dry wood snaps with fire. Shivering with cold and fighting the urge to move, I enter into the man's feelings.

Warmth soaks into his skin and melts into mine. The fire grows brighter and I see a huge dead creature with an arrow in its chest. It has golden, dappled fur and double-pronged claws.

It is the man who draws attention, even though he is turned away from me. His hair is shiny black and cropped short. He only wears breeches of leather that cling tightly to his thighs. Muscles ripple along his sleek back. Wide golden cuffs encircle each wrist.

Why is my heart pounding for no reason?

He turns to add more wood to the fire. I hold my breath. Nothing mars his striking face. It glows pale, icy purple. Ebony eyes show intelligence and defiance above high cheekbones. There is no doubt in my mind that he is an Ice Lord, only a few seasons older than I am.

Heat vibrates through every cell of my body. I struggle to stop myself from responding to this enemy.

He draws a double-edged knife from his pack. The metal handle in the middle gleams in the light. Strange symbols surround a sparkling white stone. He swaggers to the creature and slices off a sharp fang protruding from its mouth—as easily as if it is cloth.

"Great bearran, your fang is the symbol that declares my manhood and right to the throne of the mighty Ice Lords. Let Ryz-IL deny me now."

His arrogance surges through me. I want to turn away, to stop watching, but am unable to take my eyes from him. He uses the smaller end of the knife and bores a hole in the fang.

What substance can do that so quickly?

He threads the fang on a narrow silver rod in the shape of a half-circle. The tooth hangs next to a crystal jewel shaped into three stars. He inserts the half-circle into his earlobe.

I cringe before realizing an opening in his ear is already there.

He smiles and says, "To the Ice Lord heir." Caressing the fang, he proceeds to remove the fur skin from the animal.

I want to retreat, but it is impossible.

His eyes focus in deep concentration. Skill is evident in his mastery of the knife blade. Muscles bunch in his arms. Mesmerized, I catch myself falling into his feelings of confidence, entitlement, strength and desire for power.

His voice cuts off my connection. "I waste your meat, bearran. You led me far from home and I cannot carry all of you back."

He cuts off chunks and cooks them. The smell turns my stomach. I force myself to look away and carefully slip deeper into the roots of the tree, not wanting this Ice Lord to discover me. The sight of him causes my physical body to vibrate with unfamiliar, frightening heat.

I shut him out with thoughts of the coming day. He is going home. The Ice Mountains are west and he knows how to get there from the beach. I do not. I have to follow him without being seen. West is home for me, too.

Eleven: The Following

I awake to shouts and cringe from sore muscles stiffened by the damp soil. Hot pain sears through my leg. Nauseous, I pull myself up by hanging onto a sturdy root.

On the beach, the Ice Lord throws parts of the slain animal far out into the ocean. With each heave, he yells with the effort. He strides back and kicks sand on the dying fire. Grabbing his pack, he heaves it onto his back with a grunt.

I am torn between safety and my desire to return home. The ache in my leg decides for me. I need the medicinal plant. Limping and weaving between the roots, my senses tell me it is safe to leave the tree. I squint in the sun's brightness and inhale, grateful for the familiar tingles sliding into my hair.

Pebbles crumble down the rocks to my left. All the Ice Lord's feelings center on his climbing. His muscles strain with effort.

I move under the overhang of rock so as not to be seen from above. It is not long before the narrow path he has taken reveals itself, cutting up through the boulders. The Ice Lord's strength and ability to climb such a steep path with a heavy pack take my breath away. It requires every ounce of energy to follow him in my condition.

Pain hits like a thousand spikes when I start to climb. I clench my teeth, clinging to every rock. My leg wound seeps until blood flows. At least the wound is clean now. Rocks slick from ocean spray dig into my hands and feet. I climb without stopping, inch by inch, muscles screaming, breath coming in gasps.

Foremost in my mind is the fear of losing the Ice Lord. A boulder crashes overhead as I cling high above the ocean. It bounces on sharp rock, splinters, showers me with stones. I cringe with each piercing sting. Only the thought of home keeps me from crying out and letting go.

I finally reach the top and peek over the edge. Shades of green fungus brighten drab rock. Scraggly trees shaped by sea winds scrape the bluff. A brave flower here and there sprouts through cracks in the ground. The Ice Mountains loom in the distance, cold and forbidding. I shudder.

With a last look at the boundless sea, I search for Bryntar, never giving up hope.

The Ice Lord strides far ahead.

Crawling over the edge, I keep low to the ground.

Time passes in pain and determination. The cliffs turn into hills that slope to a valley enclosed by more mountains. A shining river divides a land of magnificent trees. Some stand like giants with deep green needle-like leaves. Others spread leafy shade in wide circles. I limp down the hill. Something brown and white vanishes into a tree above me, chattering in anger.

I spot one of Bryntar's medicinal plants, tear off fleshy leaves, and hide behind the massive trunk of a tree. The sticky, sharp-smelling juice of the plant stings my leg, the sores on my swollen feet, and new stone punctures. I am grateful the plant will heal my physical wounds.

The Ice Lord increases the distance between us in his desire to reach the mountains. Keeping his pace is impossible in my condition. The valley offers food, water, and time for healing. If I keep the Ice Mountains on my right, they can lead me home. The young man hurries out of sight. I ignore the slight twinge of being alone. Again.

I sidestep holes in the ground and hurry to the river. Hiding under thick bushes, I watch fat silver fish dart through flat rocks. Cool, fresh water quenches my thirst, but does nothing for my hunger. Without a knife, it is impossible to strip the bark off trees to reach the inner layer next to the wood. Waves of loss sweep through me as I remember Bryntar's lessons on finding food in the wild. Content to eat anything, I gorge on plant roots, half-rotten fruit on the ground, fallen nuts smashed with a pointed rock.

Too soon shadows slant over the valley. I shiver, wishing for a coat to cover my dress. The rolling hills offer no cave system for shelter and safety. The branches of the trees are too high to reach. My choices suddenly vanish.

A prowl of jaguarats creeps over the hills and slinks into the valley. Six large white bodies stretch over the ground. Muscles ripple under thick, wavy fur.

I cannot control the fear that lights up my hair.

The creatures stop and stare at me. Their noses sniff, long tails flicking. They screech and bound toward me on silent paws.

Terrified, I run and dive into the icy river. I stroke hard against the current to reach the far side, ignoring pain for the greater fear.

The sun disappears like a snuffed candle. My body shakes so hard my teeth rattle. Not from the water, but from experiencing the desire of the prowl as they reach the river's edge.

Moonlight leans over the mountains. Golden eyes gleam as the jaguarats race along the bank. The largest one leaps into the water. The rest follow him.

Crazy with fear, I count the splashes. Two, three, four, five, six. Two strokes to the edge. I scramble up the bank. Spot a tree with low branches. Wind sways the top. I race toward it, hoping to climb higher than the jaguarats can. Their splashes as they jump out of the water spur me on.

I trip on a mound of grass. Sucked into a hole, I scream, slide down a short tunnel, and hit bottom with a thud. Dirt sifts over me. Stench fills my nose, a creature's leavings. I frantically search for a larger tunnel and only find smaller holes.

The jaguarats shriek above. One pauses in hesitation. Desire for fresh meat wins. It scratches at the hole and shoves in its head.

The snarling mad thing horrifies me. My hair stands on end and fills with light.

The creature stops and regards me with glaring eyes.

"Leave me alone."

It screeches. Bloodlust shakes me all the way to my toes. My heart thumps erratically.

I shrink back against the tunnel wall, not knowing how to protect myself without a weapon.

The jaguarat yowls. Triple-pronged claws whip through the air, trying to reach me.

"Get away!" I scream.

The creature screeches. Digs deeper in frenzy.

I think I will go mad when an ancient awareness surges from a deep place in my mind.

You are an Enchantress with the knowledge of generations. You cannot be separated from the power of the light. Feel it and control your fear.

An unfamiliar calmness enters my mind. Wave upon wave of shimmering light courses through my body, filling me. For the first time, I experience a true connection and know how to save myself.

I am sorry, jaguarat.

I raise a finger, point it at the jaguarat's head, and concentrate on expanding the light inside me. It shrieks once when the stream of light hits it between the eyes. Agony is over in an instant for both of us. The force of the impact throws the creature backward out of the hole. Hisses and growls echo overhead as the others tear at their dead companion. Sorrow sweeps into my bones for killing a living thing.

A horrendous roar bellows from above. Raging. Continuous. The ground shakes. Shrieks and screams of a terrific battle fill the hole. My hair fades. I cover my ears and try to stop the rips and spasms of death that torture me.

Abrupt silence, until a high keening cry pierces the quiet.

Bryntar!

I claw up the hole, choking on dirt. "You are alive!"

She stares, uncomprehending for a second. Then crushes me into her arms.

I am home.

Twelve: The Homing

"Hear scream. . . afraid. . . too late." Breathless, Bryntar shakes, her chest heaving from exertion. I lead her away from the dead jaguarats. She sinks to the ground, bleeding from many wounds in her skin. Tears slide down her face and mine.

"You found me."

She sweeps her eyes over my torn dress, bruises, and dirty face. Pride shines in her eyes. "You survived."

I look toward the silent dead. "I did not want to kill."

"You killed to live. How?"

"Something inside, like an essence from long ago, told me to remember who I am. How can that happen?"

"You are Enchantress," Bryntar says.

I stare at her simplistic answer. "The light struck with such power."

"Good. You learn."

"How did you find me?"

"Seas pulled south. Fought to shore. Found footprints and another's."

"The Ice Lord's."

Her eyes flare. "He saw you?"

"No." My stomach flutters and my face burns when his image flickers in my mind.

She stares into my eyes. "Ice Lord not for you."

I never thought of having anyone in my life besides Taroc and Bryntar. Yet the faces of two young men flit through my mind, uninvited.

Bryntar interrupts my thoughts. "We leave valley tomorrow. You sleep now."

"Please, the river first," I say. The stench of blood and death smother every sense. "You need to wash your wounds."

My tattered dress reeks of things best forgotten. The cold water is welcome. I scrub hard, knowing it is impossible to feel clean.

Bryntar stands in front of the current so it cannot sweep me away and cleans herself.

Will I ever feel the need to protect someone over all else? Will I know a man, have a child, understand the depths of love? No. I am thrust into saving a world without attachment.

Bryntar carries me to a grassy knoll with views in all directions.

"Tell me your story," she says.

I curl up beside her and relate some of what happened when we were torn apart. My eyes close with warmth and sleep claims me.

It seems like only moments later when I awake, inhaling light. Sunrise glows across the mountains in orange, red, and yellow.

On the ground next to me lay leather coverings for my feet and a white fur coat. I am touched that Bryntar stayed up all night to provide me with clothes. "Thank you, Bryntar."

I wipe tears from my eyes. The fur is soft and warm against my skin. I have been cold for so long that the odor and the dampness of fresh leather seems little to bear.

Bryntar hands me a leaf from the medicinal plant. I smear the juice on wounds that are starting to heal and tend to those of Bryntar's that she cannot reach.

"Eat and walk," she says. She retrieves a piece of fruit from her bag full of fresh food and starts toward the tree-covered mountains to our west.

Sweetness melts down my throat from a crunchy piece of fruit. "How long until we reach home?"

"One day through mountains. Leg wound serious. How?"

"A sea serpent."

She stops, shocked. "You killed sea serpent?"

"I could not protect myself. Aru created a whirlpool that took it away."

"You saw beast?"

"I only felt it. Why would it spare my life?"

Bryntar shakes her head. "I have no answers. Even living for so long."

"How many seasons have you lived?"

Her answer is to lengthen her stride and pull away.

I run to keep up. "Are you ever going to tell me anything I need to know?"

"Not my place," she says. "You will learn sooner than you want."

Her mysterious comments lie next to the others in my mind.

The Ice Mountains grow distant behind us, but they still seem to watch,, to judge, to lure me.

The sun blazes overhead when Bryntar stops near a ridge of peaks. Her eyes search rocks and shrubs that cover the ground. "There." She rushes to a huge boulder and heaves it aside to reveal a deep hole in the mountain. "You first. I close."

I face the black cavity and shiver. "Tell me there is another way."

"There is not. Watch head."

We crawl inside. The boulder thumps in place, sealing us inside. Silence swallows the small space. The ridges on Bryntar's back scrape the ceiling and the noise comforts me in the total darkness. Her breath warms the confining space.

My fingers become my eyes. I touch sharp spurs of rock, slide around twisting edges ,and creep over the pebble-strewn floor. I give thanks for the protective coverings on my feet.

Bryntar's groans force me to concentrate on something else. The Ice Lord. No. The wounded young man. No. I count. One, two, three.

Seventy-nine, eighty. Dull light gleams ahead. Relieved, I push dry plants aside and wriggle into muted light.

Bryntar crawls out and collapses, heaving with fatigue.

I kneel at her side. "Are you all right?"

She sits up. "Tunnel seemed larger last time."

"When was that?"

"Nine-hundred seasons."

I sigh, and wonder how she could be that old. I will not get an answer if I ask. Maybe longevity belongs to creatures like her.

She turns around and stands in silence. Brief nostalgia tinges with love. It fills her heart and mine. "I showed this place to Taroc."

Intruding on feelings embarrasses me more and more. Will I ever have the time to practice control?

I turn to face a solid wall so high that only a tiny patch of blue sky shows far above. The white rock glitters with veins of gold. I touch the gold and, to my surprise, warmth. "Why did you bring us here?"

Bryntar strokes the mountain of rock in reverence. "Quick way home."

"This is a sheer cliff."

"Learn to see beyond obvious." She takes food from her bag. "Eat. Need strength."

"I need hooves."

She roars with laughter, smoke furling from her nostrils. A few minutes later, she heaves her body off the ground and grabs the bag. "Come."

Bryntar skirts the cliff and disappears.

I hurry after her and discover a corridor between the towering mountains big enough for me to squeeze through. "Where are you?"

She stands on a promontory high above me. "Meet farther on. Keep going." Her claws scratch rock, massive legs jumping to a higher precipice. She vanishes into clouds.

No light filters into the corridor. The cliff is smooth on either side, as if someone sliced the rock with a giant knife. I touch cool walls and move forward, wondering why every path we take leads through darkness.

At the end of the passageway, the mountain splits open. I gasp in pleasure. Several waterfalls splash into a river drifting through a narrow valley. Lush plants reflect the brilliant colors of the setting sun. The scent of flowers floats on the air. I breathe deeply and absorb the quiet peace.

Bryntar leaps down from a ledge and I yelp.

She hisses. "Be alert all times."

"It is so beautiful. We should live here instead of the caverns."

"Aru find you." She says the words with such finality that questioning her is futile. She looks me over. "Cross valley before sun sets. Strong enough?"

I long to be home and quickly answer. "Yes." Surprised, I realize I am stronger. Sore muscles and bruises have faded. The wound on my leg is smaller and scabbed over.

Bryntar smiles. "Enchantress heals fast." She thumps off.

The valley is smaller than it seemed at first. We follow the river. More peaks grow in front of us like giant guardians. They echo an awful sound. Bryntar's stride quickens. When she stops, I rush to her side. A huge hole sucks up the river.

I sense Bryntar's fear. "What is it?"

She points at the hole. "Way out."

"Another cold bath?"

Bryntar snorts.

"It does not look safe," I say. "When did you last go this way?"

"When showed Taroc."

"A tunnel can change in time. Surely we can find a path instead."

"No time. Tunnel drops through mountain. Empties into river. Before we found boy."

I shiver, remembering the waterfall that spews out of the cliff. "Why are we in such a hurry?"

A deep sadness shifts through Bryntar. "Tomorrow is day of birth.

Everything changes." She turns me to face her and points to the water. "Go."

I am confused with what she is hiding and her feelings of dread. "You first."

Bryntar touches my cheek with a claw, so tenderly my heart swells with love. She secures the bag around her neck and jumps in with a screech. The hole swallows her like a starving animal.

I inhale light and leap after her. Dragged straight down, the overpowering force shocks me more than the cold. My eyes open to slits against the surging water. It is dark again, except where light seeps through cracks in the mountain and glows green. I hit a deep curve and draw in my arms. Uncontrolled, the force slams me into walls smooth from ages of wear.

The flood suddenly slows to a stop, backing up into a pool. Submerged completely, I strain in the murky water and see the struggling white form of Bryntar, her arms pinned and useless at her sides. Her strong neck fights to jerk her horn free from the crack in the rock overhead.

Her terror sweeps into me, the panic draining her breath.

Close her feelings out. Concentrate.

I point my finger to a spot above Bryntar's head and carefully summon the light within. I could kill us with too much force. Heat and light drizzle through the water without reaching the rock. There is no time now. I glow with light and throw a beam above her head.

BOOM. Rocks explode, pieces shooting through the swirling water and stabbing our bodies. The pressure sweeps us away with mud and rock.

We fall faster, faster. Until the mountain spits us out.

I ram into the river bottom, pounded by the waterfall. My coat rips off. Rocks slash into my back.

Bryntar grabs my waist and pulls me downstream. I choke up as much water as she does. Swim away and crawl up the riverbank.

Fog smothers everything. I can barely see Bryntar, though she is right beside me. Pain stabs into my back.

She hisses. Her greater pain overcomes mine. I move close. A large shard of rock sticks in her side.

She gasps. "Too far to home. Lose much blood."

"Tell me what to do."

"Get. . . needle."

I fight to control my fear and remove the bag from her neck. I find sinew and thread the needle. My fingers are slow tying the knot. I hand it to her. She pushes my hand aside.

"Arm is broken. You remove. Close wound."

"I cannot."

"You must."

Her faith and the expression in her eyes give me strength. I grab the shard and yank it from her side. Blood gushes and pain burns through us. Holding the wound closed, I stick the needle through her furry skin. She winces, but says nothing. Over and over the needle pierces in stinging torment. I clench my teeth to mirror her bravery.

Agony stops time. The hands of a stranger sew the gaping wound shut, tie off the last stitch, and knot the sinew. I pause and cannot stop trembling.

"Thank you, Elandra."

I stare at my bloody hands and start to slide into darkness.

Her raspy voice warns. "Stay with me. Not safe until home. Wash."

I stagger through the fog, the sound of the river guiding my way. I clean rapidly in the frozen water. Rip a piece off the bottom of my ragged dress, soak it in water and struggle up the bank. Fog smothers everything.

"Bryntar! Where are you?"

"Here."

I backtrack and kneel to clean her wound, unable to remove so much blood from white fur.

"Help me up," she says.

She sits up and I put my shoulder under her good arm to help her stand. Her other arm hangs limp at her side. She hobbles off through the heavy mist, holding her wound.

"Wait. Let me help or I will lose you."

I slide next to her, hanging onto her good side. Her claws lean on my shoulder.

Trees, bushes, and rocks become obstacles of punishment as night darkens the fog and silence surrounds us. Bryntar's eyes never stop scouring the woods, but I wonder if she can see what I cannot. She keeps a grueling pace. It costs us both.

Do not feel her pain. Concentrate. Ignore the throbbing in my back.

I slip and trip on uneven ground. Twigs, dead logs, and tree branches batter in ambush. Bryntar steadies me.

I whisper. "I cannot see. How do you know where to go?"

"I smell the way."

"You will have to teach me." Exhausted, I laugh at the idea of sniffing my way home. I slip to the ground in uncontrollable giggles that turn into hiccups.

Bryntar pulls me up. "No time. Please help me."

Her weakness strikes into my heart. I drag myself up. "Oh, Bryntar, I am sorry."

Much later, the mist fades. Bryntar leads us straight to the vines that hide the stone entrance to home. She pants with fatigue and leans against the rock.

I push on the boulder and it swivels in silence. A shadow moves inside. "EEKK."

Bryntar hisses and moves protectively in front of me.

"It's me," Daniel says. Guilt flows from him as he stands there with a pack over his shoulder.

"Where are you going?" I ask.

"Out of here."

"You will be killed."

"I'll take my chances."

"Before you run headlong to your death, help me get Bryntar downstairs."

Thirteen: The Finding

"You're both a train wreck," Daniel says. "What happened?" He avoids looking at Bryntar's bloody fur.

"We were thrown out of a waterfall. She has a broken arm besides the wound in her side. Be careful."

"Jeez." He subdues his uncertainty and takes my place.

She flinches, but remains silent.

I struggle down the spiral tunnel, every step a concentrated effort not to feel Bryntar's torment.

"Where did you think you were going?" I ask.

"Home. This place is crazy. You run around with a monst. . . with her, and that Taroc guy is nuts."

I glare at him. "This is my family. Say another word and I am going to lose my temper. You do not want that to happen."

"I'm so scared."

He doesn't look scared. His eyes trail down to the rags that barely cover me.

Heat fills my body and I sway. "This is an island. How do you expect to escape?"

"Why should I believe you?" he says in defiance.

"I do not lie."

He shuts up.

When we reach the great hall, the strong odor of pine-scented candles makes me long for a childhood that is gone. How could I take my home for granted? Images flitter through my mind: Taroc chasing me through the corridors—robe flapping against his legs, the gardens of sunlight, Bryntar humming while gently rocking me in her furry arms. So many memories.

Taroc sits in the wavering shadows cast by candles. He rises with difficulty when he sees us. "Quick, put her on the chair." He hunches in stiffness over his cane, the only thing holding him upright. Wrinkled skin hangs in folds on his haggard face. He looks ancient. "Please, let me see your arm, my dear."

Taroc holds her broken arm and slides his fingers up and down. She shivers, but not from pain. When he reaches a point above her elbow, he yanks.

A yell escapes from me as her bone cracks into place.

Smoke furls from her nose, but she says nothing about my outburst.

Daniel stares at us and backs away.

Taroc frowns. "Control yourself, Elandra."

Remorse sweeps through me. "I am sorry. It will not happen again."

"See that it does not." Taroc looks at the wound in Bryntar's side and then at me with a raised eyebrow. "Nicely done. Daniel, will you please fetch a pitcher of water and cups?"

Daniel strides away, trying to hide his limp. His frustration and another feeling hover at the edge of my mind: shame, lost pride?

As he leaves the room, my fingers long to touch the golden hair that curls at the nape of his neck.

What is the matter with me? He is nothing but a stranger.

I experience a sickening pain that sweeps over Taroc. Stunned, I tremble and try hard not to feel his slow-beating heart, the sluggish movement of energy through his body, his organs shutting down regardless of his steel resolve. I know he is dying. He knows this, too.

I place my hand on his shoulder. "I am so sorry."

His eyes meet mine, dark, still alert, and piercing. "Welcome home, Elandra. You had us concerned."

Love for my teacher and mentor spreads through me like warm honey, surprising in its fierceness.

More emotions hit me, flying like trapped birds between Taroc and Bryntar. She tries to hide her sorrow about Taroc and refuses to look at him, even when he places his hand over the wound in her side. He closes his eyes in concentration. His hand trembles, yet healing takes place inside her body. Great waves of relief sweep through all of us.

She rests a claw upon his hand. "Thank you."

He strokes her arm. "It is little enough after my past selfishness."

A tear escapes from Bryntar that she wipes away. "We had lifetimes together. I am thankful."

"Are you ever going to tell me your secrets?"

Taroc studies me. "Turn around." He places his hands on my lacerations. Energy flows into the wounds like cool bubbles. He shakes with the effort. Relief flows as my pain recedes. He sags, drained and older than minutes before. Straightening slowly, he throws a blanket around my shoulders.

"I suspected that you received your unique abilities. Tomorrow will be soon enough to answer your questions. It is late and I am weary."

Excited to know there will be no more secrets between us, I hug him. "It is good to be home, Taroc."

His smile is tinged with sadness.

Daniel returns with water and cups. He pours and hands one to each of us. He looks at Bryntar. "I'm sorry I called you a monster."

"It is what I am."

"I didn't think monsters were real."

She smiles. "Who knows real truth? No monsters in your world?"

"Our animals don't talk."

Smoke furls out of Bryntar's nose.

"I'm sorry. You seem more than an animal. You—"

"You need to rest from your ordeals," Taroc says. "Until then, goodnight my dears." He turns and shuffles away. Bryntar goes after him.

"I didn't mean to insult her."

"Try harder next time."

He appraises me and offers his arm. "Let me help you to your room. You look like a three-ring circus."

"What is a three-ring circus?"

"It's where animals perform."

"What?"

"Forget it. You wouldn't understand anyway."

"Are you insulting me?"

"No. It's hard to explain my world."

"Maybe you can try, if you are not ready to run away."

Many emotions flicker through him: guilt, worry, interest in me. He says nothing.

I have trouble thinking over the stupid thumping of my heart. My throat tightens and I stomp away.

He grabs my arm. "I'm sorry, okay? It's hard not to feel like a prisoner."

I look up at him, trapped in his gaze. The gentleness of his soul hides behind his scorching eyes, confusing me. "We are all prisoners here. At least it is safer than above ground. Goodnight."

"Please, at least let me see you to your room."

"I'm going to the gardens."

He gazes at me. "They are unbelievably beautiful."

A thrill makes my knees wobble.

"What's up there?" he asks. "On the surface."

"Wild animals. Kepyrs and Ice Lords who want our deaths."

"Why?"

"I do not want to talk about it."

"The apple does not fall far from the tree."

I glare at him. "What is that supposed to mean?"

"Secrets are the norm around here."

"If you do not have secrets, tell me your story," I say.

He turns away with tortured eyes. "It took my family three years to build our ship in between school and work. Sailing around the world seemed so cool." His voice grows to a whisper. "Now I'm glad my mom and sister couldn't go at the last minute."

Horror washes through him and me.

I am determined to block out his feelings. Someday.

The words rush out of him. "I don't understand what happened. I was sleeping and thrown out of bed. By the time I reached the deck, the ship had cracked in half and was sinking. How does a ship crash into nothing? There was only an empty ocean and a strange shimmering light over my half of the ship."

He runs a hand through his hair in frustration. His voice cracks and guilt strikes through him like a dagger. "Then a whirlpool came from nowhere. It started sucking my dad and brother and their half of the ship down into it. I ran toward them and they yelled at me to stay where I was." His voice breaks.

"I am truly sorry."

"Now, I'm stuck here. Wherever that is."

I shut out his feelings. "What has Taroc told you?"

"Not much. He asked me lots of questions. I know one thing. He's dying."

A sword pricks my heart. I cannot even imagine a life without Taroc and refuse to think about it. "There must be a way to save him."

Daniel stops and turns to me. "There isn't. Don't get me wrong. I'm sorry. He won't let me leave the caverns. Says I'll be killed."

Unable to continue, Daniel stops talking and twists the leather rope on his wrist. He notices my interest. "Sailors get tattoos for luck. Mom wouldn't let me. I don't usually wear jewelry, but my sister made this to remind me that with an anchor and a compass I'll always be able to find my way home. His jaw tightens.

I have no words to comfort him and change the subject. "Did Taroc say anything else?"

"He's full of secrets."

I stop and glare at him. "I have lived my whole life with secrets."

"That sucks," he says. "You won't like this one." He takes my hands in his.

I cringe and yank away, suddenly horrified to hear his words.

"I don't get it, but somehow your life means his death."

"No. No!"

I turn back toward Taroc's study and flee, racing as fast as my heart.

"Elandra, wait."

Abruptly, the floor of the cavern heaves like a giant, continuous wave. It throws me across the corridor and slams me into a wall.

Daniel slides across the floor and grabs me in his strong arms. "Hang on!"

The ground roars under us like a raging monster. A writhing mass of black rock and blazing fire buckles the metal floors and disappears so fast I wonder if I imagine it. Aru?

The earthquake crashes us from one side of the hall to the other. The walls moan and creak, ready to burst.

My one thought is of family. Trapped in Daniel's arms, I yell. "Let me go."

"It's too dangerous."

"My family needs me." I fight to be free.

"You want to die?" Daniel asks.

The ceiling shudders. Metal splits at the seams.

"Let go!" My hair lights up. Sparks flash from my body into him.

"Ow!"

I shake, holding the energy inside so it goes no further. "I am sorry."

Terrified, he scrambles away.

The earthquake hits full force, growling, rumbling, screeching. Alive. A piece of ceiling rips off, swinging toward Daniel.

I trip across the rolling floor, fling myself at him and enclose him in my arms. We roll into a corner.

I will have control.

I cut out all thought except protection. A bubble of light bursts around us. My light deflects the torn metal that whips around and over us. Energy courses through me in waves, overwhelming all other sensation. The protection suspends us in a world separated from the chaos.

And then it is over, the stillness a jolt.

Daniel yanks away from me, dazed. His disbelief pierces into me like needles.

"How did you do that? What are you?"

Bryntar's shriek shatters the silence.

The room twists sideways on me with her terrified cry.

Daniel grasps my arm. His solidness stops my whirling world. "I've got you."

"I have to go to them."

We skirt floors gouged with holes of ripped metal. My muscles weaken as fear drains my energy. I swallow screams. Time stretches on and on. When we reach Taroc's study, the door lies on the floor like a trampled piece of parchment. We pick our way around it.

Inside, Bryntar strains to lift a huge wall off the floor, her face furious. She hurls it away. Taroc lies crushed beneath. She kneels beside him and takes his hand

Although light streams from the hole far above, I cannot breathe. I cannot think.

Taroc wheezes. "Do not cry, my dear. It is quicker this way."

I scream, the horror of what I have done crashing down on me. "This is my fault. I led the beast here. I am sorry."

My knees buckle. Daniel catches me once again. "What beast?"

I sag in his arms, afraid to look at their faces for fear it will destroy me.

Taroc's raspy voice cuts into me. "You are not to blame, Elandra. Aru came for me."

"What do you mean?"

"While you were gone, an earthquake damaged one of the metal walls that I created for protection from Aru. I am amazed the beast has not found me before now."

"What are you saying?" I jerk away from Daniel and notice the turban Taroc usually wears has been knocked from his head. His long hair spreads across the floor, silver and shining.

He breathes light.

Words stick in my throat. Until anger at his betrayal rips through me. I shut out his pain. "Who are you?"

"I am an Enchanter."

I blink, refusing to believe the evidence before me. "You have black eyes!"

"As do all males of our species."

"You lied to me!"

He struggles to breathe, his voice barely a whisper. "Only to spare you. I am the only Enchanter on this island to survive, until your birth. As soon as that happened, I started to age. Only the youngest survives when the gift is received."

"That is not fair!"

"We do not live a life of fairness," Taroc says. "We live a life of service." He turns to Bryntar. "And of love if we are so fortunate."

I am to blame. It is my fault he is dying.

"Why did you keep this from me?"

Taroc gasps, clutching his chest.

I try to block out his unbearable agony, but cannot and sink to the floor next to him.

He struggles for breath. "You deserved to know. . .the goodness of life. A thousand seasons. . . is a long time to live. I am ready to go on."

"No. Please, heal yourself."

His love spreads through me, cherishing, holding me close. "My child, I used the last of my gift to heal you."

Bryntar sobs quietly.

Tears drip down my face as I gaze at his study and the books I was never allowed to read. "You hid here for a thousand seasons?"

"As a coward."

"Taroc, no." Bryntar stands defiant. "You chose love."

"I was stupid to think I would succeed in becoming normal," he says. "I can never forgive myself for what happened to you, my beautiful Bryntar."

The raw muscles ache in her throat. She strains to speak her words. "I would do it again, to be with you."

He smiles. "As would I, my love. My only regret. . . is leaving you."

She touches his cheek, her shoulders shaking. "I want to go with you."

"You are needed here," Taroc says. He coughs without stopping and clutches his chest. His hair dulls as he struggles for breath.

Bryntar's eyes tear as she turns away.

I grasp his hand. "Please do not leave me."

Taroc's eyes shine. "Elandra. You are like a daughter. Fulfill your destiny. You have everything you need within your heart."

He takes his last breath. The small amount of light that remains slowly drains from his hair.

I watch, helpless.

Suddenly a flash of light binds us together, shutting out all else. Taroc smiles and touches the middle of my forehead with a finger. "You will be the strongest Enchantress ever born." He closes his eyes. His peace and love sweep through me. Our lights merge, stinging in brilliance.

The only father I have ever known slowly fades before my eyes.

Fourteen: The Learning

The light dissolves. My soul shrivels. Bryntar's screech sounds like a whisper. All feeling falls away to emptiness, a space with no pain or guilt or loss.

"Elandra?" Bryntar's hoarse voice filters from a lifetime ago.

I float in darkness.

Daniel's deep voice sooths from far, far away. "She's in shock."

An unclear awareness intrudes. Of warm blankets, fumbling hands, screeching metal. Then I drift into a lovely void of nothing. At the soft edge of consciousness are intangible words, prodding, yet unreachable.

Nothingness cannot last. Corrupted by muddled dreams and searing nightmares, I fight towers of ice, vicious beasts, pools of bubbling fire.

Compresses cool my burning body. I stay distanced in my refuge and ignore the voices of concern that urge me to wake. Until Taroc's words spring into my knowing. *I was stupid to think I would succeed in becoming normal.*

There is a way to rid myself of being an Enchantress?

My eyes drag open to sun shining high above. Now that I am in this forbidden study, I do not want to remain. Unbalance and emptiness pour through me. I breathe, nose quivering with the odor of dust and damp dirt. And the faint scent of Taroc. My throat tightens and I squeeze my eyes shut to stop the tears.

I am responsible for his death.

I remember his last moments, his touch on my forehead. Does he share my body? My mind searches, relieved when it is only me inside. Me with greater light and power. Dear, dear father.

Slight thuds catch my attention.

"Stupid books." Daniel sits before a jumbled stack of books. He tosses one aside and leafs through the pages of another, his urgency and frustration increasing.

Taroc's secret books.

"Those books do not belong to you."

He jumps up. "Jeez, you scared me." Shame sweeps through him.

"What are you looking for?"

"Bryntar will be stoked."

"Stoked?"

"Excited that you're awake. I thought she'd go bananas with worry."

"What is bananas?"

"Never mind. She's worked night and day on the damage to the outer walls."

"Is she all right?"

"Guess so. She hasn't stopped or talked since—"

I interrupt him, worried now. "How long?"

"Three days."

Three days?

I swing my legs over the edge of the bed, tangling in a jade dressing gown. Where did this come from? I have never worn anything that fits my curves or caresses my skin in such softness. Blushing under Daniel's gaze, annoyance surges through me. I grab a blanket and stand up, reeling, self-conscious, and totally awkward.

He catches me and whispers in my ear. "Easy does it."

My treacherous body tingles with his touch. It does not seem right that I feel anything but the misery of loss.

"I need to see her."

"Water first." He hands me a cup.

Drinking refreshes me and I pad out of the study.

Daniel catches up. He does not try to hide his limp.

"Does your leg hurt?" I know the answer, but not whether he realizes my ability to feel his pain.

He stiffens. "Yeah. Don't know if I'll walk without a limp."

Sorrow strikes me as the shame of his apparent flaw surges within him.

"You are alive."

"Big deal."

"You want to die?"

He turns away.

His bitterness, guilt, and frustration fill me. Along with a deeper feeling I do not understand, a warmth in my body that is hard to ignore. He feels it too. I gaze at his determined face, knowing he is deliberately creating an empty hole between us.

"Let's go," he says.

We creep around gaps in the once-covered ground. With the cave walls and floors exposed, the controlled warmth has disappeared. I shiver. Ruin meets us at every turn.

A pounding on walls catches my attention. Bryntar.

I turn down a long corridor toward the sound, longing to see her. I have to pass the gardens. My heart crashes as each step drags slower and slower, closer and closer. How can I bear to look?

I stop. Shake in sick horror, unable to speak. My beloved plants and trees lie in tangled destruction. My breath stops. It does not matter that the light shines from above. I fall to the dirt. Utter despair fills me as the songs, giggles, and whispers of the flowers fade into memory.

The ground aches and I with it.

"Some plants can be saved and replanted," Daniel says.

His earnest look gives me hope.

"Thank you."

Bryntar thumps in and encloses me in her arms. "My Elandra."

I clench her tightly.

She pats my back. "This is not your fault."

I stare into her eyes. "If I was not born Taroc would still be alive."

"No control over birth."

"Do I control my destiny? Tell me how to become normal, Bryntar."

Shock ripples across her face.

Daniel laughs. "You can't change into something else."

I scowl at him. "How can you say that after all you have seen?"

He frowns. "How can I believe anything? Maybe you've drugged me. I'm hallucinating and you're a bunch of loonies keeping me against my will. Or I'm in some friggin' nightmare." Anger flushes his face. Breathing hard, he turns away and begins replanting flowers.

His resentment and confusion flow into me. I sweep them aside, determined to get answers from Bryntar. "Taroc spoke of becoming normal. Is there some place to do this? Tell me."

Bryntar turns away. "No."

I grab her arm. "You would rather watch me die at the hands of Aru?"

Bryntar shakes her head. "Accept your destiny."

"Please, Bryntar. I do not want to be an Enchantress."

"Must love who you are."

"If I was normal, Aru would have no reason to want me."

Steam furls out of her nose. "Aru destroy anyway. You are only hope."

"Everyone on this island wants me dead."

Determination steels her eyes. "Their ignorance."

My skin flashes white-hot.

Bryntar hisses. "Control anger."

"How do I do that?"

"Understand the reason."

I fight the rage pounding within me. If I cannot control my emotions, how can I control my life? "Without the ability to choose my destiny, I have no life, Bryntar."

Her eyes soften. "Accept power to change all."

I ignore the growing gap between us. "If there is something that will make me normal, I have to know what it is."

"Too dangerous under Ice Mountains. I forbid it."

Bryntar has never denied me anything. I take her claws in my hands and plead. "Please, where is it?"

She says nothing.

"If you will not help, I will search alone."

"Never find."

"Maybe she has a good reason not to tell you," Daniel says. "Why go on some kind of crazy quest?"

I glare at him. "Tell me, Bryntar."

"No." Her dread strikes my nerves. She hisses and her voice cracks. "I died there." She thumps away.

Shocked and ready to explode all at the same time, I cannot move.

Daniel hands me a piece of undamaged fruit. "Here."

His thoughtfulness breaks my control. My throat clenches as I stare at the perfect ruby fruit in my hand. I take a bite with little delight in the pure sweetness.

I touch his arm and we both shiver. "Do you know what she means?"

Indecision flickers within him. "Not really."

"I need to know the truth."

"Maybe it's in Taroc's journal."

Could it be?

Excited, I jump up and hurry away.

Daniel rushes to catch up. "It wasn't there when we straightened the study."

"He hid the book in a safe place."

I run, trying to wipe out the distant pounding that echoes Bryntar's pain. She knows it is unnecessary to repair the cave. Aru can destroy anything at will. When it is time to destroy the island and me, there will be no cave, no library, and no record that anything ever existed here.

If I change, can everything be different?

I hurry through the empty doorway to the study and turn to Daniel. "I was never allowed here. Do you have any ideas of where he might have hidden the book?"

"Leave it alone. We're in enough trouble."

I whirl on him. "There is no beast waiting to take your life." Sparks crackle from my hair.

He jumps backward, scowling and a bit afraid of me. "Right, only an island of natives. You think I like being a prisoner?"

"You are here because it is the safest place."

"According to you."

"Is that why you were looking through Taroc's books when I woke up?"

"They're all in some strange language. I can't find any maps. It's like this island is in some kind of crazy time warp. Like it doesn't exist in the real world. I have to get home."

"Where is home?"

"Florida."

"How can you leave?"

"I don't know. Build a raft or a sailboat. Anything to get away from here."

"Impossible."

"Nothing is impossible if you want it bad enough. You don't understand. My mom and little sister will think we're all dead. They need to know I lived. They need me."

I block out the feelings that tear through him. "I am sorry."

His distaste and irritation hit my every nerve. "Do you think I like knowing my life rests with a. . .?"

Heat rises to my face. "With a what? A monster?"

"A girl."

"I am an Enchantress."

"Whatever. It will take courage to face Aru."

I gasp, ignoring the thought that he speaks the truth.

"Don't think I'll help you, either. I want to get off this stupid island." He stalks out of the room.

Daniel cannot possibly know the burden of what it means to be me. Refusing to think about him, I focus on finding Taroc's book.

Isolation soaks into me once again.

Fifteen: The Writing

I slowly turn in a circle. Where would Taroc hide his treasured book? Since Daniel said he looked at the books on the floor, I dismiss them. Broken bookcases and twisted metal walls only cover stone and dirt.

Thoughts about Taroc and his life filter into my mind as I slump on the bed. He spent years of loneliness until he met Bryntar. He would have finished reading the books in the library in a few years. What else did he do with his time?

What if he wrote more than one book? He would need a larger hiding place.

My eyes dart around the study. Unless Taroc buried the books, he had only one place that offers the space and protection, his huge bed. I get on my knees and run my fingers along the smooth frame of dark wood. My heart thumps in my throat while I crawl around the bed. On one side is a small button. When I press it a panel slides open to display hundreds of books.

The idea of living a thousand years has meant little to me until now. Hesitating and feeling like an invader, I open the cover of the top book. Inside is a notation—*The End*. My hands tremble knowing I will soon have the answers I crave.

Someday, all of Taroc's words will be etched in my mind. Now, I want to find the diary written when he and Bryntar met. She mentioned nine hundred seasons on our trip home. Book after book passes through my hands until I find the one I want.

My twitchy fingers turn the pages of yellowed parchment. I scan the heavy, precise handwriting. Taroc's loneliness echoes mine. Then his regret changes. I immerse myself in his story.

"After painstaking experiments with metal, I finished forging armor to shield me from Aru. It was my first scouting excursion away from the caverns in a long time. Stupidity caused me to wound my leg. I paid no attention to the fact that someone tracked my footprints. While I was hiding under a rocky ledge to attend to the cut, Bryntar discovered me. She registered great surprise when she saw me healing the wound. I had never encountered a female Ice Lord and gasped at her stunning beauty. Raven hair as wild as a summer storm framed high cheekbones and eyes to rival the blackest cloud. Even the tint of purple skin enhanced her loveliness."

Bryntar was an Ice Lord?

"You do not look like a myth," she said.

"I laughed. She raised the sharp blade in her hand. I had lived a hundred seasons alone and with fear. Yet, I jumped up and bared my chest, ripping off my armor. "Kill me and take the power you think it will give you, savage. It is not as if I have a life to look forward to living."

The lump in my throat makes it hard to swallow when I realize he felt as I do. Suddenly, the handwriting changes to a flowing script and a thrill courses through me knowing it must be Bryntar's.

"I was born warrior. Feared little. Taroc looked like any male, but for the turban and armor. I lowered my weapon. Stories of Enchanters inhabiting my island were part of our culture. I even wanted to meet one as a child.

"He stood there. Arrogant. Powerful. No different from Ice Lords. Yet the intelligence in his face captured my heart. Breathing stopped as our souls spoke to each other. There could be no other for me. Not even my impending marriage could interfere. Planned since birth, I had no desire to be Queen. Nor did I like the Ice Lord King who swore his love. The freedom to live with a man of my choice intoxicated me.

"Taroc helped me plan my accidental death, a cliff edge overlooking the northern ocean. My people knew of the sea creatures and never swam there. I hid clothes to take with me. My family died many years earlier in an avalanche. No one ever knew when they saw me fall that Taroc was in the water, ready to save me."

Her words shiver through me along with a great sadness. I will never know that kind of love. Shutting that desire deep inside, I skip pages.

The handwriting changes to Taroc's.

"It never occurred to me that there might be a way of getting rid of my powers, to have a chance of becoming normal, rather than living a thousand seasons alone. Until I found a story hidden in ancient writings. It told of

a misty lagoon deep inside the Ice Mountains that transformed matter by using desire.

"Bryntar knew of the tunnel leading into the interior of the Ice Mountains. My fear of being discovered by Aru disappeared with new hope. I believed my dearest was more excited than I. We would live out our lives together. What have I done to deserve such unselfish love?"

I read faster.

"We have worked hard to prepare for the strenuous trip. We must avoid the Kepyrs. Care has to be taken to evade the Ice Lords that patrol the mountains. I built a canoe to take us along the shoreline for greater safety.

"When we return, I will cover the walls of these dank caverns for my beautiful Bryntar. She deserves so much more than living underground. I am still in awe that she would give up her life as an Ice Lord Queen to be with me."

I swallow the lump in my throat and carefully turn the pages. No maps or charts indicate a way to find the lagoon. Only a long passage when they reach the misty pool. These words are difficult to read, as if smeared by water. My fingers touch tiny, rough grains. They smell like salt.

"What a fool I am. My Bryntar. Gone. GONE. She does not blame me. How can she be grateful? I would kill myself, but cannot leave her now. She shed tears of joy to know she would live as long as I. An angel in the body of a monster. I curse myself."

His emotions slash through me, but I cannot stop reading.

"In the event that an Enchanter follows in my footsteps, I record what happened. I shall not record how to find the lagoon or what we encountered during our journey.

"If any Enchanter reads this, beware. Accept your destiny with courage. Leave the waters unmolested or risk the sacrifice that will be made."

His words of warning make no impact. Frantic, I strain to decipher the fading script.

"Ready to immerse myself and change my life, I gazed at the silver mist. It hovered over the charmed water, the atmosphere sacred. My heart pounded.

"Bryntar stood behind me under an overhang of blue ice. I removed the shirt of armor and lifted a foot to step into the lagoon. A roar pierced the stillness, bursting into my ears. Aru. Ice shattered like a thousand flying birds. A chunk smashed into Bryntar. She screamed, sprawling on the ice. I raced to her and cradled her bleeding head in my arms.

"Only silence greeted me, but I could feel her heart beating against my chest. Her eyes flickered open and she said, "Too late for me. Enter the waters, my love."

"*Tears dripped down my face as I entreated her to stay with me. She was silent, her wounds too severe for my abilities. Desperate, I carried her to the lagoon and placed her into the water without touching the liquid myself. There was no way of knowing if I could help. I had to try.*

"*I placed my hands on her head, ignoring the profusion of blood. The waters roiled. Frigid mist consumed us. I thought of nothing except healing Bryntar and my desire that she never leave me. That was my mistake, my selfishness in wanting her to live as long as I would.*

"*Mist condensed, writhing as if alive. I could see nothing, but did not break contact with Bryntar. Cool, healing energy surged from me into her, more than I had ever known.*

"*Would I have continued if I had known what was to come? Never.*

"*She shrieked in agony—a cry so horrific I shall never wipe it from my soul.*

"*I did not know what was happening, but dared not let go of Bryntar's jerking body. Her soft skin transformed into fur and scales beneath my fingers. Her screams mingled with those of grinding bones.*

"*The energy expanded to such a degree that I thought we would both explode.*

"*Then came deathly silence. The mist dissipated. A monster lay in the water beneath my hands. The white fur covering she wore became her skin, the nail-studded helmet, a horn on her forehead. Her leather boots were the feet of a lizard.*

"*Everything transformed, even the color of her eyes. They blinked open, bluer than the sky. Stunned, I stared.*

"*She tried to speak, but only succeeded in emitting guttural croaks.*

"*I had unknowingly made her into a dragon-like monster with my desire to be together—the only creature that could live as long as I would. I did not understand until many seasons later that her desire to be with me was the cause of her radical transformation. The lagoon fulfilled her wish in the only way possible. Even so, I shall always blame myself.*

"*I released her and backed away, guilt and horror swarming like a sickness through my body. Remaining as I was would be my punishment. I would never leave her.*

"*Bryntar rose from the water on two legs and hovered over me, trembling. She saw her reflection and...*"

Taroc's words become black smears across the page. I close the book, shaking and unable to read more. Stunned, I stare down at my dressing gown and know it belonged to my dear Bryntar before she became a monster.

Sixteen: The Seeking

I lock away the terror of Bryntar's transformation. It happened a long time ago and will not sway my decision to find the lagoon. The possibility of becoming normal becomes a deep longing: never feeling someone's pain or thoughts as if they are my own, never needing to control my energy, never worrying about causing damage. I wonder about withstanding the pain of transformation. Surviving a battle with Aru is more frightening.

Darkness slips into the study unnoticed while thoughts collide in my mind. Is the lagoon still hidden deep within the Ice Mountains? How can I convince Bryntar to take me to the place that changed her life? Without her, I can never find it.

I finally understand the reason for all the secrets. I hope Taroc can somehow hear me. "Thank you for allowing me an innocent childhood."

My hand absently brushes my skirt as I get up from the floor, another puzzle to uncover. Where does Bryntar hide the clothes I wear? I leave the study to find her, concentrating on creating light to find my way in the dark.

The silence of the caverns sends shivers up and down my spine. Shadows slink over slits and cracks in the walls with my passage. Even repaired, my home will never be the same without Taroc. I cannot stop the unanswered questions in my mind concerning life and death. How can I save the island from a beast that creates earthquakes? How much time will pass before it comes after me? Can I find the lagoon and become normal so I am free?

Arriving at Bryntar's room, I knock on the door and hear soft, uncontrollable sobbing. "I am coming in, Bryntar."

She is not in the room. I circle around, tuning into her feelings. They come from behind an undamaged wall. More secrets. My fingers slide along the cold, textured metal. A lever moves and the wall swivels out to uncover elegance inside the hidden room. Hundreds of candles flicker like tiny, warm stars. Furniture carved in intricate patterns decorates the ancient room.

Bryntar stops crying. The sanctuary rests in unspoiled silence. I touch the rich wood of a wardrobe and sense that Taroc built it.

She lies on the floor next to the beautiful bed she shared with him, too large for it now. She clutches the blue and gold fabric that drapes over the bed and I die a little inside.

Centuries have passed since she shared this room with Taroc. I struggle to block her feelings and lay down next to her, taking a large claw in my hands. She shudders, but says nothing.

We remain there until most of the candles burn out and she sits up, hunching over her knees as if to ward off pain.

"Thank you, Elandra."

"I am so sorry about what happened."

She lifts her head. "You found his books."

"Yes, dear Bryntar."

Her eyes grow soft and wistful as she gazes around the room. She keeps her deepest sorrow buried now. The silence stretches.

She finally speaks. "You still want the lagoon?"

"I realize the lagoon chooses the transformation. That I must be exact in my desire to be normal."

Bryntar searches my face and nods. "More danger in finding lagoon now."

She rises and shakes scales and fur, still covered with the dirt of her cave repairs. I follow her as she stalks from the room and closes the door to her past.

Sudden drumbeats bang into my head and I grab a wall for support. Overwhelming reminders of my mother's death stagger me.

"What is it?" Bryntar asks.

"Drums. In my head."

"Where?"

Confusion muddles my thoughts as I try to locate the source of my feelings. The drums seem farther away now, yet they intermingle with something familiar. Daniel? His heartbeat throbs next to mine.

"I do not understand. I feel Daniel and the drums together. How can that be?"

Bryntar looks at me sharply. "Quick. Search caves."

She bounds ahead and I hurry to keep up, hampered by the gown around my legs.

Tension knots in my body. "Daniel. Daniel. Where are you?" He must be here somewhere. Maybe the library. He wanted a map of the island.

Dread daggers into me. I remember his frustration at being a prisoner, his grief at the deaths of his father and brother, his determination to get back to his mother and sister.

Bryntar runs to me. "Not in the lower caverns."

"He is gone."

She stops abruptly.

Not once did I consider the trauma he experienced, the heartbreak it must have been for him to land in a world so different from his own.

"I should have cared more about him. This is my fault."

"Feel him," Bryntar says.

I close my eyes and concentrate. Daniel's feelings are so clear it is almost like his eyes are mine. "He runs despite his leg pain. Scared at what chases him." I cry out when he falls, which breaks the connection. His last feelings of regret linger.

I can hardly breathe. "Something happened to him. I feel nothing now."

"You feel trees, grass, ice?"

Reliving Daniel's last feelings, dry dirt, cracked leaves and broken sticks become clear. "No ice."

"Caught by Kepyrs."

I shudder and must ask, though I do not want to. "Did they kill him?"

"Ceremony first."

"Do you know where he is?"

"Sacrificial pit is one day away."

Images of sacrifices from books I read as a child make my skin crawl. "Tell me they will not bury him alive."

"Burn alive."

Screams bounce from the walls. Mine. I choke, gasp in dry heaves from an empty stomach.

"We will save him."

Instant relief spreads through me. I vow to myself that if we succeed, I need to find a way for Daniel to go home.

New thoughts overwhelm me as I hurry after Bryntar. What if the Kepyrs catch her? How can I save Daniel without being captured?

Bryntar passes Taroc's study and leads the way to the storage room. She opens the door. "Pack food." She throws me three bags with straps.

I gather fresh and dried fruits and tubers, stuffing in as much as possible.

Bryntar moves large bins to uncover another door. Darkness gapes inside. She hauls out a canoe for two people made from a hollowed-out log. A strange metallic shirt rests in the bottom.

"Take. Protects heartbeat from beast."

"It did not protect Taroc at the lagoon."

She glares. "He took it off."

"I needed protection before we explored the island. It would have hidden me from Aru and stopped the earthquakes. Taroc would still be alive and…"

Smoke steams from her nostrils as she interrupts. "Aru needed to awaken your powers."

Horrified, I cannot believe she purposely exposed me to the beast. "You knew Aru would find me?"

"It is your destiny."

"I will change it."

"No choice over destiny." Her voice cracks with emotion.

My throat is so tight swallowing is impossible. Marveling at the lightness of the fabric, I snatch the protective shirt and complain. "This is too big."

"Remake to fit." Bryntar throws the bags of food inside the canoe with a few blankets and lifts it over her head to push past me.

"Wait. Where are you going?"

"To the study."

My legs falter when we reach Taroc's chambers, memories fresh in my heart.

Bryntar's steel resolve astounds me. She collects Taroc's boots, fur-lined coat, pants, hat and gloves, and throws them in the canoe.

"How can you shut out your feelings?"

She hisses. "To save Daniel."

I have controlled my thoughts and feelings too little to think I will ever be able to save anyone when their lives depend on me.

She lifts the canoe once again. "Stay inside. Get warm clothes. Back before daylight." She disappears past me. The thumping of her feet fades to nothing. I am alone in my destroyed home for the first time. An icy coldness seeps into me.

Determined to change my destiny, I return to the storage room, grab the protective shirt, a heavy circle of rope, a knife. I haul everything past the broken ridges in the stone path to Bryntar's room.

When I open her secret chamber, it is hard not to feel like a thief. Relief sweeps through me when I fling off the flimsy dressing gown and search her drawers for the warm clothes needed for the Ice Mountains. I find the most delicate undergarments ever seen and put them on. The softness and warmth of the fur lining of pants and boots warm my freezing legs and feet. The heaviest coat, vest, and hat are made from thick jaguarat fur. I find Bryntar's sewing kit and try to ignore thoughts of the revulsion Bryntar must have experienced after she transformed. I hurry from the chamber.

She leaves a candle that flickers high above the staircase. I stumble up the curved stairs and slump to the floor. My body screams for rest. I sink to the floor and thread the needle with slow fingers, refusing to think about what is happening to Daniel. My stitches take forever as I adjust the metallic shirt to fit my chest. When I twist the last knot, sleepy warmth seeps into me from the softness of the fur coat. I lean against the wall and close my eyes.

It seems like only seconds later that Bryntar shoves through the door. The wind whips like an icy claw. Her face glows, the purple cast more pronounced against her white fur.

Only once have I seen her more frightened, when she thought I was dead. She hollers over the wind. "Protect yourself. Hurry or Daniel dies."

Seventeen: The Rescuing

I wipe sleep from my eyes. "What happened?"

Bryntar stuffs the metallic shirt in my hands. "Must go. Now." She throws the rope coil around her shoulders.

"Tell me."

She rushes back out the stone door without a word.

I hurry to put on the metallic shirt under the fur coat, pull on the hat and shove the knife in my belt. I look down the curved staircase wondering if I will ever see my home again and slip out the door.

Wind slams me to the ground. Bryntar disappears among the dark trees.

"Wait." I strain to stay upright and center on the power within. Every cell tingles with energy, giving me renewed strength. I lean into the blasts of wind, keeping Bryntar in sight until I catch her.

"Control yourself," she says.

I follow her eyes. My body glows with light. Surprise causes it to fade.

"Please, tell me what happened."

"Witch controls Kepyrs."

Bryntar hisses, smoke from her nose dissipating in the wind. "She tells tribes you create Daniel. They kill at sunrise."

I cannot stop shaking. "If Daniel dies, I am to blame. This is my fault. I should have talked to him about his problems."

"We are to blame. Come."

"Can we make it before. . .?" I cannot say the words.

"Now."

Tiny whirlwinds of dust and dead leaves bounce around my legs. I control my rising panic by shutting my mind to all thoughts of Daniel. It will be impossible to continue if his fear overwhelms me.

We clear the forest to see a wide plain before us. Storm clouds swarm overhead. Bryntar lifts me to her back. I straddle the ridges and hang onto her neck as she bounds forward in great lurching strides.

"Do you have a plan to rescue him?" I ask.

"No."

Soon rain spills from the sky like a veil. Heavy winds throw raindrops as hard as pebbles against our faces. My nervousness increases. The vast open spaces leave us exposed to unknown dangers. I scour the terrain but see only immovable dark shapes through the downpour. It gives me little comfort to know anything out here has the same problem in this blinding storm.

The rhythm of Bryntar's great strides lulls me. The scent of sweet spring flowers drifts from the dampness of the fur coat. I close my eyes.

Much later, Bryntar stops running. I slip off and land on the ground.

"Ouch."

She pulls me up. "Stay alert. Kepyrs over mountain."

The rain drizzles. I gaze up at a mountain of rock. Boulders and sharp ledges jut through thick mist as if disembodied. I try not to lose Bryntar as we climb over uneven rocks, cling to clumps of grass, slide in sticky mud. Over and over. Higher. Harder.

Breathless, I long for light to replenish my hair, yet strain to reach the top before the sun rises. Severe pain shoots through my head and into my right arm. Daniel. I grab my arm and slip on moss, tumbling backward.

"Bryntar!"

Sharp rocks sting as I roll down the mountain. My knees bang into a ledge and I tumble off into mist.

I am going to die.

I hit the swaying branches of a large tree. Their sharp needles stab me, but I cling in desperation.

"Elandra. Where are you?"

"Here!"

I lose control from the pain, the loss of time, and especially the thought of more climbing. Light flashes from me in every direction. Bushes burn. Rocks split. Trees topple. I stare at the destruction in despair.

Bryntar leaps into view on the ledge above me. "Smart to use light."

How can I tell her I lost my temper? That I have no control at all? I balance on a slippery branch and reach for her outstretched arm.

"Hurt?" she asks.

"Not enough to stop."

She tosses me to her back. "Hold tight."

I grasp a ridged plate as she lunges upward.

The clouds disappear and the moon shimmers in a sky grown lighter. Bryntar eventually reaches the peak. Tension tightens every muscle. It will be sunrise sooner than I want.

I climb off her back and flatten myself on the ground, heart thumping hard. In the village below, the dark shapes of hundreds of huts squat in a wide meadow. Large fires burn on three sides of a dark pit in the center. I know Daniel is in the pit because his terror bites into me.

"Are the fires for protection?" I ask.

"Place to burn sacrifices. Cover with dirt."

My skin crawls. "You mean Daniel is standing on buried victims?"

Bryntar hisses. "Barbarians."

I creep down the mountain after her, bile souring my throat. A glint of a knife in the moonlight catches my attention. Guards lurk in the shadows. I plan a route to avoid them so I can remove Daniel from the pit before the village awakens.

Bryntar stops. "Stay. Hide here."

I try to remove the circle of rope from her arm. "You cannot go down there." She resists. "I can hide easier. Please, Bryntar."

A puff of steam rises from her nose. She sighs and releases the rope. "See the river?"

I locate water on the far side of the village.

"Any trouble. Go there. I come."

I heave the rope to my shoulders and sag with the heaviness. I keep low to the ground, knowing my white clothes do not blend with the darkness. My heart thumps. I sneak into the center of the village and avoid stepping on anything that would alert my presence. Flames roar like wild animals around the pit and I hide in their grasping shadows. My clothes stick to my body from the heat. The aversion to the pit crowds the edge of my mind. I force myself to concentrate.

Find Daniel. Find Daniel. Find Daniel.

I sneak toward the throne at the far end of the pit, lift the heavy rope to the ground and tie it to the stone pillar underneath.

I crawl fast. Unwind the rope and fling it over the edge of the pit, hoping it is long enough. "Daniel. It is Elandra." Please hear me. Please hear me. "Daniel. I am at the end of the pit by the throne. Climb up the rope."

Sweat pours down my face. I dare not go down to find him.

How long can I wait?

A sudden jerk on the rope startles me.

"Elandra?" His voice is raw.

"Come on. Hurry. We have to get away before the sun rises."

Daniel climbs up the rope.

My arm throbs and my head swirls with his pain. It does not stop him.

I hurry back to the stone pillar ready to untie the rope we will need if we make it to the Ice Mountains.

When Daniel appears, I pull hard on the rope to help him over the edge. "Come on."

His breath comes fast and hard as he crawls toward me.

I remove the rope, coil it and slip it over my neck and under my arm. Its weight burrows into my shoulder. Fear overrides the throb in my right arm and it fades. I wish the same for Daniel, for he has experienced too much pain on this island.

Drums split the air.

I drown in old memories and cannot move.

"Run," he says. He grabs my hand and drags me toward the river.

Kepyrs flow from their homes: families with noisy children, elders, and leaders.

The witch, Laruna, hobbles out of her hut in a robe of blood red. An elaborate headdress denotes her elevated station as Priestess. She sees me and shrieks. "Enchantress!"

Children cry amid the confused shouts of their parents.

Laruna screams again. "Catch her. Bring her to me."

My stomach grinds. I do not understand the fear that slams into me from these strangers. My legs shake so hard I cannot move.

Daniel hauls me forward. "Come on."

I force my reluctant legs to move. I do not look back, but feel the warriors and guards closing in. Arrows and spears strike the ground around us.

Eighteen: The Escaping

We dodge between and around hut after hut. Unarmed villagers and children flee from us, screaming.

Daniel stumbles, pulling us both down on the rock-strewn dirt. "I'm holding you back."

"Do not give up." I pull on him, my nerves raw. "Our only chance of escape is the river."

Laruna screeches behind us, issuing commands that echo through the valley. "Kill boy. Bring me Enchantress."

I shut out her voice.

Daniel trips again. "Sorry."

An arrow whizzes into the rope on my shoulder. I yank it out. "Stay low."

The sun rises in crimson glory. My hair floods with light and I streak ahead with renewed energy. I cannot control a circle of light to protect us while we run.

Daniel lags, holding his head. He gasps. "Save yourself."

Exhaustion reflects in his pale face and I snatch his hand. "Not without you."

"I was wrong about you not having courage."

"You were not."

"Only a girl would argue at a time like this." He smiles and a little light of hope shines from his eyes.

"Unless you want to die, run faster," I warn.

Blood oozes from his right arm.

"Are you hit?" I ask.

"Do you count the arm and head wound when they captured me?"

I laugh, despite everything. It feels good to release a little of the knot twisting in my stomach.

A muscled warrior leaps in front of us. "Do not move." His drawn arrow points at Daniel's chest.

We do not move. I feel the vibration of pounding feet through my boots and know there is not much time before we are surrounded. I point my finger at the warrior, struggling to control the energy. Thin light blasts into his chest. He screams and crumples. I hope he is not dead. There is no time to find out.

A dozen warriors rush us whooping and screaming. They halt when they see their downed companion.

I throw a bolt of lightning on the ground to warn them.

They still circle, their weapons aimed at us.

I whirl around, sweeping my finger across each one. They shriek and collapse, surprise frozen on their faces.

"Wow," Daniel says. "I'm impressed."

"Come on."

We dash around a larger, elaborate hut. A huge warrior guards the entrance, his crossed arms holding a dagger. My light flashes into him. He grunts and sinks to the ground. We run past and Daniel picks up his knife.

I can feel the surge of the river, even though it hides behind a hill.

Daniel slumps to the ground. "Too dizzy. Can't make it."

Many more warriors rush over the hill, shouting. I cannot take the chance that they will kill Daniel before I can hit each one. I enclose him in my arms.

He pushes me away. "Go. Leave me."

An arrow thumps into the fur of my sleeve before I can protect us with light.

A fierce shriek pierces the air. Bryntar jumps out from behind a huge rock on the other side of the river. She splashes through the water in rapid leaps.

The villagers shriek, terrified.

The warriors turn and see her. A massive warrior releases his spear. The silver-pointed tip of the shaft glitters in sunlight before it thuds into her shoulder. She wrenches out the spear as if it were an annoying twig. Blood spurts, bright against her fur.

Fury surges through me. Bolts of white-hot energy sizzle from my hand and blow the warrior apart. I whirl around, ready to kill everyone.

Bryntar screams. "No, Elandra!"

I concentrate on her face, wondering how I could live without her. I shake in barely controlled anger.

"Do not shoot another arrow or I will kill you all!"

I glare at each Kepyr. Lightning bolts fly from my fingers on the ground between the warriors. The deafening explosions of light, dirt, and rock make them prostrate themselves before me.

Bryntar grabs us and runs to the river. "Swim." Ripping the rope from me, she throws us into the water.

The cold makes my bones ache instantly. Without the rope to weigh me down, I fight to stay submerged. Arrows slice through the water and float away on the swift current. I strain to see Daniel far under me, kick hard toward him, and seize his shirt. We rise to the surface.

Daniel gags and coughs up water.

The witch screams. "Kill. Kill. Kill."

Warriors run alongside the river. Spears slash by our heads.

I yank Daniel underwater.

He swims hard next to me. We dare not surface and stay under until he pulls on me and shoots to the surface.

"Don't you breathe?" Daniel gasps, coughing up water.

"Not air."

"Leave it to me to fall for. . ."

Rough hands drag me underwater. I fight to free myself. Arms crush me tight against a muscled chest. I reach for the knife in my belt. It is gone. Instead its sharp edge touches my throat.

A warrior drags me to the surface. "Fight me, I kill you."

"You are dead," I say.

He laughs and presses the knife into my neck.

I ignore the slight cut of the blade, knowing my power can kill him, especially in the water. I worry the shock will kill Daniel, too. I sag and let the warrior haul me to shore, trying to think of a way to get free.

Suddenly, the river bleeds. Arms release me and I float away from my captor. Daniel releases the dagger that sticks through the warrior's throat. He gathers me close and I wonder why I want him to hold me forever. "Did he hurt you?"

"Not much."

He trembles. "We have to get farther away."

The current takes us quickly and I wish we could ride it all the way to the ocean and far away from the island. Guilt bites deeper than the cold. Daniel killed to save my life. I killed from uncontrolled anger. I am a murderer and it sickens me.

We float away from our destination. The Ice Mountains mock me before they disappear. I hope Bryntar escaped and is not far behind us. I watch the shore as the river curves away, taking us farther and farther downstream.

Daniel grows weaker. "Sorry. Not gonna' make it."

His hand slips from mine. Frantic, I snatch at his fingers.

Water whaps me in the face and fills my throat. I cough, reach for him, and grab his wrist. It takes all my strength to drag him ashore.

The bitter wind hits my skin. I cannot stop shivering as I haul Daniel through tall, thin trees and behind dense bushes. Drained, I cover our trail and stumble back to him.

His face is white, green eyes dull with pain. He smiles faintly. "Even with your superpowers, I would have taken you on a date."

"What is a date?"

He closes his eyes.

"Daniel!"

Nineteen: The Surprising

I place my hand over Daniel's chest. Nothing. I cannot feel his heart beating over the thumping of my own.

"Daniel. Please wake up." I lay my head next to his heart to hear its faint, erratic beat. "Tell me how to help you."

My every nerve aligns with Daniel's. I smooth the wet hair from his face and touch the swollen bump on his head. An unfamiliar chill streaks to my fingers and I yank back in surprise. The sensation disappears. I touch the throbbing wound with my whole hand and feel nothing. Try my fingertips again. Icy tingles stream into Daniel. I tremble and blink in disbelief as his wound begins to heal. When my fingertips start to burn, I jerk them away. The heat fades.

A clear vision of Taroc's finger touching my forehead tightens my throat. The light was so bright before he died, I had forgotten until now. Did he transfer his healing power to me? My choice to become normal washes me in doubt.

My fingertips run along the jagged cut on Daniel's arm. I am grateful to feel the warmth of his blood, the connecting of tissue and muscle, the sealing of his cut. When the burning starts, I know the healing is finished. Tears drip down my face.

"I'm not dead, yet." He sits up and wipes a tear from my cheek.

Relief rushes through me when his color returns. His eyes penetrate my very soul. My heart beats in time with his. He leans over and his lips touch mine, so gently I think I am melting. The island, the cold, the fear vanish in the safety of him.

He stops the kiss.

My lips part in desperate need. He pulls me into his arms and kisses me again. The melody of my heart sings as we spiral into an unknown peace.

I am confused by the need to be one with Daniel and never want to stop kissing him. A precious joy intermingles with growing heat and scares me. Yet there is also purity. And with that knowing comes the calm acceptance that I love Daniel. With everything that I am. I do not know when or how it happened. I only know it is true.

Daniel caresses my hair. "You are so beautiful."

I ache with fierce longing.

Feelings of being less than a man and the inability to protect me rise in him.

"Please do not feel unworthy."

He chuckles in surprise. "It's almost like you can read my mind."

I lower my eyes, a needle of fear shooting into my chest. "It is similar."

He stands up, wobbles, and gains strength. "What do you mean?"

I cannot lie to him. "I can feel you."

"What's that supposed to mean?"

"I cannot read minds. I feel thoughts, even physical pain."

"Why didn't you tell me?"

"We had no time. Then you ran away."

"You should have told me."

I drown in his growing anger. "I cannot control it."

"Learn how. My feelings are none of your business."

He starts to walk away. "Don't think our kiss meant anything to me."

"Where are you going?"

"Away from you."

How can you leave me after what we shared?

Hurt, then slow anger flares. I choke on my words. "You want to leave the one who risked her life to save you? To heal you?"

His eyes dart to his arm. Pride overruns his feelings. "Stay out of my head."

"I am sorry. I cannot help the way I was born. It is hard to separate my feelings from those of others."

He stares into my face with a stranger's eyes. "Try harder."

I shudder at his disgust.

"Can you read my feelings now?" he asks.

I do not answer.

"Control yourself." He stomps off.

Is this the same Daniel who kissed me? We shared a moment I will never be able to forget. I do not understand how his feelings can change when mine have not. A heavy darkness wraps itself around me.

I think of Bryntar. How can she cope with the loss of Taroc after loving him for nine hundred seasons?

A faint drumbeat flows on the wind. I cringe, abruptly aware of movement in the trees. I push Daniel behind a bush and clamp my hand over his mouth. He shoves me away.

Bryntar leaps out of the trees.

I jump up and throw myself into her arms, the only real place of safety I have ever known. I do not care that the rope around her shoulder rubs my face.

She winces and pulls away.

I reach up to touch her bleeding wound. "Do not move." Cool energy streams into the gash.

Her eyes fill with silver tears. "Taroc gave you his gift?"

"Only in my fingertips."

"That is enough."

"Super girl kills with a single blow and heals the sick," Daniel says. "Why not fly us out of here while you're at it?"

I avoid his eyes. "Only birds fly."

"Not in my world."

Bryntar glances at us. "Kepyrs not stop."

"We need a safe place to rest," Daniel says.

"How can we hope to escape them?" I ask.

"We outsmart," Bryntar says.

The endless beat of the drums increases in volume.

"Let's get out of here," Daniel says.

Bryntar plunges through the trees.

Daniel ignores me and hurries after her.

The drums batter my broken heart.

Twenty: The Hiding

There is no escape from my connection to Daniel. No matter how hard I try to dismiss it. I pretend to ignore him.

The sun pours heat from above and dries our wet clothes. Too soon, I wish for the cold river and take off my coat and boots. I dare not remove the metallic shirt that protects my heartbeat from Aru.

The constant beating of drums makes me want to scream. I trudge after Bryntar. "How much farther?"

"Until dark," she says.

My stomach grinds in emptiness. I cannot swallow for the dryness in my throat.

Spindly trees change into barren hills and sparse grass. I am more nervous than ever, being so exposed. I hate the hot metallic shirt, the next hill, the sharp rocks, the drums, and Daniel, for he talks only to Bryntar.

Smothered in sweat, I am relieved when fluffy clouds swarm over the sun. Their giant shadows give me the illusion of protection. Will I ever feel safe again?

The drumbeats stop abruptly. Silence is welcome, yet my bare feet still feel the vibration of our pursuers. "The warriors are not far from us."

"Terrific," Daniel says.

"Run." Bryntar leaps up a hill and disappears. Daniel vanishes after her.

I rush to the top and look down in dismay. Bryntar and Daniel stand before a wide impression that spreads as far as I can see, as if something massive fell from the sky and crushed the land. Thousands of trees grow like deformed bones and carve through tangled marsh and brambles higher than my head.

Heartbeats from within the swamp crowd my senses. Of the places I have seen on this island, this one scares me the most. I hurry down the hill.

"We cannot go in there."

"Have a better plan?" Daniel asks.

"It is too dangerous, Bryntar."

"I know," she says. "Only chance."

Daniel points to the Kepyr warriors racing over the rise. "Our chances for survival just hit zero."

My skin crawls.

"Stay alert," Bryntar says. She plunges downhill through a gap in thick, mangled trees.

Daniel moves faster than I do and disappears after her.

I glance back at the advancing warriors and push through the trees. My bare feet squish into warm mud and decay. The droning of insects saturates the air. I slap away the stinging bites.

"Wait," Daniel says. He stares at the clothes in my arms. "Put on your boots. They can protect you from snakes and ants."

Pleased that he has any thoughts about me, I slip my muddy feet into the soft fur and take a step. It is difficult to walk. Mud sucks with every step.

"What if we get lost?" I ask.

"I will get us out," Bryntar says.

"Unless we die first." Daniel snatches a branch and bats away a large colorful frog that leaps toward me.

I wince. "Why did you do that?"

"Stay away from anything with bright colors."

"Why?"

His shoulders slump. "Color means poison where I live."

"How will we escape the warriors?" I ask.

Bryntar shakes her head. "They do not follow. Surround bog and wait."

"Great," Daniel says. "Why trudge through this muck and get killed when we get out? Let's end it. Where's the quicksand?"

"What is quicksand?"

"You're going to save the island? I feel so much safer now." He glares and adds, "Enchantress."

I flush at the hated name and scowl at him. "Do not call me that."

"Since you can't fly, I'm not sure Angel fits."

Bryntar pushes between us. "What is problem?"

"Nothing," Daniel says.

I turn from him so he does not see my face. I will not give in to tears.

"Stay close. Walk in my footsteps," she says.

"Ladies first," Daniel says to me. He bows.

I stomp past him. Sour air stings my nose. I swipe away a swarm of buzzing insects. Dense vines choke reeds, roots, and plants. A sudden shaft of light brightens the many patterns of green and brown, unexpected and beautiful. Until the ground looks like it moves. Spiders and bugs crawl everywhere. I shudder when a bird shrieks in agony.

Daniel laughs. "Welcome to the bog."

I glare at him. "Do you know how it feels to experience death?"

"Only the loss it brings. That never goes away."

I try to detect a glimpse of sympathy. There is none or he hides it well. I wish I knew how he stops his feelings.

Rain trickles overhead and pours in a sudden deluge. The sound is a welcome relief after the continuous buzzing.

"Drink while you can." Daniel opens his mouth to the rain.

Bryntar and I do the same.

When I finish, an unexpected pink flower catches my eye. I take a step to breathe its fragrance.

"Stop!" Daniel yells.

Slime sucks me into a mucky hole so fast that I barely close my eyes and mouth in time. I sink fast. Brown sludge smothers me. I cling to the heavy clothes and sink deeper, unwilling to give them up in hopes of reaching the Ice Mountains. There is a sudden tug on my hair. Please, please be Daniel. I move slowly upward.

Something brushes my boots with tentative curiosity. I flinch, chilled that I cannot open my eyes to see. My heart flutters like a trapped insect as the creature moves up my leg.

Get away, get away!

I drop the clothes and kick against the ooze. A body slides up my side. I panic, jab a finger of white-hot energy into it. Mud explodes around me and I am thrown up and out of the hole.

I hit Daniel and we roll across the marsh. I wipe my eyes to see him covered in slime. He gags and struggles to breathe. Bryntar wipes mud that clings to the top half of her trembling body.

"Almost lost you both," she says.

The marsh ripples under us.

"Run." I yank on Daniel. We stumble away.

A gigantic snake rises out of the sludge, scaly body as big around as a tree. A forked tongue flicks under beady eyes.

Daniel stares in disbelief. "Snakes don't grow that long."

Bryntar snatches us and races away.

"You can't outrun it," Daniel says.

The snake glides over the ground so fast that I know we cannot escape.

"Put me down."

Something in my voice makes Bryntar stop and release me. I spread both hands and send small hot flashes from each finger into the reptile. Tiny fires sizzle into the glistening scales.

The snake hisses. Huge coils twist over our heads and slam into the ground. Muck and plants spray over us. Daniel and I trip and slip away to avoid being smashed as the coils wind over our heads and pounds the ground again. Scales twist around Bryntar and squeeze.

"Kill it!" Daniel yells.

The rope around her neck saves her momentarily. She claws to free herself but the snake tightens its grip.

"Leave her alone!" I blast the snake between the eyes. The coils loosen and the snake slithers back into the murky water.

Daniel grins. "Way to go!"

I run to Bryntar. "Are you all right?"

She breathes deeply, her eyes shining. "You will save island."

I fall to the ground, unable to stop shaking. I almost lost her.

"The snake is not dead."

"You kill Aru."

"I do not want to kill anything. Or save people who hate me. I do not want to be an Enchantress." I plunge through the swamp.

"Wait." Daniel catches me and grabs my arm.

Angry, I pull away. "Leave me alone. Your feelings for me are quite clear."

"Hey. Who pulled you out of that hole?"

"So I can save you, too?"

His face flushes. "C'mon. It's almost dark. We need water, food, and a safe place to sleep."

"Nothing is safe on this wretched island."

"We survive," Bryntar says. She gazes into my eyes. "Take more care." She pats Daniel on the back. "Thank you for saving Elandra."

"Anyone would have done the same."

"No," Bryntar says. "Few choose courage over fear."

For the first time since we argued, I feel Daniel. Embarrassed, he looks at me. "Now we're even. I still owe Bryntar."

"Not owe," she says. "Survive together. You know swamps. Choose place to rest."

His feelings change before he locks them away. A new resolve of confidence floods through him.

We eventually reach a higher, dry patch of land that suits Daniel.

"I gather food." Bryntar hurries deeper into the swamp.

Fatigue fills every part of me. "I am thirsty."

"We can't drink the water," he says. "These vines have liquid." He takes an instrument from a place in his pants and flicks open a small knife.

"What kind of knife is that?"

He turns it over in his hand with care. "My dad says everyone should have a Swiss Army knife." His voice catches, but he shows me the different parts.

The construction and different tools amaze me.

He cuts a slit at the top of a vine and one at the bottom. "Put your mouth under it." He holds the vine.

Tart, sticky liquid dribbles into my mouth. The bitter taste puckers my mouth.

Daniel laughs.

"You might have warned me."

"It's better than dehydrating." He cuts more vines until we have our fill.

"You need to burn this area to get rid of bugs," he says. "I'll gather leaves for a shelter."

Bryntar returns with reeds and tubers. "No, we keep going."

"No way. Not at night."

She shoves the food at us. "Warriors rest. We do not."

We eat, each caught in our own thoughts. I am too tired to feel anything, but I smile when Daniel makes a funny face while eating stringy shoots.

"Frog legs taste better," he says.

"Eeuww."

He smiles at me. "I do cook them."

I melt inside, but control my expression.

Bryntar rises. "Come."

"We'd better cover up with more mud," Daniel says.

"I already smell horrible," I say.

"Not to the bugs." Daniel smears mud over his skin.

I do the same and try not to smell the rancid odor.

Bryntar leads us through strands of moss that hang like green hair. I almost cry out in joy to see the broad pool ahead. Anything is better than the weight of dried mud on my hair. I kneel over the water. Its warmth soothes me. My hair shines silver once again. I cannot wait to get away from this swamp and be thoroughly clean.

Birds suddenly shriek overhead.

"Croc!" Daniel yells and races toward me.

I push dripping hair from my face. "What is a croc?" Two large bumps the size of plates stick out of the water and glide toward me.

"Crocodile." Daniel snatches my arm and drags me into the trees with Bryntar.

"Too small to worry about," I say.

"Those are its eyes. Come on."

I look back at the pond and gasp. A giant crocodile leaps out of the water, half as long as the snake. It flicks its tail, mashing plants. Huge teeth protrude from massive jaws.

Daniel yanks me through bushes, heedless of their thorns.

"Ow. Ow. Stop."

"Don't you have regular-sized animals here?" He holds my hand so tight it becomes numb as we stumble through the swamp.

Bryntar rips through trees and bushes to make us a path.

The crocodile hisses, lunging through the bog, trampling everything in its path to get to us.

"Watch out!" Daniel pulls me into his arms. A wild boar plunges through the bushes. One tusk grazes my leg before the boar disappears into the undergrowth. My heart slams in my chest when its death squeal pierces the night.

Deep growls from the crocodile shatter through my pain. I sense the overpowering lust for more food. I yank away from Daniel. "Get out of the way, both of you." I run in the opposite direction and see the creature sniffing the air. I shoot a small bolt of light to distract it.

It twists toward me, massive claws squishing into the ground.

I leap into the branches of a tree. Slip on damp moss. Scramble up, ignoring the rough bark that digs into my hands.

"Higher!" Daniel yells.

The crocodile rams the tree, knocking me through the branches.

I scream and snatch at any tree limb. Crash into vines and cling desperately. The tree shakes as I scramble up a larger branch, terrified.

The crocodile leaps on the trunk and claws the tree.

Fear saps my energy and slows me down.

Daniel shouts, "You have to kill it!"

I straddle a branch and point a shaky hand into the jaws snapping under my feet. A trickle of heat wavers from my fingers into its mouth.

The reptile shakes its head. It lunges up higher, front claws ripping out huge chunks of the tree.

I leap for a high branch and dangle over its head.

Maddened, the crocodile emits a horrible hissing growl so loud it shakes the tree.

The hairs on my neck quiver. The tree cracks and slams to the ground. I fall into a mass of slimy branches. The crocodile bellows, catches my scent, whirls toward me. Entangled, I cannot free myself.

"Over here," Daniel yells. He throws mud to capture its attention.

Bryntar hurls large branches that bounce off its leathery hide.

The crocodile lunges toward them.

I wrench myself free. Raise my hands and spread the fingers of both hands at the crocodile. Instead, white heat blasts in two shining columns from the center of each palm. They bite into the back of the crocodile's head. With a shrieking growl, it plows into the ground. I tremble with pain that is over in an instant.

Daniel runs toward me. "You're really something." He starts to help me up until I see the halo of light surrounding me reflect in his eyes.

"Do not touch me. I could hurt you."

He pulls away and I am reminded once more of how different I am. If I do not succeed in becoming normal, I will never have any other life, and never one with Daniel.

Shafts of moonbeams turn Bryntar's eyes silver. "Energy builds. Good you learn control."

The glow around me fades. "I-I do not k-know how to control a-anything. It just happens." Furious that I cannot stop shaking, I force myself to stand still and wipe my face. "Get me out of here." I do not look back.

Bryntar leads me away, around black eddies of foul water and hanging vines sticky with sap. I stumble in exhaustion.

"We can talk about the croc if you want," Daniel says.

"What about you killing the warrior?"

He swallows hard and turns away. "I don't want to talk about that."

I know exactly how he feels.

Bryntar finally stops before a quiet, narrow lake. Moonlight glows green on the mat of tiny plants that cover the surface of the water. I jump when a frog peeks its head out of the tiny fronds.

Daniel laughs.

I glare at him.

"Sorry."

He is not sorry about anything.

"How do we get across the lake?"

"Swim," Bryntar says.

"There could be poisonous snakes and more crocodiles," Daniel says. "Can't we go around?"

"End of swamp is across lake," she says. "Only chance. Kepyrs not travel in dark."

I say nothing and hope I do not have to kill again.

Bryntar shifts the rope to her other shoulder. "You hold onto back. Elandra, use feelings to protect."

"I'm on the swim team at school," Daniel says.

"You swim in teams?" I ask.

"Individually and for overall team points."

"Safer together." Bryntar strides into the lake.

Daniel and I wade in, grasp a ridge on her back and float next to her as she swims across. The warm water glides over me. My body relaxes. It would be so easy to fall asleep. I concentrate and let feelings seep in: wind through the wings of night birds, Bryntar's confidence in my ability to save the island, the darting of fish below us, Daniel's unguarded sadness. I sense no danger underwater. A bright colored snake slithers away from us, leaving a curved line of black water through the lake's green cover.

Bryntar strokes hard, her power propelling us through the water quickly.

I slip into another's feelings outside the swamp, directly in our path.

Twenty-One: The Meeting

I whisper. "Someone is beyond the swamp."

Bryntar shakes off the lake water. "Impossible." She slips through the tangled trees without making a sound.

I rise from the lake, leaving behind the foul-smelling swamp.

Daniel and I follow Bryntar's trail and creep next to her prone figure to survey the grassy meadow before us.

The stark Ice Mountains draw my attention to the north and west, still distant and foreboding. I shake off their distraction and look toward the warmth of the fire and the warrior who sharpens a large curved knife in front of it.

"Kepyrs not travel at night."

"Looks like your guy doesn't follow the rules," Daniel says.

I touch her arm. "No more killing, Bryntar."

She nods and removes the rope from her shoulder.

"I'll distract him while you sneak up behind," Daniel says.

"No," I say. "I am going alone."

Bryntar nods in approval.

"You can't," Daniel says. "Look at him."

Muscles bulge on the tall man as he removes his shirt.

"He is smaller than the crocodile," I say.

Daniel touches my arm. "Be careful."

Warmth tingles up my arm. Why did he do that?

I stride forward into streaks of moonlight.

The warrior hears me as soon as I step from the trees. He raises his knife, but does not turn toward me.

I move closer and cringe. Deep scars ravage the dark skin of his entire torso. Some scars look like the claws and teeth marks of animals. Others are more uniform and unfamiliar.

He turns to me with the weathered face of a man older than the young warriors we fought at the Kepyr village. Shock changes to joy in his deep brown eyes.

Where have I seen eyes like his before?

"You live!" He sets his knife down and kneels before me. "Forgive me, Elandra."

He knows my name?

My throat tightens and I can barely speak.

Bryntar leaps between us. "Move away, Kepyr."

The warrior looks up in surprise. "Forest Spirit is not a legend?"

She laughs and clutches her throat for the pain it causes her.

The warrior turns to Daniel. "And a foreigner? I see why the Kepyrs pursue you."

"Why didn't you see us at your village?" Daniel asks.

"I was on my way to hunt at the Sunken City until I heard the drums calling me to guard this place."

Bryntar glares at him. "Liar. Kepyrs not hunt at night."

"Some of us do not believe in the old ways."

"All Kepyrs are barbarians."

He smiles. "Like Forest Spirit is a legend?"

She hisses and turns away.

Questions itch my mind. "Who are you?"

He rises with pride. "I am Kydaka, older brother of your mother."

The arrow that killed my mother pierces my heart once more. He cannot possibly be family. "If you speak the truth, how could you let her die?"

Kydaka's eyes darken and fade into the past. "When the birthing woman told the tribe about you, I was captured and beaten for information. His voice breaks. I recoil to feel the whip that lashed his back until it was raw.

He lifts his chin. "I never betrayed my sister. Or my family." He shudders with unbearable grief. "Priestess told us you were dead, showed us a piece of your hair."

"What are you not telling us?" I ask.

He looks at me sharply. "My mate was heavy with our first child when I was declared a traitor. No one helped her and they both died when the baby came."

Bryntar growls. "Savages."

"Why are you alive?" Daniel asks.

"Kepyrs value strength and courage. Dead, I am less useful."

Bryntar towers over Kydaka. "You make up stories."

He meets her eyes without flinching. "You save Enchantress, the flesh of my ancestors. I thank you." He smiles at me. "You are our savior."

I look away, unable and unwilling to believe his words.

"Should have killed you all," Bryntar says.

Kydaka turns to her. "Many do not believe the ways of our ancestors. Now there is hope that Elandra can fulfill the plan of my sister."

I stalk away, furious. "What about my plan? You think it is all right to create a child and sentence her to death? I will not save this island. I am going to a magic lagoon hidden in the Ice Mountains to become normal. Aru will not want me then."

Astonished, Kydaka stares at me. He starts to speak then changes his mind. "You must leave while it is dark, before the other warriors come."

"You do not fear the dark?" Bryntar asks.

"There is more to fear on this island than the darkness of night," he says.

"Pretend you did not see us," I say.

"I do not lie."

"We could tie you up," Daniel says.

Kydaka shakes his head. "Failure means death." He picks up his knife. "I will go with you. Guard Elandra with my life."

"I protect her," Bryntar says. "Not trust you."

"You can." Kydaka winks at her and slices his arm from elbow to wrist.

I cry out and grab my arm.

"Jeez," Daniel says looking at both of us.

"You feel my pain?" Kydaka asks.

I nod and remember that his pain is not my own. I succeed in redirecting my thoughts to the patterned thunderclouds over our heads. It dulls the ache and that is enough.

Kydaka drips his blood over the ground.

"What are you doing?" Daniel asks.

"They will think I am dead."

Bryntar tightens, but says, "Clever."

I strain to hear her, but noises are muffled. I am consumed with concentrating on the growing storm to rid myself of the pain shooting through Kydaka's arm.

Bryntar returns, struggling with a large crocodile. Her claws clamp its jaws closed. It whips its tail to free itself.

"I admire your great strength," Kydaka says to her.

She blushes under her icy purple skin. "Your shirt?"

Kydaka rips his shirt into pieces and rolls them on his bleeding arm. He tosses the scraps on the ground near Bryntar's feet. "Get away."

Daniel and I move far away before she releases the crocodile. It lunges when it smells the blood-soaked scraps, snapping them between its teeth. Then it rushes her.

Kydaka grabs a burning stick from the fire and touches the crocodile. The reptile hisses and plunges back into the swamp, leaving a distinct trail. He follows the crocodile, letting his arm bleed on the ground.

"Smart move," Daniel says.

I take Kydaka's arm when he returns and slowly run my fingertips down his knife wound. His eyes grow in awe as he watches the cut heal. He prostrates himself at my feet.

"I am yours to command, Enchantress."

"Do not kneel before me."

He rises. "How can you save the island with healing power?"

If anyone talks about me saving the island again, I will scream.

Smoke rolls from Bryntar's nose. "She has greater power than any."

Kydaka drops his knife near the fire.

"You're going to need that," Daniel says.

Kydaka shakes his head. "A warrior does not leave his weapon unless he is dead."

Bryntar scowls at him. "You still earn trust." She throws the rope over her shoulders.

He watches her stride off and I sense the interest he has in her.

I remove my boots and wipe off the caked swamp. Soft blades of grass cool my feet. Unexpected longing for home flutters through me.

Oh Taroc, how I miss our gardens.

I shut off my mind, preferring to concentrate on following Bryntar. I do not know whether I am getting better at controlling my thoughts or if I am too tired to care.

We travel over flat land and reach a meadow with fruit-bearing trees. Bryntar shakes one and we have our fill.

"Better than soggy tubers," Daniel says. He smiles at me.

Confused by my feelings, I do not smile back.

We travel through the night. I plod along, weariness heavy in every step. Shadowed hills poke up in the distance. The Ice Mountains lure my eyes. Especially when our travels take us toward them.

"When can we sleep?" I ask.

"Daylight. We hide in Sunken City," Bryntar says.

I long to talk to Kydaka about my mother, but the darkness holds me apart. I look for any resemblance to her but see only her eyes and her courage in him. Perhaps that is enough.

The night grows blacker as storm clouds track us. Thunder splits the air. My skin prickles and energy swirls through me.

"Get away from me!" I scream. I run from my companions as fast as I can.

Bryntar stops Daniel and Kydaka from following me.

Safely away from them, I raise my arms as small flashes of lightning shoot toward me.

Daniel yells. "Watch out!"

Jagged bolts explode in a shattering crack over my head. White-hot shafts of power sear through my body. Again. Again. Again. I burn, until I feel the need to accept my oneness with the light. Love overpowers me and I relax. More energy strikes, but the heat cools to a delicious tingle. I open my eyes to a halo of brilliance that illuminates me and turns the entire sky a deep blue.

A drop of rain sizzles on my skin. Then another. My light fades as sheets of rain flow over me. I drink in huge gulps and relish the cleansing.

Bryntar and Kydaka rush toward me. My chest tightens to see Daniel remain apart.

Kydaka kneels. "Oh, magnificent Enchantress. I am your humble servant."

I pull him up. "Never."

"As you wish." His words do not reflect his feelings.

I am concerned with how Daniel feels as I walk toward him.

"I can't believe it. You should be dead."

"I did not choose this. I want a different life."

"If you really can save this island. . ."

"Would you like this burden?"

He looks down. "I don't know."

"That answer is an excuse for not thinking."

"At least our trail washed away," he says.

I give up trying to understand him and trudge toward a silhouette of angular hills.

Much later, the night changes to muted rays of rose, lavender, and gold. The colors spread across a flat expanse of land sparse with patches of vegetation. A bright creature with three green and yellow striped tails scuttles into a hole.

The hills become distinct architectural forms. Soon the sun brightens huge chunks of iridescent gray stones protruding from the ground like living beings. Smoothed by centuries of wind, hundreds of sharp-angled pillars reach to the sky or lean against each other, crossing, crisscrossing, and creating an intricate maze of dark rooms in the forgotten city.

"Cool. It looks like an abstract sculpture," Daniel says. "Who built it?"

"The creators are not known," Kydaka says.

Bryntar leads us down a narrow path under fantastic slanted arches. Fleeting impressions of foreign life flick through my senses, too faint to capture.

"We rest before reaching the ocean," Bryntar says. She climbs up the crenellated sides of an eight-sided pillar and disappears.

"Forest Spirit is amazing," Kydaka says.

"Her name is Bryntar."

Kydaka scales the slanted column quickly.

Bryntar peers over the edge. "Climb. No wild animals in here."

Overcome by the massive structures, I have missed the feelings now gnawing at my nerves. I gaze around and see indistinct shadows hiding in the multitude of dark alcoves. My body quivers.

This ancient city is home to hundreds of jaguarats.

Twenty-Two: The Watching

"Hurry," I say. The fear in my eyes spurs Daniel up the pillar. My boots slip on the dry sand that covers the surface.

He leans over and reaches for me. I take his hand and he pulls me up and into a high, six-sided room.

"Thank you."

"My pleasure."

I ignore the confusion his smile causes and confront Bryntar. "You could have warned me about the jaguarats. We cannot kill hundreds of them to keep everyone safe."

"What's a jaguarat?" Daniel asks.

Kydaka points across the overlapping shafts of stone. "Look there."

Daniel stares at the animals and whistles. "I suppose they're meat-eaters?"

His unguarded fear slithers through me. "Why did you bring us here, Bryntar?"

"Kepyr not expect us here. Also quick way to canoe."

"If we survive." I look at Kydaka. "You hunt here alone?"

"When a hunter knows his prey, he knows how to kill it," he says. "They hunt at night and the young ones are overconfident."

"You and Daniel have no weapons to protect yourselves."

Daniel pulls his knife out of his pants. "I have this."

I laugh. "Their claws are longer than that."

His face reddens. "How would I know? Dumb island is crawling with monsters."

"You have no monsters in your world?" Kydaka asks.

"Our monsters are the human kind. We have advanced weapons that can kill anything."

"You must tell me of these weapons."

"Enough talk about killing." I stomp to the back of the dust-layered room.

The bleached bones of the long dead crunch underfoot and I kick them away. Darkness cools my anger. It does not help to know that anger covers my fear. Longing for my safe childhood clashes with the danger of my quest to become normal. I stride to a corner and lie down to rest, shuddering with fear for what faces us when we try to escape this city.

...

I awake from images of blazing fire and colliding ice to see Daniel scraping a long bone with his knife.

"That is a good sharp point," Kydaka says. He pats Daniel's shoulder and lifts his own spear. "Now we have protection from the jaguarat. I will show you how to use it."

I stand and sweep past them. "Take care. They hunt together."

Daniel hefts the spear in his hand, trying to ignore his nervousness.

I move to the edge of the room and sit next to Bryntar. The sandy floor warms my fingers. I blink in the intense sunlight striking the maze of stone pillars.

"It is time," she says.

I study the structures. Jaguarats lie in rooms, large white shadows stretched out in sleep. Some prowl the rims of the columns. The younger cubs emit tiny growls and hisses in tumbling play.

Why does anything have to die?

Daniel moves beside me. He stares at the jaguarats, then at his spear and sighs.

A huge male jaguarat jumps to the top of a wider pillar across from us. Power flows from his golden eyes, eyes that stop at Bryntar and then stare at me.

"He is their leader," she says.

"Do we have to kill him?" My stomach clenches waiting for her answer.

"No," she says. "Leader protects us."

"Yeah, right," Daniel says.

Bryntar glares at him. "Jaguarats fear-share."

"You're kidding, right?"

"For continuation of species."

I stand up and brush off the sand, wanting this day to be over. "They know we killed some of their kind?"

"Let me get this straight," Daniel says. "One jaguarat is going to keep the others from killing us? I don't believe it."

Kydaka moves toward Bryntar. "How can we use this to our advantage?"

"Stay close together. Elandra leads. Then Daniel, you, me."

I cannot lead us. The jaguarats are ready to tear us apart.

"There are too many for me to kill. You will all die." I stare into the leader's eyes and am surprised to feel his confidence.

Bryntar turns me to face her. "We protect Kydaka and Daniel between us. Watch females."

"I agree," Kydaka says. "They might disobey the leader to prove their worth for mating." He lifts his spear. "I am ready."

Daniel squeezes my hand. "I'll be right behind you."

I do not know whether to laugh or cry. Somehow his words reassure me. I take a deep breath of sunlight. "Do I need to know anything else?"

Bryntar warns, "Do not run or slow pace. Do not speak."

"Don't get eaten," Daniel says.

We slide down the pillar. Daniel and Kydaka stay so close that I can hear their breaths in the deathly silence. If I make one mistake and the leader loses control, some of us cannot hope to survive. I step onto a footpath that twists through the broken city.

Opening my feelings, I reel in the wave of anger, ferociousness, and curiosity that surround me. There is no more time to be a girl at the whim of emotions. With unwavering resolve, I think about Taroc: his calm, but sturdy discipline, his power as strong and unwavering as that of the jaguarat. I hope the creature senses my intent. Light suddenly radiates from my body in every direction.

Snarls, hisses, and yowls echo off the stone hills. The uneasy pacing of many paws slams into my senses. I dare to lift my head.

The leader bounds from pillar to column to stone arch. Along the way, he bats an overeager youngster, snarls at a male who challenges him, and ignores the nervousness of the older jaguarats. He stays on the edge of the city heights next to us. There is comfort in his steady heartbeat.

I focus on the next step, the rock in the path, the unexpected curve, keeping firm control over my feelings. Sweat trickles down my face and neck. The dry day stretches on and on. At last, the sun sinks lower in the sky. Shadows deepen the Sunken City, making visibility difficult.

A sudden wind gusts through the pillars blinding us in a cloud of dust. Daniel grabs the back of my jacket and I hope the others connect to him. I shield my eyes and search the path with my boot to move forward. Terror tightens my chest. I feel the bloodlust of three hidden, hungry jaguarats.

"Spears ready," I whisper. Dust dries my mouth. An annoying tickle rises in my throat. I swallow, refusing to cough.

The fast heartbeat of the jaguarat leader thumps next to mine. I see the shadow of his massive body jump the arch over our heads. Terrifying growls and screams split the air as he fights for domination.

"Go." Bryntar pushes us forward.

Daniel grabs my hand. We stumble over the path. Trip, bump, and scrape stone blindly. My heart races faster than my feet. The dust whirls away revealing the edge of the city. Kydaka and Bryntar drive us on. I spit sand and cough, not believing that we are almost through.

A deafening screech shatters the silence. A huge female jaguarat jumps in front of us, fur ridging her back in warning. Her ominous growl displays her long fangs. Her tail flicks back and forth, muscles tense, ready to spring and tear us apart.

Twenty-Three: The Parting

Daniel drags me behind him. He and Kydaka raise their spears.

"Wait," I say.

In a tremendous leap from a tower, the jaguarat leader crashes into the female. They roll across the rock-strewn ground. Relief surges through me to know the leader is alive, even with a gash down his side. Growls and screeches soften to moans and purrs.

I avoid eye contact with the female jaguarat, but glance at the leader. *Thank you.* Then I run, the others by my side, without stopping until my sides heave and my muscles give out.

The sun fades below the horizon, the waning rays sending scraggly shadows of scrub brush and dry grass over the high plain. The shadows soon succumb to darkness. Even the sliver of moon and sprinkling of stars do little to light our way. In the deepest part of the night, I drop onto the sand.

"I thought you'd never stop," Daniel says. He stretches out on the ground and I avoid looking at his muscular body.

Kydaka uses the end of his spear and topples a thorny plant. He slices off the juicy leaf pads. "Remove the skin before you eat it."

Daniel uses his knife to peel the prickly skin from the pads and hands one to me.

"Thank you."

Why does Daniel think of me before himself? He has made it quite clear that the kiss we shared means nothing.

Confused, I take a bite of the thick leaf. My nose tightens with the tart odor. The sour flesh refreshes my dry throat, although I am almost too tired to chew.

"I guard first," Bryntar says.

Kydaka nods. "I will relieve you."

"How much farther do we have to go?" I ask.

"We reach ocean tomorrow," Bryntar says.

I have lived a lifetime of tomorrows and wonder what another will bring. The sand is cool and smooth, the tiny grains molding to my curves. The metallic shirt itches and I long to remove it, to be free from its weight and its meaning. I imagine Aru deep underground, waiting for me, and swallow my bitterness.

Bryntar's dark form etches the midnight sky. Kydaka rests next to me. Somehow, they offer safety. The warm summer breeze wraps around me like a blanket. I close my eyes and the world disappears.

...

A rodent chatters in my ear and I jump, instantly awake. It skitters away, spotted tail held high. The sunrise encircles Daniel in rays of rose and gold as he stands on the hilltop.

Oh, Daniel. My body cannot forget the feeling of your arms.

I join him and watch the Western Seas sparkle in the distance.

He turns to me, a faraway look in his eyes. "Home is across the ocean. I hope."

Because there are no words to comfort him I say, "You did not awaken me for my turn."

"You needed the rest."

"You did, too."

"I didn't face what you had to."

I touch his arm and thrills course through me. "You saved my life. The snake—"

"Forget it."

What? The event? Your feelings for me? I wish I could ask what you mean.

"I have not been on the water," I say. "Only in it."

"I was born on a boat. My mom insisted on going with my dad on his last race."

He heaves a great sigh. "This canoe Bryntar talks about isn't exactly my choice for an ocean-going vessel. Tides and currents can be treacherous."

"You stay close to shore," Bryntar says as she moves behind us.

Kydaka offers me another leafy pad to eat. "We can be seen easily on this open plain. We must go quickly."

I feel Bryntar's grudging respect for my uncle. She takes off down the hill toward a stand of trees, their mottled bark and silver-green leaves brilliant against blue sky.

I eat while running after her.

Our journey is uneventful, which makes me more nervous as I search for hidden danger behind every tree and rock. When we reach a rocky bluff overlooking the wide expanse of ocean, the sun already blazes high overhead. It turns the water into a rippling reflection of light. Wind tiptoes across it in white froth.

"This way," Bryntar says. She leads us down a narrow animal trail between gray and black boulders washed smooth by sand and sea. She reaches into a long cleft above the waterline and drags out the log canoe, the paddles and our supplies.

Starving, I immediately grab a sack of food inside the canoe and distribute some.

"I don't suppose you have any meat?" Daniel asks.

"I will hunt on the trail," Kydaka says.

"Here are some warm clothes," I say and throw the bundle to Daniel.

"Thanks." He takes it and changes behind a large rock.

"I am sorry we have no warm clothes for you, Kydaka," I say.

"I will manage."

Bryntar turns to me. "You and Daniel rest. Leave when dark."

"You are coming with us," I say.

Daniel laughs. "That canoe only holds two people."

Nausea clenches my stomach. "I cannot go without you."

"I travel inland," she says.

Fear stops my breath. I cannot imagine ever being away from Bryntar again. "Not without me."

"No. You slow me. Terrain is rough."

I hold down panic. "There must be another way."

"Only way for you."

I know by the stubborn tilt of her head that she will not change her mind.

Kydaka places a gentle hand on my arm. "She is right. I will travel with her to ensure her safety."

Smoke seeps from her nose. "You cannot keep up."

Kydaka smiles at her.

I feel her confusion when he does not argue with her.

The sun sets in fire. A damp and salty wind breathes down my neck. I hunch behind a boulder in silence and ignore the conversation between Daniel and Bryntar about how to reach our destination. I only want to get to the lagoon and become normal. When they finish, Daniel gives her his spear. He repacks the canoe and secures everything with the rope. He and Kydaka carry it to the beach.

Bryntar does not have to tell me how she feels.

"I know the dangers in the sea," I say.

She turns away.

I cannot bear for her to leave, and throw myself in her arms. "Be careful."

She hugs me and I hear the rapid beating of her heart. "Go."

"Promise you will meet us."

Her eyes become soft. "You must reach the cave before dawn."

"Can we?" I ask Daniel.

He looks out to sea. "Not if that storm hits us first."

Heavy black clouds hang on the horizon. I look toward the rugged rocks that line the ocean and lead under the Ice Mountains.

Kydaka gazes at the sea, concern in his eyes. "Our worry will be for you."

Control. Do not let them see you cry. I walk away from my only family.

Daniel and I roll up our pants and put our boots into the canoe. We wade into the ocean. The frigid water seeps into my heart as well as my bones. The breakers splash us as we push the canoe over them. I swallow a mouthful of salty water and cough.

Daniel laughs. "Better keep your mouth closed." He climbs into the canoe and reaches a hand to help me.

I ignore it and climb in, careful not to tip us both into the sea.

He takes a paddle and hands me the other.

I search the shoreline for Bryntar and Kydaka. They are gone.

Twenty-Four: The Paddling

Daniel puts his paddle in the water and the canoe glides over the surface. The contracting muscles in his shoulders, back, and arms mesmerize me. He fights the tide to keep us near the coastline without coming too close to the breakers, alternating paddle strokes on each side.

"We'd make better time if you'd help," he says as he turns to me.

I snap out of my appreciation of his body, glad he cannot see my face. "Tell me what to do."

"We each paddle on a different side," he says. "I'll take the left side first. We'll rotate sides when our arms get tired. Skim the surface of the water with the paddle. Go ahead and try."

I push the paddle through the water several times and succeed in going in a circle and drifting toward shore.

Daniel laughs. "You've got the idea. Match your stroke to mine. Together. Now."

We paddle and I concentrate on his rhythm.

The canoe skims across the water, even though the tide fights our forward momentum.

The night becomes a lullaby of wind whipping the sea, paddles swishing through water, waves caressing the sand.

"What happens when we reach our destination?" I ask.

"An underground river will take us to Bryntar's meeting place."

The water turns a sparkling bright blue as if millions of stars fell from the sky. I forget to paddle.

Daniel stops. "What's the matter?"

I turn to him. "What is that shining in the water?"

"Bioluminescence. From tiny marine life."

"It is beautiful."

"Very." But he is staring at me and I look away, unable to stop the burning heat inside.

Crashing waves fill the silence between us until he adds, "I didn't like you knowing my feelings."

"I understand. You block them now."

"It takes a lot of effort. I don't know how you cope with everything you are. I'd be crazy."

I will be if I do not know how you really feel.

"Why did you kiss me? Curious to be the only one to get close to an Enchantress?"

"It wasn't like that and you know it."

"I know what it meant to me. You cannot admit what you felt."

"It's not that I don't care."

I want to slap his face, but turn away. "Coward."

"I risked my life for you."

But you do not love me.

Despair wraps around my heart. The brewing storm matches my mood.

His voice fills with regret. "You have to understand. I don't know what's going to happen to me. I can't commit to anything or anyone."

My heart throbs. I paddle harder.

"Listen, I don't blame you for wanting to be normal. I think you should change your mind. We're all going to die unless you—"

"It is my choice to make."

"Is it?" he asks.

"What do you mean?"

"You don't face Aru, we all die, right? If you become normal, won't the island still be in jeopardy? You'll die, too."

"I am going to find a way off this island."

"Right. Who's going to build the ship when they all fear you? You don't have a choice. That's what sacrifice is all about. One life for many."

Anger pulses behind my eyes. "You want me to die?"

"You don't know if you'll die when you fight Aru."

I yell at him. "Thank you for telling me your real thoughts and feelings."

Daniel paddles hard. He squints through the darkness at the towering cliffs on our right. "I don't know if we can make the cave. It's on the other side of that promontory."

"Paddle faster." My voice is as cold as I feel.

We synchronize our movements. Sheer chunks of ice form the glacier. It juts into the sea, gouged and jagged. Frigid wind slams into us and tosses the sea. Larger swells surge under our canoe.

"This island isn't normal," Daniel says. "How can you have glaciers, swamps and deserts in such proximity?"

My muscles ache from paddling. "I know nothing about island history."

"Change sides," Daniel says.

It does not help. I want to scream from the constant ache and clench my teeth instead. As long as Daniel paddles, so will I.

As we round the glacier, the wind throws rain in our faces, making it even harder to see the coastline.

"We need light," Daniel says, "or we'll miss the entrance."

I keep paddling and concentrate on creating light. My hair glows.

"We have to go ashore," Daniel says. "I can't see well enough in this storm." He turns the canoe toward the breakers.

I feel the fear that shivers down his spine when he sees rocks jutting up from the sea.

"You can do it," I say.

He lets the tide shoot us toward shore. "Whatever you do, hang on to your paddle."

"Watch out!" I push my paddle against a slab of floating ice, but a huge surge of the sea flips the canoe. A tangle of twisting waves drags me into freezing darkness. I barely hang onto the paddle and kick hard to the surface. Gasping with terror, I scream. "Daniel! Daniel!"

His head pops up through the smashing waves.

My heart explodes with relief.

The tide hurtles us to shore and throws us onto rocky sand. We stumble through biting water to retrieve the canoe. Luckily, it is still in one piece and somehow our supplies secure under the rope.

"Where is your paddle?" I ask.

His embarrassment flickers for a moment and is gone. "Lost it."

I am too tired to comment.

"Help me carry this." He slips my paddle under the rope and flips the canoe over his head.

I take my place at the front, straining to maintain the glow that provides our only light in the drenching rain.

Sentinels of stark ice rise high above us and I barely keep from falling into the foaming sea. My hope that we find the entrance of the cave soon dwindles.

Much, much later, I stagger and wade into a yawning hole in the glacier, clothes a soaked burden. The numbing sea reaches my waist. Do I always have to be wet and freezing?

"Let's put it down," Daniel says.

We flip the canoe over. I stretch cramped hands. "I need rest."

Daniel climbs inside. "Can't. Tide is on our side until it meets the river. Unless you want to paddle against the outgoing tide."

I glare at him and climb inside, handing him our only paddle.

"Fair enough," he says, grinning.

My light offers a small glow in the giant chasm. Chilled, I try not to think about the weight of ice over my head as the darkness swallows us.

Twenty-Five: The Paddling

The constant drip of water is the only sound that echoes in the silence, except for the quiet swish of the paddle. I hate being swallowed by blackness. If I fail in becoming normal, I will know every inch of this island and avoid all the horrid dark places.

Guilt hovers over me at my relief from paddling the canoe. "Let me help," I finally say.

Daniel sighs as he hands me the paddle. I moan as my muscles cramp with the first stroke. "I am not getting anywhere."

"We've joined the river. It's flowing against us. Our arms are pretty much useless. We're going to have to get out and push."

Wet clothes are rigid with cold against my body. "I am cold enough."

"Keep your voice down. We don't know how sound carries. Or what's at the other end."

I shut up and paddle in circles.

"I could tie the rope to the canoe, swim ahead, and pull you through."

"I will help." Removing my boots, I crawl over the edge and grit my teeth against the coming shock of icy water. I gasp in pleasure. "The water is warm. Part of it anyway."

Daniel jumps in. "What a break. Hot springs must feed the river. I wasn't sure how we were going to make it."

"Thanks for keeping that to yourself."

"Sarcastic, aren't we?"

I do not have the energy to respond and do not want to fight with him.

Warmth rises to my waist and I can finally wiggle my toes. Soon we are sweating with the effort of pulling the canoe against the river current.

"Did Bryntar say how far we have to go?" I ask.

"I'm hoping we're almost there."

Soon, we are. I am stunned when we stand at the end of a tunnel covered by thick green trees with leafy branches that droop over the water. I peek through the branches. Sunlight shines from far above. Pink, orange and gold reflect like jewels on the towering monoliths of ice. The light is so brilliant I shade my eyes and am amazed at the large grassy meadow growing in the middle of the glacier.

"How is this possible?"

Daniel pulls me back quickly. "Ssh."

Yells and laughter echo through the air. Seven young men stand naked on top of a high glacial tower. Ice Lords. I cannot take my eyes away. A waterfall spews out of a large hole in the glacier beneath them. The torrent plunges into a small, steamy lake.

"You first, Oh Mighty Leader," shouts a shorter, young Ice Lord.

Voices join in a loud chant. "Jyrr, Jyrr, Jyrr."

Jyrr strides out of the group, laughing. When the star symbol and fang hanging from his ear catch the light, my traitorous body responds and heat rushes to my face. He is the Ice Lord from the cave, in line to inherit the throne. Tall and confident, his icy purple skin ripples with muscle. He is even more striking in contrast to his friends and I understand why he is their leader. What I do not understand is his influence over my body.

"Who are those purple guys?" Daniel does not hide his discomfort.

"Ice Lords. They must not know we are here."

"Get back or they'll spot us."

He tries to pull me back, but I resist. "I want to hear what they say."

"Then hide under here."

We crouch under a thick branch of leaves.

Jyrr dives off the ice slab and into the crushing waterfall. I unconsciously hold my breath. It is a long time before he surfaces to the wild cheers of the others. They screech like wild animals and leap after him. To my surprise, they all survive and climb out of the river, laughing and congratulating each other.

Daniel whispers under his breath. "Jerks."

The shorter Ice Lord says, "Come on or be late for the feast."

"You do not order me," Jyrr says. "Remember your rank."

The boy bristles.

The others laugh and race out of the water, pushing the short one back. They put on their fur clothes and reach for their knives, arrows, and spears.

The shorter Ice Lord glares at their backs and leaps out of the water. He dresses and hurries after the rest who disappear between the spires of ice.

When they are gone, I step into the light and take a deep breath. Energy soars through me.

"It's obvious you know Jyrr."

"I do not."

"You lit up like a firecracker."

"What you are talking about? We never met. I was hiding in a tree when he showed up. Then I followed him to find the way home."

"You're pretty defensive about a guy you don't know."

"He is nothing to me but an enemy."

"If you say so."

Mortified, I yank the canoe into the grass and rummage for food. It is bad enough that my body responds to the Ice Lord without Daniel knowing it. "Is this where we are supposed to meet Bryntar and Kydaka?"

"Yeah. Let's hope they don't run into those pretend warriors."

I whirl on him. "Ice Lords rule this island and train their young well. Jyrr killed a giant bearran with one arrow."

"Now it's Jyrr?"

"I learned his name when you did." I tramp cross the meadow to be closer to the waterfall and the lake. My bare feet sink into glorious soft grass. Memories of my garden at home bring unexpected tears and I wipe them away.

Daniel removes our supplies from the canoe. He hides it under a bank covered in golden flowers and hefts the sacks of soggy supplies over his shoulders. He tries not to limp as he strides toward me. "Bryntar warned me about the severe weather we're going to face. We should dry our clothes."

"You expect me to take mine off?"

"Only if you want to be dry." He grins and throws me a blanket. "Rest while you can."

I remove my coat, cover myself in the blanket and wiggle out of fur pants. It takes longer to take off the shirt next to my skin. I leave the metallic armor and my undergarments. I lie my clothes in the sunshine and curl up under the blanket.

Daniel strips off his clothes down to very short pants. His muscles send flutters through my stomach. What is the matter with me? I turn my back to him, hating my uncontrolled responses to young men.

The peace and solitude of this hidden oasis seeps into me. I close my eyes, sore and weary, and never consider that other life forms may roam these glaciers.

Twenty-Six: The Gathering

A hand clamps over my mouth. I fight against the heavy body on top of me. Daniel whispers in my ear and my body relaxes. "We've got company." His warm breath soothes my thumping heart. "Get into the lake."

He moves off. I slither out of the blanket and we slide into the water.

A deafening roar pierces the night, louder than the crashing waterfall.

Even though the water is warm, I shudder when the moonlight shines on four beasts bounding across the meadow. Their golden dappled fur gleams. Bearrans. Two are young and race after each other, growling and tumbling through the grass while their mother watches. My attention fixes on the huge male who rises on hind legs and sniffs loudly. His fangs glow in the light. He catches our scent and lumbers toward us, trampling through our supplies. Fascinated by his size and grace, I can only stare.

Daniel takes a deep breath and yanks me underwater as the bearran leaps toward us. The beast plunges in over our heads, displacing massive amounts of water. It crashes into Daniel and I feel his pain as the force of the animal hits him in the back and knocks him away.

I plunge through the water to reach Daniel and pull him deeper underwater.

The bearran swims after us, great arms and legs pounding over us.

We swim farther away into darker water.

Daniel rises to the surface, gasping for air.

"Are you all right?" I ask.

"I'll live."

The bearran surges toward us.

"I cannot shock him while you are in the water."

"I'll swim for that shore." He vanishes underwater.

I strike out on the surface toward the waterfall. "Hey!"

The bearran turns its massive head toward me. Water slides off his thick fur in waves. He swims fast for his size. I look toward the glacier walls, expecting to see Daniel. He is not there. I swim closer to the waterfall.

Where are you Daniel?

Almost on top of me, the bearran growls, hot breath blowing through my wet hair. I dive underwater and his claws snag my vest. The beast pulls me closer as I struggle to free myself. Huge arms thrash, trying to rip me apart. An edge of whirling water catches us. I take a chance that Daniel is out of the water. Twisted in muscle, fur, and water, I stick my finger into the beast's chest. He bellows. A huge paw swats me into the air. I splash in the lake away from the churning waterfall and pop to the surface.

The bearran fights the power of the waterfall and his great strength pulls him to freedom. He swims to the shore and cuffs the cubs that jump on him.

Daniel rests on the far edge of the lake in safety. I sigh in relief.

The bearran growls and raises his head.

Screams and shouts come from the top of a glacier. Dark figures slide down the icy sides with torches of fire. Bryntar and Kydaka. They reach the bottom and run straight at the beasts, yelling and waving their torches.

The bearrans bolt out of the meadow.

Thrilled to see my family, I hurry out of the water. "You could have been killed sliding down the ice."

Bryntar folds me in her arms.

Kydaka smiles and lays down his spear. "Very exciting."

Bryntar shakes her head, but I see her tiny smile.

I wrinkle my nose at the smell of uncured leather. Then I notice his fur coat. "You encountered a bearran, Kydaka."

"Could you call me Uncle? Bryntar displayed amazing bravery." He grins at her.

I wonder how she blushes under her icy purple skin and whisper, "Do you like him?"

Respect flickers and is gone. "He is a man. Where are clothes?"

My face flushes when I remember I only wear the metal shirt and flimsy underwear. I hurry to get dressed. While my clothes are intact, our supplies are scattered or eaten.

"Boy, am I glad to see you two," Daniel says as he joins us.

Bryntar glares at him. "Where are clothes?"

"Drying."

Smoke furls out of her nose, but she says nothing.

He leans over to grab his clothes and winces.

I take the torch and shine it over his back. A swollen, ugly bruise travels down his spine. "You are hurt."

"Just a bump."

"You have much luck," Uncle says. "Not many survive a bearran."

"Let me help." I run my fingers over the bruise and down the muscles of his back. Music sings in my heart. Entranced, I am lost until the burning in my fingers startles me.

"Are you all right?" Uncle asks.

I flush and pull away from Daniel. "Of course."

Daniel pulls on his clothes. "Thanks."

Uncle hands me fur gloves and a hat. "To keep out the cold."

I take them eagerly. "I am grateful."

He shoves a bag at Daniel.

Daniel smiles as he takes out dried strips of meat. "Finally, some real food."

Uncle grins. "Fortune smiled on us when the bearran thought we were the food."

Daniel laughs. "Tell me what happened."

Uncle picks up his spear. With leaps and jabs, he acts out the killing of the animal. The torchlight stretches his shadow in wild movements across the meadow.

I try not to listen and watch Daniel's entranced face.

When the story is over I turn to Bryntar. "Did you see the young Ice Lords?"

"No. Not allowed here."

"Kids break rules." Daniel says. "Part of growing up."

"Not here. If caught, the penalty is severe," Uncle says. "To be branded an outcast is worse than death."

I am an outcast. But for the love from Bryntar and Taroc I would not be here now.

"What if the Ice Lord is the heir to the throne?"

Bryntar hisses. "He should not be heir."

"Justice and knowledge serve a leader," Uncle says.

"How about arrogance?" Daniel asks. His unguarded jealously surprises me.

"He has courage as well," I say.

"If he gets caught by the elders, it will not matter," Uncle says.

"Finish eating," Bryntar says. "We leave."

"We have this delicious dried meat," Daniel says, holding out a piece to me.

I pay no attention to him. "Will we find other food on our journey?"

"Nothing you would eat," says Bryntar. She stalks to the lake, pulls up green plants with pulpy brown pods and stuffs them in a bag.

I fold up blankets and shove them inside another bag. Daniel shoulders the rope and we follow Bryntar's torch as she leads us to a small trail through the ice. I gaze back at the meadow and wonder how many more dangers face us.

"I will protect you with my life," Uncle says as he trots behind me.

"Hope that it will not be necessary," I say.

Walls of ice rise above us. We walk single file. I dislike the confining silence. "Tell me about your life, Uncle."

"I roam the island. My home is the land, even though I am still under orders when the Kepyrs need me."

"After what they did to your family?"

He hides his underlying anger well. "I accept my destiny."

I touch his arm. "I cannot tell you how sorry I am. It is not your fault that my mother chose to disobey the law. You should not have suffered."

"Was it not her destiny?" he asks.

"I do not believe in destiny. She made her own decisions."

"You can choose to believe what you want. That does not make it the truth."

I refuse to think about his words. I have to believe I have a choice for my life.

The gorge narrows. Giants of ice hover in cold silence, so close I can touch their frozen, unmoving surface. The twisting, confining passage closes in on me. Flashes of torch fire do little to relieve the depths of complete darkness. A shiver strikes deep into my bones.

Twenty-Seven: The Crossing

We plod along the narrow path. Fog closes around us, wet and heavy. I walk in silence, unable to talk. Tension grips my chest. I wait for the sun.

Bryntar stops when we reach the entrance to a wide cavern. "Be careful. No talking." She holds her torch high.

The cave is a fantasy of ice. Magnificent spires fan out like the spiky petals of a gigantic flower. Folds, layers, and twists of ice texture the cave in majestic grandeur. Strange markings on the walls in a language I cannot understand glimmer under the ice. Across the floor, clusters and pillars of blue ice turn purple in the red glow of the torch. Mist curls around, making everything look like a magical kingdom floating in clouds. I touch the clusters in awe of their beauty and watch a drop of translucent liquid slide to the floor.

"This cave is unstable," Daniel whispers.

Uncle says, "Spread out to balance our weight."

I step inside the wonderland. The ice is firm under my feet although tiny fractures design the floor like delicate vines. We separate and cross the cavern.

I do not breathe or think of anything except getting to the other side. I take a small, slippery step. Balance before taking another. Another. My shadow spreads across the wide expanse in the wavering light: around fantastic formations, under heavy icicles, and between jagged shards that hover over our heads. I shiver in the eerie silence.

Bryntar stops before a gaping hole. She crawls under icicle teeth. Daniel and Uncle slide in after her.

I take a last look at the fragile beauty of the ice cave and push my bag through. Sun filters from far above, making the icy teeth look like shiny knives.

I bump one small icicle and gasp. No. Visions of the whole cave crashing down upon us flash through my mind. I quickly slide my boot to catch the icy shard. It drops and sticks on the fur. I do not breathe as it slowly melts.

Chills shiver down my back. I creep into an icy tube that rises to the surface. I suck in light, but there is little to fill my hair. I shove panic away.

Bryntar claws up the wall of jagged crystal. "Follow me." She scales the column of ice with ease.

Daniel throws the end of the rope to Bryntar and wraps it around himself. "Tie this around your waist." He passes it down to me. He uses his knife as leverage and moves up the ice with skill.

Uncle secures the rope around us. "You first."

I grab a frozen icicle that juts out of the wall and start to climb. Lacking light, I sway in dizziness. My boots slide on slick ice. I hit my elbow and bite back a cry.

Uncle catches me. Shoves me higher. "Keep going."

My hair hangs, lifeless and nearly empty of light. Breath stings in sharp gasps. I strain to see through blurry eyes.

"I cannot make it."

"Do not give up now," he says.

My fingers slip. I swing in air, shadows closing in on my mind. Pain crushes my waist when I am yanked up and out of the hole.

Sun blazes across the ice in piercing brilliance. I inhale the brilliance of light in ragged pants and close my eyes.

Daniel removes the bag from my neck and encloses me in his arms. His heart races next to mine. "You okay?"

This is where I belong.

"Are you all right?" He wipes bright strands from my face.

"I think so. Thank you."

His worry fades and barriers close around his feelings.

Uncle heaves himself over the edge. "She is well?"

"Her super-self." Daniel's warmth disappears. "We need to stay tied together." He moves as far away from me as the rope will allow.

The Ice Mountains stand in silent glory before us. Glaciers glisten among protruding black rocks. They rise above remote Kepyr villages, ridges, valleys, forests. I gaze across the seas. There is only endless water in every direction.

I will never escape this island.

"Where do the Ice Lords live?"

"There." Uncle points to a higher summit in the distance. Anger sears through him.

"You do not like the Ice Lords?" I ask.

"They hold Keprys in slavery. We need freedom."

"Kepyrs cling to old ways," Bryntar says. "Your leaders like control."

"You take their side?" he asks.

"Laws must change," she says. "Not happen. Unless. . . "

"Do not say it." I turn from her gaze. "Where is the lagoon?"

She points toward an outcropping of black rock. "Stay in my tracks."

"You order like an Ice Lord," Uncle says.

Bryntar glares at him. She strides toward the outcropping. An inch of snow crunches under her taloned feet.

"Did I say something wrong?" Uncle asks.

"You do not know her story," I say.

"I'd like to know," Daniel says.

"It is for her to tell."

Daniel strides away, being careful to walk in Bryntar's tracks.

"Watch out for crevices under the snow," Uncle says.

We plod ahead while the sun moves through the sky. I am thankful for the bit of warmth, although it is still so cold that the ice does not melt. Daniel and Uncle chew on meat as we walk. I eat one of the green plant stems. It is fibrous, the brown pod sweet. I need sleep more than food, but there is no safety on this exposed mountaintop.

Large spikes of ice push through the frozen ground in shades from lightest blue to deepest turquoise. Frozen snow spreads under our feet in wide, tiered curves, rutted with cracks and dirt.

It is the black mountain and the lagoon hidden in its depth that draw me forward. Events have pushed me to this place, this glacier of bitter cold.

Bryntar trudges ahead. Even with her growing dread, she is determined to give me my desire. Daniel is in no better place than I am—a stranger to this island, unable to return home or be free from the threat of death. Uncle is sworn to me, an allegiance of blood.

I slow my steps and my uncle joins me.

"Am I selfish to want a life without fear?" I ask him.

"All life faces fear," he says.

"Not when they are born."

"That is true. We must live fully for as long as we can."

"How do you do that?"

Regret fills his face before he smiles. "You choose your life by your thoughts. The people of this island lack control to create good. Their evil formed Aru. Your mother and father wanted to save life. Is it fair that they created you for that purpose? Not to you. Because they did, you are tied to the life or death of this place and everyone and everything here."

"I hate the burden."

"Life exists. We create the meaning."

His words cut into me. There is nothing to say that excuses my selfishness. For the first time, I realize darkness resides inside me. I am no better than anyone on this island. My heart feels like the glacier beneath my feet—cold, scarred and torn with cracks and ridges.

The sudden tug on the rope around my waist makes me stumble over unexpected bedrock.

"Run!" Daniel shouts and runs back to me.

Huge golden-brown wings block out the sun and flap in great gusts of wind. Sharp claws snatch my hair. I jerk into the sky.

Twenty-Eight: The Descending

The bird screeches and shakes me. I bite my tongue and warm blood drips down my chin. The sour smell of fear fills my nose.

"Don't let go," Daniel shouts.

The wind whips me back and forth. Wings whap in great gusts. My hair stings and I clutch it with both hands. The rope tightens around my waist. I cry out as I am pulled in two directions. The bird falters, but does not lessen its grip.

"Let go! We catch you!" Bryntar yells.

I release one hand and aim a shaking finger at the taut rope. Bright light severs it. I stab a wisp of light into the bird's foot. It screeches and releases me.

Shouts assault my senses. Bitter wind tears across my face, but flashing visions capture my attention—of Bryntar's gentle touch, Taroc's lessons, Daniel's kiss. I close my eyes and wait for the inevitable.

Three sets of entwined arms break my fall. We hit hard. I cry out as our bones grind into unmoving ice.

"You all right?" Daniel's worried eyes meet mine.

"I think so."

He gently pulls me up.

Bryntar's relief sweeps through me.

"Why didn't you shoot it down?" Daniel asks Uncle.

"It is forbidden to kill a Golden One."

"It could have killed her!"

Uncle hangs his head. "Forgive me. It is hard to change old ways."

I watch the giant bird soar away.

"Everything dangerous on this island is too big," Daniel says.

A thousand needle-like pricks throb in my head. I inhale light and relax.

A loud crack splits the air. The ground trembles under my feet. Great heaving chunks of ice break through the surface and split the glacier.

"Jump!" Bryntar sweeps me into her arms. She leaps the fissure that divides the glacier like a curving black snake. "To the mountains. Stay together."

Uncle races close behind, gathering the rope that used to connect us to the others.

Daniel trips on a fissure that opens under him. He disappears with a yelp.

"Daniel!" I wiggle out of Bryntar's arms and run to him. "Pull, Bryntar!"

Uncle leaps for the rope.

I run and peer down into a bottomless hole. Daniel clings to a small ledge. He is safe.

Bryntar and Uncle pull Daniel up and over the edge.

The ice shifts with an air-shattering boom. We bolt away. The hole closes as fast as it appeared.

I cannot stop shaking.

"It's not done yet," Daniel says. He grabs my hand and we scramble with Bryntar and Uncle over ground that grinds and thunders under our feet as if alive. Then all is still and silent, as if there had never been such deadly movement.

We gasp for breath, but do not stop running until the black outcropping of rock rises before us.

I collapse on the ice, heart thumping and unable to breathe in light.

Bryntar retrieves the torches from her bag. "Light them."

I sigh with exhaustion and ignite the torches. She gives one to Uncle.

"Deep breaths. Only darkness below." She vanishes between the rocks.

I suck in as much light as possible.

Daniel takes my arm. "You still want to do this?"

Any other time I would long for his touch. There is only one thing on my mind now. I can almost feel the lagoon beckoning me.

"I have come too far."

"It's okay to change your mind."

Ignoring the reproach in his voice, I bite my lip and turn away. Before me are many dark caves and gaps in the mountain. One small irregular hole radiates Bryntar's faint light. I lower my head and crawl through. The torch gleams on an oval of shiny, black rock that expands into a long corridor of warmer air. Voices carry behind me.

"You cannot change her mind," Uncle says.

"Do you know what's going to happen?" Daniel asks.

"No. I can only hope."

"That's not good enough to stake my life on."

"Then why did you come?" Uncle asks.

"She saved my life."

I hurry to catch Bryntar, ignoring the regret that keeps growing stronger in my heart.

She takes one look at me and says, "You need rest."

"I need the lagoon."

She turns me toward walls so glossy that my reflection stares back at me—a stranger drooping with fatigue.

"Maybe a short rest." I slump to the floor.

Daniel and Uncle join us and I am thankful for their companionship.

Beads of sweat drip down Bryntar's face. I feel her emotions as she fights her memories of the last time she was here. Her love for me pushes her through them.

Deep shame spreads through my soul to have no words of comfort.

Uncle runs his hands over the walls and turns to Bryntar. "How long have you lived?"

"Nine hundred seasons."

He blinks in surprise. "Has the mountain ever erupted?"

"Not in my life."

"These walls were formed by a volcano," Uncle says.

"How do you know?" I ask.

"I saw one in your father's books."

My stomach lurches. "You knew my father?"

"Not his name. Your mother kept that secret. She talked about him and their dream for the island. He was in line to be the Ice Lord leader."

"Line changes with greed," Bryntar hisses.

"Who is their leader now?" And what if he is my father?

"Ryz-IL," my uncle says.

Daniel jumps up and paces. "If he is your father, would it change your mind?"

"I do not know."

He glares at me. "I couldn't save my family. I sure can't save this island. Tell me. What's so good about being normal?"

"You cannot understand."

"Don't you get it? You're risking all our lives." He snatches the torch from Uncle and disappears down the tunnel.

Unable to look at Bryntar and Uncle, I jump up to follow him.

"Daniel, wait."

His torchlight flickers far ahead as he sets a grueling pace over jagged stones that fill the tunnel floor. Bryntar rushes past me since they are still tied together. I walk slower to conserve my breath and Uncle stays at my side.

"Tell me about my mother."

"She was gentle and kind, yet her inner strength far surpassed most Kepyrs. She carved wood and was considered an accomplished artist. Kadiya was braver than any warrior, than anyone I have ever known."

Her name was Kadiya. I shudder with the memories. "Bryntar saved my life."

"It was meant to be."

"Do you believe something greater controls us?"

"Perhaps. I do not know. My people worship Aru—a creation of Kepyr and Ice Lord. They bind us to the old ways to keep the power. What created them? Why is it against our laws to create someone like you?"

His questions confuse me more. "Why would my mother risk our lives?"

Uncle takes a deep breath and shakes his head. "She and your father believed in his vision. They loved the island and knew that darkness affected its life."

"Do you believe we are going to be destroyed by Aru?"

"I believed in my sister."

It is hard to control my rising anger, but somehow I do. "That is not an answer."

He sighs. "I believe it is possible."

"Maybe it is better to let Aru destroy the island."

Uncle grabs my arms and turns me to face him. "All life is precious. Even to the end."

His conviction slams through me.

"You must think me horribly selfish."

I am surprised there is no judgment in his feelings.

"Life offers us many challenges to overcome. To master destiny is the most difficult."

I cannot master my destiny.

A long time later, we catch up to Daniel and Bryntar. They stand on a high platform of solid rock that juts over a large cavern far below. Broken stone and boulders scatter across the cracked floor. Uneven walls sparkle with iridescent flakes that flicker red in torchlight. I do not see the lagoon and panic.

It cannot be that patch of swirling mist in the corner? I risked our lives for that?

A few shimmers of lagoon peek through the fog, striking me with a sensation of great age—as if something under the silver water surges with intelligence.

A shudder jerks through Bryntar. "The ice is gone."

Daniel points to a stream of molten rock that curves around one side of the cavern and vanishes into the ground. "That's because of the lava flow."

Dreams of fire and ice quiver through my mind.

Daniel removes the rope from his waist. "Undo your ropes so I can knot the pieces together."

Daniel ties one end of the rope to a sturdy rock.

"I have not seen that kind of knot," Uncle says.

"It's a bowline knot, a sailor's best friend. Easier to untie when we leave."

Daniel's fingers tie one knot after another down the length of rope. "These are half-knots." He reaches the end of the first rope and joins the two pieces in a different knot. "This is a stopper knot. So it won't come out."

"What are the half-knots for?" I ask.

"Your hands and feet. Easier to support your weight so you don't slip." He throws the rope over the edge and peers down. "Don't think it's long enough. We'll have to drop the last few feet."

Uncle says, "I will go first." He smiles, hands his torch to Bryntar and throws his spear over the edge. It clatters on the rocky floor.

My heart jumps into my throat when he disappears over the edge. I lean over and watch his body descend into darkness. He lands with a small crunch of rock.

Bryntar throws the torch to him.

"I'll go next." Daniel grabs the rope.

My throat constricts in a lump.

He climbs down with ease.

Bryntar clasps my arm. "You go, Elandra." Her face is rigid, the purple tint almost white.

"I cannot leave you alone," I say. "You next."

She hesitates.

I touch her arm. "Thank you for bringing me. I know how you feel about this place."

"Reconsider," she says.

"I cannot save the island."

"Conquer fear." She throws her torch to Uncle and heaves her huge body over the edge.

Darkness swallows me. I control the panic at the edge of my mind, but am unable to conquer the deeper fear of my unknown future. Hurry, dear Bryntar.

She thumps when she lands.

I snatch the rope with both hands and slowly climb over the edge. My arms still ache from rowing. I move carefully before releasing a hand or foot.

A sudden vibration rumbles through the rocks. The rope starts to swing. I slip a few feet and cling to it with my legs. "Help." A whispered terror as I dangle in darkness.

Twenty-Nine: The Shocking

Daniel yells, "Grab the rope, Bryntar!"

The rope jerks and stops. I cling in terror.

He calls up at me. "You okay?"

His voice is so far away that I look down. Shadows leap in torchlight and swirl around and around and around.

His voice penetrates my panic. "Move one hand at a time."

I do not want to move. I cannot move. I can barely breathe.

A sudden weight on the rope makes me squeeze tighter. I hold in screams as it swings back and forth. Sweat slides down my neck and inside my gloves, but I cannot control the chills.

And then I am in Daniel's arms, his warmth surrounding me.

"You're okay. We'll go down together."

I hold in tears that will burst if I say a word.

"I've got you. Move one foot down."

"How? We are using the same knots."

"I'm not using the one where your foot goes."

My voice squeaks. "Where are your feet?"

"I'm only using my arms."

"We are going to fall!"

"Calm down. Sailors are good with their arms."

And their hands and their lips. Concentrate. I block out everything except Daniel's whisper in my ear. "Slide your foot down. It's not far."

The shaking toe of my boot touches the small knot.

"Good. Hold on. I'm moving down."

"No. Please."

"You're going to be fine. Listen to me."

He lets me go and before I can feel his loss, he says, "Move your hands down."

I close my eyes, think only about his words, and slowly inch lower. When we reach the end, Daniel jumps first and lifts me down. The ground is solid under my feet, but my knees buckle.

Daniel grabs me by the waist. "Easy there."

"Thank you." My voice cracks.

His smile hits me full force. "Don't make it a habit, okay?"

For a moment, he does not guard his feelings of real concern for me. I welcome the flutters in my chest.

Lava hisses in the corner.

The hairs on the back of my neck prick. "There is something alive in there."

"Relax," Daniel says.

I watch the molten lava sizzle around boulders and feel stupid. Except when Bryntar's nervousness seeps into me.

Uncle moves to my side. "Are you sure you want to do this?"

"Facing Aru is certain death."

"You don't know that," Daniel says.

"Your control grows," Bryntar says. "When time comes . . ."

"I will still not be ready."

"Is this transformation dangerous?" Daniel asks.

Bryntar whispers, "Unbearable pain."

"What!" Daniel stares at her, horrified. "Have you been in the lagoon?"

She closes her eyes, remembering.

I quickly shut off her feelings and experience Daniel's hot anger instead.

He whirls on me. "You're ready to become a monster?"

"Accident," Bryntar says.

Daniel paces. "What difference does that make? Elandra has no clue, no guarantee that she'll get what she wants."

"Taroc saved my life," Bryntar says.

Daniel yells. "Look at the cost!"

She turns away, trembling.

"Who is Taroc?" Uncle asks.

"My mentor. An Enchanter." I choke up and cannot continue.

"There is more than one of you?" Uncle asks in surprise.

I push my guilt deeper. "He died."

"Not your fault," Bryntar says.

"Does that matter, now?" I ask.

I step toward the lagoon. It is larger and more menacing than I thought. Writhing shadows of mist shift over the surface. An ancient intelligence surges beneath the still water with detached interest. It makes me more nervous.

Daniel grabs my arm. "What happens if you die?"

"I can die either way. Why does it matter to you? You made your thoughts about me perfectly clear."

"I care."

"For your survival."

His face reddens. "Not true."

"What is the truth, Daniel?"

"I-I don't want you to change."

Yet you are afraid of me. Although maybe you are as confused as I am. I shrug off the thought and turn to Bryntar.

"Should I remove my protective shirt?"

Daniel whips me around. "Please don't do this."

It is difficult not to respond to his pleading eyes. I struggle against my feelings for him and don't react.

He turns toward the lava river. "I give up."

Bryntar glides a hand down her leathery face. "Remove everything. Might become permanent." Waves of horror pulsate through me until she shuts off her feelings.

My hair and body shoot unbidden flashes of light that disappear into the fog. "What is happening?"

"Perhaps a reminder of what you are and what you will not be," Uncle says.

I flinch, never once considering the repercussions of my decisions. "Is that supposed to make me feel better?"

"It is to make you realize what you are giving up," Uncle says.

Every heartbeat in the cave starts to magnify in my head: mine clawing its way out of my chest, Daniel's beating with worry, Bryntar's erratic thumping, Uncle's steady beat, and suddenly, many more.

"We are not alone," I say in warning.

Sturdy, pale-skinned animals slither out of crevices in the walls. White, unseeing eyes revolve in their sockets over long noses that sniff the air. Sharp claws scratch rock as their stubby legs stalk toward us.

"Sloats," hisses Bryntar.

Daniel shakes his head. "Let me guess. They're blind and dangerous."

Uncle lifts his torch and his spear. "Be careful. Their bite is deadly—if they do not shred you to pieces first."

"Great." Daniel opens the blade on his knife.

"Use this to keep them away." Kydaka tosses his torch to Daniel.

"Thanks," Daniel says.

"Can we make them leave?" I ask.

Uncle backs toward us. "They hunt together but have no leader. Form a circle back to back, and do not take your eyes off them. Our only chance lies in their blindness."

We prepare for the attack, our arms touching. The animals creep closer and screech in such high-pitched howls that excruciating pain shoots through my head. Their hunger almost overrides my concentration. I know there can be no mercy. I shoot a beam of light at the largest one. It moves so fast that I miss and lightning crashes into the walls, shattering rock. It leaps for my throat.

Bryntar snatches the creature midair and flings it against a boulder.

The next few moments whirl by faster than I can think: lightning, flashing torch, jabbing spear, shrieking. A sloat leaps from the top of a boulder, so close I can see black venom drooling from its fangs. Terrified, I disintegrate it.

I cannot discern the screeches of the creatures from the yells of my companions. My only comfort comes from the knowledge that I can feel they are alive.

Soon, burned flesh permeates the air. In an instant, silence comes like a blow. The creatures that survive back away from us and vanish into the crevices.

I whirl away from the dead. "Is anyone hurt?"

Uncle's bleeding hand hangs limp. "One bit me." Venom drips from the blackened tip of his little finger.

Bryntar screeches and snatches his hand.

"You do care for me," he says.

She rips Daniel's knife from his hand and knocks Uncle to the ground. Pins his finger and severs it in one hard blow. He screams once.

I shriek, pain slamming through me. The cavern blurs.

"Seal it!" she yells at me, tossing the poisoned finger into the lava.

I stagger in agony.

"Elandra! Control!"

Daniel shakes me. "Now. He could bleed to death."

Barely able to focus, I lurch away from Daniel, ignoring the pounding of my heart to shut out everything else but the light within me. I touch the bleeding wound and a tiny, hot ray closes it.

Uncle passes out without a word.

I crumple to the ground next to him.

Bryntar barely croaks, "Heal him. In case poison spread."

Taking his strong, weathered hand, I touch Uncle with my fingertips. Overflowing love fills me for this man who has risked his life for my dream. Icy energy surges with greater strength than I have ever experienced. Thank you, Taroc.

"I could have saved his finger."

"No," says Bryntar. "Poison spread too fast."

"He's lucky you could heal him," Daniel says. "Why do you want to waste your talent on some stupid dream?"

Uncle opens his eyes. He staggers to his feet, but does not show the suffering and loss we both feel. He faces Bryntar. "I would not be alive but for your quick action. I am your grateful servant."

Bryntar blushes. "Good it was not your head."

Uncle chuckles and she actually smiles at him.

"Let's ditch this place before something else happens," Daniel says.

"How can I leave when we have come this far?" I look at my uncle. "And sacrificed so much?"

"Are you nuts?" Daniel asks. "You don't get it. If you don't value who you are, you don't deserve to be an Enchantress." He turns away in disgust.

I never thought about losing my abilities to protect and heal. Guilt pricks my conscience. "Maybe Aru will disappear once I become normal."

Daniel glares. "You're kidding yourself."

Bryntar hugs me and chokes on tears.

"Be sure you are ready to lose your gifts," Uncle says, his face grave.

"Get it over with." Daniel marches toward the lava river.

The lagoon ripples, attracting my attention.

Bryntar shudders and backs away.

Every step toward the misty water takes me further and further from help and closer and closer to the unknown. Muscles clamp tight against my chest.

This is the right decision for me. Bryntar did not die. I will die if I fight Aru.

The water beckons with an undercurrent that laughs at my fear. Breath squeezes out of me. I lean over and barely touch the smooth silver surface with a fingertip. Instant desire and greed pierce my feelings. They are not my own.

Bryntar suddenly rips me away from the lagoon. "NO."

I struggle against her tight hold on me. "Let go. I need to do this."

"No," she says.

I glare at her. "The choice is mine. Do you think I came all this way and risked all of our lives to give up now?"

Her blue eyes flash. "Hoped heart would change mind."

"You were wrong." I pull away, anger jabbing through me.

"We will die."

The ground shakes under my feet. I jump away. A wide gap rips across the floor, trapping Uncle on the other side.

He yells, "Watch out, Daniel!"

I look up to see a molten cloud growing out of the lava—a writhing lump of rock, smoke and fire. It explodes and throws Daniel to the ground. Smoke spreads, obscuring everything.

"Run to the rope," I scream to Uncle. I race over the rolling, groaning ground to find Daniel.

Flares streak out of the bunching cloud like a hundred fiery eyes. It this Aru? I struggle in the foul smoke.

The cloud swarms toward Daniel.

Too late, I remember the words from Taroc's diary, Leave the waters unmolested or risk the sacrifice that will be made.

I touched the water.

Daniel cannot die because of me. I shoot a burst of light into the cloud. A yawning mouth of hungry fire consumes it. I dive to snatch Daniel's hand before he disappears in the billowing smoke.

He grabs my hand and jumps up. We stagger over undulating ground through choking fumes. Sparks bore into my coat and Daniel snuffs out the flames.

"I cannot see Bryntar," I say.

The swelling clouds spit hot rocks through the air. Lava overflows its banks.

"Bryntar! Where are you?"

"HERE," she roars.

I yank away from Daniel and run.

"Stay with me," he yells.

Bryntar's shadow wavers in the haze. I scramble over cracks that split the ground. In an instant, molten rock blasts through the fissures under her. Thrown into the air, she crashes over a boulder and disappears in the steam.

"BRYNTAR!"

I plow into the blinding ash, disintegrating anything in my way. Stumbling around the boulder, I stop and stare in horror while Bryntar's unconscious body slides into the lagoon.

Thirty: The Transforming

"Bryntar! No!" Please. No.

I kneel next to her and long to touch the one clawed hand that rests out of the water, to let her know she is not alone. Even though Taroc held her the first time, he was a greater, more experienced healer. I dare not touch her. My stomach churns to think that she can die from being exposed a second time to the waters of change.

Can she transform while unconscious? How will the lagoon know what she wants?

"Dear Bryntar. I never should have made you bring me here. I am so sorry." Tears pour down my face unheeded. I deserve to pay the ultimate price for my selfishness. Please, not at the cost of her life.

I jump up and yell. "Take me, Aru. I am yours. Please, spare her."

With a bellow, the tangled clouds slither into the broken ground and vanish leaving silent, falling ash.

"Elandra! Elandra! Where are you?" Daniel appears, frantic, covered in soot. "What happened?"

"Daniel, Bryntar could die in the lagoon!"

"Let's pull her out."

I grab his arm. "We cannot interfere or it might kill her."

Daniel coughs and rubs ash from his face.

"It should be me," I say. "I cannot escape my destiny."

"You believe that?" he asks.

"There is nothing else to believe."

Uncle appears through the fog with his torch. "Believe in yourself. We all have a special purpose."

Sorrow and resentment boil inside me. "What is Daniel's purpose in being stranded on this island?"

"Maybe saving your life," Daniel says.

"So I can die?"

Mist smothers Bryntar.

"If transforming is painful, better control your feelings," Daniel warns.

I will not let her go through this alone.

Bryntar suddenly shrieks, a long, unending, terrifying howl.

I crumple to the ground. Strong arms enclose me, but overwhelming pain stops all thought.

Her body writhes in convulsions.

Stop. Please. No more.

Bones grind. Marrow freezes. Nerves scream and burn, hotter, hotter. I cry out in scorched agony.

Muscles squeeze away my breath. Erratic heartbeats slam into mine. Tendons rip, rebuild. Skin stretches, tears, and reforms. I feel it all and screech in anguish. Please, please. Let me die. Tears cannot drown the pain. I am hopeless, mindless, breathless.

The torture sweeps us closer and closer to death. My heart stops beating. Weakened, I feel energy float from my body. I am so sorry, dear mother. Daniel forgive. . .

Bryntar roars, a cry so mournful, I think our hearts will break.

Then there is only silence.

I gasp, heart beating into life. And breathe in painless relief.

Dazed, I awake in Daniel's arms, worry and horror in his eyes.

Barely able to speak he whispers, "Y-you okay?"

Uncle holds my hand. Shaken to his core, he has no words.

A moan filters from the mist, a sound completely unlike Bryntar. The vapor shifts and uncovers a small, clawed hand lying out of the water.

I crawl forward. "Please forgive me, dear Bryntar."

A perfect hand appears. Shocked, I can only watch as the mist lifts to unveil a stranger.

"My God." Daniel's face is whiter than the ash.

Uncle bows his head. "Never did I expect to see such a miracle."

I whisper, my throat raw. "Do not touch her until she is out of the water."

Bryntar emerges from the lagoon on shaky legs, no longer the monster I know. Long black hair hangs in her face. Leather boots and fur clothes cover her body. She is what she once was, a statuesque Ice Lord, though her blue eyes remain. They meet mine as she pushes the hair from her breathtaking face with a wan smile.

"My Elandra." Her voice murmurs in unaccustomed softness.

Torchlight flickers over a line of delicate, shimmering scales that trail down one cheek.

I clasp her in my arms. "You are alive."

She hugs me, her love thrilling every cell of my body. She sighs when she sees her small, clawed hand.

"I am sorry, Bryntar. Part of your cheek and hand were not submerged in the lagoon. I was afraid to touch you in case I interfered with the transition."

She touches the scales on her face. "A small reminder of my past." She speaks in a whisper as if afraid to form the words. Her legs tremble and I catch her before she falls.

Uncle passes his torch to Daniel. "Give her to me." He lifts Bryntar into his arms.

"It is not necessary," Bryntar says. "I am quite capable."

"When you regain your strength," he says.

"You still planning to transform?" Daniel asks me.

I stare at the lagoon and remember the all-consuming greed when I touched the water. The entity that resides within wants me. I can withstand the pain, but cannot be sure my powers will not kill me in the direct transformation process. I also cannot guarantee what will happen to everyone if the lagoon gains my powers.

With resignation and the finality of letting go of my dream I say, "I will not enter the lagoon."

Daniel sighs. "That's a relief."

Uncle carries Bryntar toward the tunnel. "Let us leave this place."

Lava bursts out of the wall behind the lagoon and spills into it. The cavern rumbles. Rocks crack and smash into the water.

My mind touches the defeated intelligence in the lagoon before it rises into the fog and vanishes in envy.

Daniel snatches my hand. "Come on!"

We hurry across the uneven ground, coughing through the thick smoke. The wide crack in the ground blocks our way of escape.

"How did you get over that?" I ask Uncle.

"Jumped."

"Bryntar cannot jump in her condition," I say.

She moves out of Uncle's arms. "We jump together. It is our only chance before the cavern collapses."

I look back at the lagoon. It gurgles and disappears under hot rock.

"Me first." Daniel hands our one remaining torch to Uncle.

I hold my breath when he yells and leaps the chasm.

Uncle throws the torch to Daniel.

"You next," I say to Uncle and Bryntar. If they cannot make the jump, I do not know if I want to live. Until I see Daniel's face.

How could I leave him alone on the island?

Uncle takes Bryntar's hand. They back up. Run. Jump.

My heart leaps with them.

The ground gives way under Uncle's feet as he lands on the edge. Daniel grabs his hand causing Bryntar to dangle over the abyss.

"Do not let go!" I scream.

Bryntar claws her way up the side of the chasm still holding Uncle's other hand. Daniel heaves them over the side.

Rocks explode from the walls.

"Come on, Elandra!" Daniel races to the rope.

Dizzy with fear, I stare into the dark crack and jump. It almost seems as if hot air propels me over. I run to the others who are barely visible in the increasing smoke.

"I will haul you both up," Uncle says, "then send the rope down for Daniel." He jumps to the end of the rope and climbs quickly. I feel his refusal to acknowledge the loss of his finger.

"Go," Daniel says. He lifts Bryntar up to the end of the rope.

Her muscles shake as she takes it and starts to climb.

A shattering explosion bursts overhead. The rope drops and Daniel barely catches Bryntar. The ledge hurtles toward us. Daniel shoves us against the wall and covers our bodies with his. The ledge shatters when it crashes into the ground. He flinches as pieces hit his back. Then all is quiet and so dark it is impossible to see anything.

I summon the light within, but my hair radiates little light. Large rocks fill our escape tunnel. "Uncle, Uncle! Where are you?"

The ground rolls under our feet.

"If the sloats got in here, we can get out," Daniel says. He pulls our rope from the rubble and gathers it together. "Come on."

"We have to find my uncle!"

Bryntar lays her hand on mine. "He is gone."

"No. He is alive. He has to be."

Daniel grasps my arm with an iron grip. "Come on. Let's check that hole and hope it goes somewhere."

I yank away. "You expect me to leave without him?"

Tears glisten in Bryntar's eyes. "I would want you to leave if it were me."

She takes my hand.

Tears slide down my cheeks. How can I leave Uncle behind?

Daniel drags us around fallen rock to a small crack in the wall.

"We're in luck. I feel a draft of cold air."

"What if those creatures are in there?" I ask.

"The lava is rising," Bryntar warns.

"What if Uncle is trapped and still alive?"

Bryntar's regret sweeps into me. "We cannot know if he escaped. Try to feel him."

Desperate, I close my eyes and search for any feeling from him. Uncle. Uncle. My heart sinks. "There is nothing."

"Let's go while we still can," Daniel says.

"We cannot desert him."

"Your uncle wanted you to save the island."

I glare at him. "He never said so."

"He hoped you would change your mind."

Uncle died because of me. I will never forgive myself.

My light fades, leaving us in darkness. Never again will I put myself before those I love. Ever. Facing the consequences of my selfishness is a brutal kind of dying.

Daniel pulls me into the narrow fissure. "We need some light."

"You go first," I tell Bryntar. Dull light encircles my hair. I am thankful the lagoon transformed her, for she would not fit in this rock cleft otherwise.

Daniel leads the way deeper into the passage. To freedom or death?

The dead cold shocks me. Thoughts tumble through my mind of Uncle, my new Bryntar, getting trapped under the ice. Starving instead of fighting Aru. I am too numb to feel anything. Behind us, rocks burst in the quickly rising lava.

"Climb!" Daniel yells.

Thirty-One: The Climbing

We squeeze farther into a crevice that is little more than a slit of space with ledges, rocks and cavities lifting to unseen heights. Only wind sweeps in unrestricted.

"You expect us to climb these steep rocks?" I ask Daniel.

He ties the rope around his waist and hands it to me. "Yep."

"I should go first so you can use my light."

He shakes his head. "Me first, Bryntar, then you."

"Why?"

He fingers my lackluster hair. "We'll pull you up to conserve your breath."

Bryntar and I tie the rope around us, binding our fates together once again.

"What if we cannot get out?" I ask.

"We will."

"You cannot know that."

"I'm not going to die on this dumb island." Daniel searches for handholds and pulls himself up until he reaches a small ledge. "Hold the rope tight at the bottom. Use your feet against the rock, Bryntar."

She grabs the rope and makes it look easy, although she hunches her tall body.

I gasp with the effort of conserving my breath and providing dim light. As soon as I put my boots on the rock, they haul me up. Our climb becomes a repetitious trial of straining muscles and frayed nerves, bangs and bruises. Rock does not forgive mistakes.

We finally reach a split in the passage.

"Stay here," Daniel says.

He disappears into a dark recess and my senses alert for danger. Over my weariness, I feel his steady heartbeat and relax.

"Can't get through this way," he yells.

It feels like forever until he returns.

"Elandra needs rest," Bryntar says.

"How long does she have if we don't get out?" Daniel does not wait for an answer and continues up the other passage.

I worry about Bryntar's exhaustion. "Are you all right?"

"There is much to think about." She turns to me. "Did you control your feelings during my transformation?"

"I could not bear to let you go through it alone."

She touches my face. "I would not wish that kind of pain on anyone. Especially you. I am sorry. It was so unexpected. I never dreamed. . ."

"Are you sad that you changed?"

"No. It is strange after such a long time. I almost forgot what it feels like." She looks at her clawed hand and touches her face. "Am I hideous?"

"You will always be beautiful."

She frowns. "I cannot protect you in the same way."

"It is time I protect you."

"We have no weapons. Until we reach the surface, I do not know where we are. It will be dangerous to return home."

Home. Waves of longing fade. There is no home for an Enchantress.

Her next words slam into me. "You must learn total control or there is no hope for any of us."

"I do not know how."

"Find something to hold onto that makes you strong enough.

Daniel tugs on the rope, his voice echoing off the rocks. "It's a tight squeeze. Go slow and be careful."

Bryntar pats my arm and vanishes.

When I crawl inside the cramped space, the wind howls and whips my face. I look up at a maze of gaping black holes and sharp stone walls covered in slick ice. Unable to see Daniel or Bryntar, I am thankful for the insistent tug on the rope for I do not want to imagine being stuck in this narrow, tangled mass of rock. They can no longer offer help in lifting me. My heartbeat thumps in my head as I worm through a tight hollow tube. It is barely big enough to squeeze through and I bump my knee on an unseen rock. I twist and wiggle on my back over a flat shelf, the ice inches from my nose. How did Daniel do this?

I breathe heavily, the light diminishing quickly. The small light around my head shines on a mass of beady red eyes. Thick, furry creatures squeal and leap at me. I scream and cover my face, but instead of attacking me, they run over my head and down my body. I shiver in revulsion.

"Elandra?" Daniel's voice sounds far away.

"I-I am all right." Reeling and light-headed, I slip through another gap. A straight shaft rises to a tiny wedge of light.

"Hold on. We're pulling you up."

"Wait." My legs are sluggish and unable to tighten around the rope. The air brightens around me. I float into a strange land of quiet murmurs. A figure materializes and I smile in recognition. "What are you doing here, Taroc?" I try to hug him, but cannot seem to find my arms.

He scowls at me. "What are you doing here?"

"Where are we?"

"Do not think you can leave your responsibilities behind, Enchantress. What you have faced is nothing compared with what lies before you."

Weightless, I giggle. "Did you know I tried to become normal and Bryntar was thrown into the lagoon instead?"

His black eyes grow even blacker. "No!"

"She changed back into herself. Well, almost."

He cannot hide his relief. "Thank you, Enchantress," he says gruffly. "Go back and complete what you were born to do."

"I still cannot control my feelings."

"Detach yourself from them. Observe yourself as if you were someone else." He shimmers and blows blinding light into my face. "Live."

I choke and awake to sunshine and biting cold.

Daniel hovers over me while Bryntar holds my hand.

"Thought we'd lost you," he says, collapsing next to us.

"I saw Taroc."

Bryntar flinches.

Daniel wipes the hair from his face. "An illusion, due to your lack of, light."

"He was as real as you are. We talked before he sent me back."

"Back from where?" Bryntar asks in a whisper.

"I do not know. There were others, too. I heard their voices."

"They tell you where to find food and water?" Daniel asks.

Frowning, I say, "I can provide water."

Careful to control the heat in my finger, I melt ice that forms a small puddle. It takes several times to quench our thirsts, for the water freezes fast.

A flat plain of ice stretches before us with only a few rocks or pieces of glacier protruding from its surface. The mountain home of the Ice Lords looms closer than I thought possible. "Can we return to the canoe?"

Bryntar rises. "Too far." Her voice quivers with rawness. "The Ice Lords patrol here. We need to find a suitable hiding place."

"You know where to find food?" Daniel asks.

"There is a protected valley to the south."

"Let's go."

I drag myself up, muscles protesting, and trudge after them.

The ice is so hard that we do not leave prints. Freezing wind throws clouds across the sky and worms its way through my fur clothes. I stop abruptly when it also carries faint rumblings, whoops and yelling voices. Bryntar and Daniel look at me and we start running.

Thirty-Two: The Storming

Daniel tugs on the rope that connects us. "Hurry. Hide in those ridges!"

The wind blows harder, tossing snowflakes in a gray sky. I slip and crash to the ice.

Bryntar reaches out her hand.

"You are as tired as I am," I say. "How can you keep going?"

"To ensure our survival."

The glacier vibrates with the thundering of hundreds of hooves. A herd of strange creatures appears out of the snow and dashes toward us. Huge horns curve and twist to sharp points over their backs. Shaggy brown hair hangs over and under their massive necks and covers long muscular legs.

The yells and whoops behind the creatures grow louder.

"Hurry or we will be trampled," Bryntar says. She drags me up and I cling to her hand.

We race to the stark ridge ahead of us. The creatures run faster than I can imagine. Their hooves smash through snow, snorts fill the air, hearts beat into mine.

"We are not going to make it," I say.

Daniel sprints back to us and grabs our arms. "Faster!"

The herd thunders closer. We leap over a lower ridge and hit hard. The creatures split and race around us.

A voice whoops behind the herd. "Come on, Jyrr! Before the blizzard swallows us."

I cringe and hope we are concealed in the ridge.

Jyrr laughs. "That was more fun than attending Council."

"Not if they find us missing. Beat you home."

I peer through the snow to watch two shadows race away, riding on the same kind of creature that almost trampled us. "What kind of animal allows a rider?"

Bryntar eyes gaze into her past. "Khorbocks are quite gentle when domesticated."

Daniel sits up, breathing hard. "That was the same jerk we saw at the waterfall." He shivers. "It's below zero. We've got to find shelter."

Bryntar wipes the snow off her face. "This is all there is for many miles."

Muffled moans and snorts startle us.

"Wait here," Daniel says.

"We are tied together," I say.

"Yeah. Come on."

Bryntar and I follow him as he climbs over mounds of ice to the other side of the narrow ridge. A layer of snow covers an injured, male khorbock struggling in a deep trench. Fast-falling snow covers his black body.

Daniel shakes his head. "He looks pretty bad."

For once, I concentrate on blocking out the creature's pain by thinking of how to help him. "His front legs are broken."

Daniel's face lights up. "Luke Skywalker survived freezing weather in *The Empire Strikes Back.* This guy's so big I can gut him and we can climb inside the carcass to keep warm."

"What is *The Empire Strikes Back*?"

"A movie."

Bryntar's face looks as confused as mine feels.

He takes out his knife.

"Stop!"

"We have to put him out of his misery," Daniel says. "I'm sorry, but it might give us a better chance to beat the cold. And I'm hungry. Aren't you?"

"Not enough to kill. I can heal him."

"C'mon. He has two broken legs. He's huge and dangerous."

"Bryntar, please."

"Daniel makes sense," she says. "You are more important than this unfortunate khorbock."

"You will not kill him!" Light bursts from every cell of my body with such great force that they are thrown backward. My shock immediately diffuses the light and I run to them. "I did not mean to hurt you."

Daniel helps Bryntar up. "Remind me not to make you mad."

"What happened to me?"

Bryntar smiles. "Something to remember. Strong emotion controls the light. Come. I shall hold the horns of this creature."

"You're both nuts."

I want to touch his arm, but he backs away. How can I blame him? Energy still thrums through me. "Daniel, let me save him."

"Fine. Unknot your ropes. I'm tying him up."

He secures the rope to a chunk of ice, makes a large loop and throws it over the khorbock's neck. He tightens the loop after he wiggles the rope past the huge horns and wraps the end around another solid piece of ice.

The creature struggles to get up. Its great body crashes into the ice. Over and over.

How I wish I could block out his pain.

Daniel uses the end of his rope to throw another loop around a hind leg.

The leg strikes at Daniel, but he jumps back quickly and pulls the rope tight which stretches the khorbock's body. Its muscles tremble from the effort to move.

"Can't get to the leg under him. You'd better heal him before he kills himself."

"Be careful, Elandra." Bryntar holds one of the horns while I kneel next to the great head and sweep off the snow.

The khorbock rolls his huge brown eyes in terror and tries to strike me. The hooves hang useless. I remove my gloves and stroke the cream-colored spots on his nose with my hands, surprised with our connection.

Once his fear lessens, he transfers his feelings to me: of other creatures, grassy fields, and warm water. I close my eyes and let him sense my calm purpose. He snorts and stills all movement when my fingertips touch his broken bones. Holding the knee in place, I feel tremendous amounts of icy tingles stream into it. Trembling with the effort until my fingers burn, I hold fast. To reach the other leg, I hang over his shoulder. When the healing finishes, the creature heaves a great shudder.

It is snowing so hard I cannot see anyone. I call out, "I am finished."

Bryntar appears immediately at my side. "We need to let him up. If downed for too long, a khorbock has the will to die."

Daniel touches my shoulder. "I can't see well enough to take off the ropes."

I move closer. "Step back and stay together. Do not talk and do not move."

He nods and moves away with Bryntar.

I again open myself to the feelings of the khorbock and loosen the loop from the great head. When reaching over to remove it from the magnificent horns, warm air from his nose snuffles against my cheek.

"Easy. Good."

I concentrate on sending the feeling of stillness and crawl over his body to unhook his hind leg. As soon as he is free, the khorbock leaps up. I fall to the bottom of the trench and roll under him. He shakes his head and looks down instead of leaping to freedom and crushing me.

Daniel snatches me as I crawl up. "Are you crazy? You could have been killed." He pulls me away and reties the rope around my waist.

The creature shakes off the snow and bounds out of the hole. He is so tall that his shoulders reach my head. I am surprised when he does not run away.

Bryntar hands me my gloves. "You have earned his loyalty. He will not leave unless you want him to."

I pat his neck and the silky hair hanging over his shoulder.

"We'll be warmer in the trench," Daniel says. He jumps in and lifts us down.

Relieved to be out of the stinging wind, I sink to the frozen ground. The khorbock folds his legs and lies above us, tucking his nose in his chest.

"Will he be all right?" I ask.

Bryntar nods. "He stores much fat and his hair keeps him warm."

"We should be so lucky," Daniel says. "Without blankets or wood for a fire, I don't know if we can make it through the night."

Thirty-Three: The Discovering

The blizzard shrieks over our heads, leaving us in a world of white. Pillars of ice overhead block most of the snow from reaching us.

Daniel pulls us together into a corner. "We have to share our warmth."

I insert myself between them and Daniel closes me in his arms. We huddle in silence, knowing this trench is our last resting place. Without a fire, we cannot survive the night. I shiver, but not with cold, with the knowledge I am responsible for this by saving an animal instead of those I love. What was I thinking?

"It is done, Elandra." Bryntar says. "You cannot regret who you are or decisions that are past."

"I am beginning to think you can read minds," I say.

She smiles. "Only your face."

"Am I missing something?" Daniel asks, looking down at me.

"I am sorry for sacrificing your lives for that creature."

"You were thinking about saving a life," he says, "not about dying."

"How can you not hate me when we are going to freeze to death?"

He winks. "By hoping for a miracle."

My heart races sheltered in his arms. Even though I know he cannot feel it, my love pours into him. I close my eyes.

Bryntar sits up abruptly. "What are you doing?"

"Going to sleep."

"You did something else. Your body emitted heat instead of light."

"I felt it, too," Daniel says.

My face flushes. "I was thinking."

Bryntar strokes my face. "With that kind of heat, we might survive this night. Try it again."

Heat radiates through my clothes with thoughts of Daniel.

He hugs me. "Wow. That's terrific."

"What if I cannot maintain the heat we need?"

"Maybe I can help. What are you thinking?" he asks.

I cannot tell you that.

"I-I need to concentrate to make it work."

"Don't let me stop you. I'd like to be warm."

"What if I fall asleep?"

"We'll take turns keeping you awake," he says. "I'll go first.

I take Bryntar's hand. She relaxes and closes her eyes. Her feelings of relief flow through me.

Daniel whispers in my ear. "You can tell me. What thoughts can make you do that?"

My toes tingle. More of my heat soaks into him. "I cannot concentrate and answer your questions."

"Right." He chuckles. "You might have to keep me awake." His arms tighten around me and I feel safe in a trench in the middle of a blizzard.

He falls asleep quickly. My eyes never close, not when their lives depend on me. Instead of waking Bryntar, I let her sleep. She deserves it after spending the second-worst day of her life helping me. The night passes with thoughts about what it would be like to be far away from here and loving Daniel for the rest of our lives.

…

The blizzard blows over during the middle of the night. The silence is complete, broken only by deep breathing and the loud snuffles of the khorbock. My uncle's death sneaks into my mind. I send the thought away and begin reciting long passages that Taroc made me memorize in order to say awake.

Thank you, Father.

Long after, the sun brightens the sky in shades of pink. I am grateful to see another sunrise.

The khorbock grunts as he rises and shakes off snow.

Daniel releases me and jumps up. "I can't believe I fell asleep."

Bryntar stretches her legs. "You did not wake me, either."

"You both needed sleep more than I did." I stagger up, so tired I sway.

Daniel catches me and teases. "Guess you like it in my arms."

I pull away, embarrassed. "Only to save your life." I think I feel his disappointment, but it is gone in an instant.

Bryntar climbs out of the trench. "Let us go. We all need food."

I climb out stiffly while Daniel gathers the rope.

The khorbock rubs his nose against my hair and I pat his shoulder. "How far do we have to go?"

"Too far for you without sleep." Bryntar says. "You ride the khorbock."

"What if I fall off?"

"A khorbock is easy to ride."

"What if he runs away with me?"

"He can carry all of us." She hands me the rope and I stare at it.

"Let me," Daniel says. He hands me a length of rope and loops it around the creature's nose.

"I will ride him first." Bryntar takes the rope from him and grabs the mane.

Daniel hands her the other end and holds his hands together. She steps on them and lifts one leg over the creature to settle on his back.

"Stand back."

The khorbock snorts and hops to the side, trembling

She pats his neck and hums a song I have not heard since I was a baby. The melody drifts in the air. His ears twitch. She squeezes his sides gently and guides him in a circle.

"This is an extremely intelligent khorbock. I have never seen one so gentle."

"It's the Enchantress's touch," Daniel says, winking at me.

My heart thumps faster. I wish he would not do that.

"Or he has belonged to another," she says.

"I'm glad he's here. Let's go." Daniel locks his hands together for me.

I lightly step into them and straddle the khorbock's wide back, careful to avoid the long horns. Daniel jumps up behind me.

"Hold on," Bryntar says. "We can make the valley before dark."

I grab her waist and Daniel encloses mine.

She makes a clicking sound and the creature strides forward in a long-legged gait. The movement is so smooth that I lean against Daniel and am instantly asleep.

...

I awake when the khorbock hops sideways and snorts, almost dumping me on the ground. I gently loosen the tight grip around my waist and turn to Daniel. "Thank you."

"Anytime," he says.

Violet, purple, and red streak across the deepening sky like giant wings. "Where is the valley?"

"Beyond that cluster of rocks," Bryntar says.

"Why did we stop?"

"Something spooked the khorbock," Daniel says.

"I need to get off and walk," I say, slipping down the hairy side. My legs buckle and feel like I am still riding the creature.

Daniel and Bryntar dismount and she hands me the rope.

The khorbock jumps again when a slight breeze carries a faint, "Help."

"Did you hear that?" I hurry forward across the hard ice, pulling a reluctant khorbock.

"Help. Help me!"

It is Jyrr.

The khorbock stops near a great fissure and refuses to take another step.

I start forward, but Bryntar grabs my hand. "As soon as he sees your hair, he will know who you are."

"What about her eyes?" Daniel asks.

She slumps. "We cannot hide her."

Daniel hands me his hat. "This can help a little."

"It is too dangerous," Bryntar says.

I breathe deeply and stuff my hair inside the hat.

She sighs. "What about my clawed hand and scales?"

"Your hair covers them," I say. "You can hide your hand."

"Any islander will know Daniel is an outsider," she says.

"They all probably know by now," he says.

He takes the rope off the khorbock. "We'll just have to tie him up and leave him where his people can find him. Agreed?"

"How are you going to do that?" I ask. "He is taller and outweighs you."

"You know who is down there?"

"I recognized his voice."

Daniel shakes his head in disgust. "The jerk?"

"I think so."

"He won't be expecting an attack." He turns to Bryntar. "You have any way to knock him out?"

"My pleasure."

Daniel grins. "He might get some sense."

"Do you think that is a good idea?" I ask. "He is powerful."

"What else can we do?" Daniel starts to crawl to the crevice. "Do I need to know anything else about Ice Lords that could help me with this guy?"

"They respect strength and fearlessness," Bryntar says. "Although the female warriors are held in great esteem, male Ice Lords rule."

"Great."

I wonder why that matters until I remember the books of my childhood. Few civilizations give equal status to women.

Daniel reaches the edge of the fissure and peers over it.

Bryntar creeps behind him.

"Get me out of here." Jyrr sounds far away.

Daniel removes the rope from the khorbock and tosses it over the edge. "Tie this around your waist."

I pace. Why am I so nervous? It seems to take forever before two large hands toss up a jeweled bridle and carved saddle. When the dark hair of the Ice Lord appears, Bryntar punches him in the face. He sags and his weight pulls Daniel toward the crevice.

"Daniel!"

"Grab me," he yells.

Bryntar and I snatch his legs and pull them both to safety. My heart thumps so hard I think it is going to jump out of my chest.

Daniel smiles sheepishly. "Should have thought that one through." He separates the two pieces of rope, gathers one and uses the other to tie Jyrr's wrists behind his back. He secures the arms by wrapping the rope several times around Jyrr's chest and waist and down to each ankle. He leaves only a small amount of rope between the prisoner's feet. "That should do it." He sits him up.

The Ice Lord moans. He opens his eyes and glares at Daniel.

"You assaulted the heir to this kingdom. Release me at once."

"I don't think so."

Jyrr smiles. "Since you saved my life, I can be lenient."

"I am not going to untie you," Daniel says.

"You shall be tortured and killed for your actions!"

Daniel smiles. "Is that any way to treat your savior? No one else is riding to your rescue." He picks up the saddle and bridle. The jewels sparkle in the waning sun. He turns to me. "I think these will be perfect for my khorbock, don't you?"

Jyrr tightens. "Those belong to me."

The Ice Lord's anger streaks through me, hot and ragged. I am speechless and do not understand why Daniel provokes him.

"There are two dead khorbocks at the bottom of the crevice," Daniel says. "Anyone else down there?"

Defiant, Jyrr's eyes flash. "No."

"What is the penalty if an Ice Lord is caught lying?" Daniel asks Bryntar.

"The tongue is ripped out," Bryntar says.

Jyrr's icy purple skin pales. "My friend and I were caught in a blizzard and fell into the crevice. His khorbock crushed him."

Daniel's eyes flare. "Where I come from, we don't leave our dead behind."

The Ice Lord flinches and lowers his eyes. "He lies under the khorbock. I could not free him, even with my great strength."

"If we free you, bring your people to return the body to his family."

Jyrr sneers. "Who are you to order me?"

"I'm the one who decides whether you live or die." Daniel hauls him to his feet.

Jyrr is a head taller, but there is no fear inside Daniel. He walks without a limp, but I feel the strain on his knee. He looks at us, winks and leaps up on the khorbock. "Mount up. I'm hungry."

I am about to argue with Daniel when Bryntar whispers in my ear. "Do not interfere. It is important for Daniel to gain respect."

Daniel reaches a hand for me and while he settles me behind him, he stares at Jyrr. Chills race up and down my body at the disdain in the Ice Lord's eyes. Something passes between the young men and I feel Daniel has somehow claimed me as his property. I am not sure if I like this.

Bryntar mounts behind the saddle.

Daniel secures the rope. "Let's go."

Jyrr scowls. He raises his chin in defiance and almost trips with the rope tied between his ankles. "You expect me to walk like this?"

"I can throw you back into the crevice. Or leave you for the bearrans."

I am confused with the laughter Daniel feels and the opposition of his curt words.

"Who are you?" Jyrr asks.

"Your enemy. Be a good boy."

Jyrr utters a few unknown words of anger, his hatred shivering through me.

Daniel turns the khorbock south. To his credit, he keeps the khorbock at a slow walk so Jyrr does not stumble too much.

We eventually reach an ice wall painted with the last brilliant rays of sun. The khorbock steps onto an almost hidden trail. Around and down we wind on a thin path of melting ice and crumbling rock. The khorbock is sure-footed and does not miss a step. It is difficult for Jyrr to keep from falling.

"Are you trying to slay me?" he asks. His face does not mask his rage and frustration.

Daniel looks at him with arrogance. "With your great strength, I am sure you're quite capable of walking this simple path."

The Ice Lord yells more unfamiliar words.

Bryntar's fear shoots through me.

I lean over and whisper, "What did he say?"

Her worried eyes meet mine. "He vows to kill Daniel with his bare hands. An Ice Lord always keeps his vow."

Trembling, I look down at Jyrr. Black, defiant eyes rake across me, his intent clear. I will belong to him. I shudder and wonder how my body could ever have reacted to him.

Thirty-Four: The Charming

My khorbock lowers his head as we pass under a low-hanging arch of rock and enter a small meadow nestled between two mountains. A small pond shimmers red in the sunset. The smell of sweet fruit makes my mouth water in anticipation.

Daniel dismounts. "You may rest, Ice Lord."

Jyrr sits on a large rock. His wrists bleed from the rope wrapped under the golden cuffs, but he does not speak.

Bryntar and I slide off the khorbock. He immediately munches grass.

Daniel puts his hands on his hips and looks at us. "Make a fire by the water. Bring me food."

I hesitate, unused to this Daniel.

Bryntar hurries to gather fruit. "Do as he says."

I pick up twigs, leaves and dry branches, placing them in a pile near the pond.

Daniel lifts heavy rocks to form a circle.

"You are stronger than you look," Jyrr says with a smirk.

Daniel laughs. "I admire strength of character."

Jyrr's face darkens with the insult.

Bryntar puts the fruit by the rocks and kneels beside me. She hides my hands from the Ice Lord and pretends to strike two rocks together to start the fire while I ignite it. Soon the flames crackle with heat.

Daniel pulls me to his side and whispers in my ear. "I don't trust him. Please pretend we're together until we can get rid of him."

I wish we were together.

"May I feed him?"

"Only after you eat. He needs to know his place as a prisoner."

"How do you know these things?"

"Movies."

There is enough on my mind without worrying about what 'movies' are.

"Whatever you do, be careful," he adds.

"Yes, Daniel." I bite into honeyed fruit, thankful to fill my hollow stomach. When I finish, the pure water in the pond quenches my thirst.

Choosing a piece of fruit, I walk toward Jyrr, feeling Daniel's eyes on me. "Do you wish to eat?"

Jyrr smiles. High cheekbones and icy purple skin make him strikingly handsome. His cropped black hair is the opposite of Daniel's blond waves. The bearran fang hangs from his ear with the crystal stone in the shape of three stars.

"Thank you," he says. His soft mouth touches my hand and shivers streak through me. Juice dribbles down his chin. "Forgive my clumsiness."

I rip a leaf from a plant and wipe his smooth face.

"Another fruit, please?"

I feed him another and another, unable to stop my body from thrilling to the lure of his voice.

What is the matter with me? How can I react this way when I know he will kill Daniel if given the chance?

Ripping a large leaf, I dip it in the water and put it to Jyrr's lips.

"Please, on my wrists."

I walk behind him and pour water over the caked blood. When finished, I make the mistake of looking up. His eyes lock onto mine. "I did not expect the Enchantress to be so young or so beautiful. What is your power?"

My heart thuds to my feet and I back away from him.

He chuckles. "Your eyes are stunning."

I cannot stop shaking.

"You tremble," he says with a smile. "Do not fear me. The younger Ice Lords and I do not believe in the old ways of destroying your kind. Become my mate and I shall rule this island without challenge."

Bryntar steps behind me. "She is not for you, Ice Lord."

He turns disdainful eyes on her. "Have we met?"

"Never."

"Still you look familiar. I know I have seen your face."

"You are not worthy of her."

His eyes flare. "You do not know me, woman."

"Who is your father?"

"I am ready to inherit the throne."

"Unless you are challenged," Bryntar says.

Uncertainty shudders through him, but he says, "No one would dare challenge me."

"Are you ready to face Aru?" she asks. "For that is what it will take to save this island."

He smirks. "I do not believe in Kepyr superstition."

"You would be wise to heed the old prophecies." Bryntar steps behind me and rips off the hat. Hair falls down my back and over my shoulders, shimmering with light.

Jyrr cannot hide the surprise in his eyes. "Truly beautiful."

"Be warned Ice Lord," she says. "She can kill you with one finger."

He laughs. "You have the claws of a beast, woman. How is that?"

Bryntar flushes with anger. "Rest Elandra. I guard first."

"Elandra. . . as lovely as the girl," Jyrr says.

Heat rushes to my face.

Daniel pushes through us. "You do not have permission to talk, prisoner."

"My name is Jyrr," he says. "There is no fear in talking to me. Since I will rule this island, I am interested in learning about all of you."

Daniel sneers. "Enough talk."

I turn to stoke the fire, but Daniel yanks on my arm and pulls me into the darkness of the trees. "What are you doing?"

"Keeping the fire going."

"You're flirting."

"I do not know what you are talking about."

"You like him."

"I do not know him."

"I've known lots of guys like him. They think they own the world and can have any girl they want. He wants you."

I tingle with his warm breath on my neck.

He takes my hands and I can hardly breathe. "If the Kepyr trackers are as good as your uncle was, I'm sure the whole island is after us. Our ace in the hole is Bryntar. They won't be looking for her."

Oh, Uncle. I wish you were here. You would know what to do.

"He wants me to be his mate so we can rule the island."

Daniel cannot hide his jealousy. "Don't be a fool. Once he gets what he wants, he'll kill you. Believe me, you can't trust him."

"You do not have to worry, Daniel. There will not be any man in my life."

He flinches and turns so I cannot see his face. "We have to decide what to do. We could use Mr. Ice Lord as a hostage, but there is more danger for us that way. Or ditch him and find a place to hide until Aru rears his ugly head."

Aru. In our struggle to survive, I have forgotten my destiny. "What is the difference? We are doomed."

Daniel takes my shoulders. "Not as long as we are breathing. I have faith in you. Get some sleep. I'll relieve Bryntar in a few hours." He strides back to the fire.

Bryntar glares at Jyrr as he pretends to sleep.

I lie down as far away from Jyrr as possible and watch the fire breathe. Flames twist in the darkness, like my emotions. Daniel worries about me. Bryntar distrusts and dislikes Jyrr with unreasonable passion. Jyrr strains against his ropes, furious to be helpless.

The fire is hypnotic and I close my eyes. No pillars of ice or molten lava mar my dreams as I float away. . . until darkness sucks the light from my hair. I scream, gasp for breath and wake up from the nightmare.

Something feels wrong. Frantic, my eyes search the area. The khorbock rests in the shadow of a tree. Daniel hunches by the fire.

Where are Bryntar and Jyrr?

Thirty-Five: The Condemning

Knots of panic twist in my stomach. I lurch toward Daniel. "Where are they?"

He raises his head, the despair in his eyes clear. "Bryntar's gone. She took Jyrr with her."

"It is the middle of the night. Why would she leave?"

"So his people can find him and we can be safe."

I feel enclosed in a horrible nightmare. "How could you let her go?"

He stands up and gently takes my shoulders in his hands. "We agreed it was the safest way to protect you."

I yank away from him. Sick chills crawl through me. "You planned this together?"

He paces, running his fingers through his hair. "She knew the Ice Lords would send out a search party. We couldn't let them find you."

"It never crossed your minds to include me in your decision?"

"C'mon. We knew what you'd say. Besides, he has some kind of power over you."

"Are you jealous?"

"Don't be silly."

My knees shake so hard I fight to keep standing. "I would never agree to put the only mother I have ever had in such danger. Especially not with Jyrr."

"She's lived nine-hundred years and knows every inch of this island."

"As a powerful monster. What do you think they will do if she is captured in her condition?"

"I'm sure she can take care of herself."

"She does not even have a weapon."

He plops down in front of the fire. "She knew the risks. How upset you would be. She wanted you to forgive her. To understand this was the only way to ensure you could survive and save the island."

"It has always been about saving this island!"

He leaps up. "Are you blind? This is about saving the one person she loves more than life itself."

"Do not say that."

"Face it. It's true."

I would rather die than be the cause of her death. Unwanted tears blur my eyes and I blink them away.

"I'm really sorry." He puts his arms around me.

I push him away. "Do not touch me. If she dies, I will never forgive you for letting her leave without me."

"It was her idea. I couldn't have stopped her even if I wanted to."

I disregard his frustration and stalk toward my khorbock.

He catches my arm and holds it tight. "You're not going anywhere. You don't even know where she went and it's impossible to track her in the dark."

"You are hurting my arm."

He drops it. "Sorry."

I glare at Daniel. "Stay here and be safe."

"You think it's safe now that Jyrr knows about this place? He'd kill me without hesitation."

"You need to go your own way."

"I don't have a way. I want you to save this island so I can go home."

I dismiss all the emotions slamming through me, his and mine.

"Goodbye, Daniel."

He grabs me from behind and traps me in his arms. "Listen to me."

I struggle against his hard chest. "Let me go."

"Not until you agree to hear what I have to say."

It is impossible to escape without hurting him. "Talk."

He does not release me, but loosens his grip. "We're going to meet Bryntar. She will join us as soon as she can."

All the fight drains out of me. Their betrayal still hurts.

"You could have told me sooner."

He throws up his hands. "Like I had a chance with you flying off the handle."

I do not try to understand his words. A sudden urge to see Bryntar and know she is all right overtakes me. "We need to leave now, while it is dark."

"I agree. It's safer." He gazes into the clear sky. "I can use the stars and my compass. I'll need daylight to find her landmarks."

"Where are we going?"

He puts the fire out. "South, to avoid the Ice Lords."

"Into Kepyr territory? It will be just as perilous."

"Yeah, but this place isn't safe now."

He helps me onto the khorbock. My legs protest, but the saddle is designed to make the ride more comfortable.

"You take the reins so I can get our direction." He mounts and I wish he did not have to wrap his arms around my waist.

The creature starts up the steep path and I am thankful he knows the way. Except for the rhythmic click of hooves, the night is silent. Cold once again becomes our constant companion, for my nerves are raw and no heat radiates from me.

"Did you really mean what you said?" Daniel asks. "About never forgiving me?"

"I did."

"I can't be held responsible for Bryntar's decisions. I am only responsible for my own."

"That may work in your world, but not here and not for me. I am responsible for everyone."

"It doesn't work in my world either. Everyone wants to blame someone else for their problems."

We reach the ice plain and Daniel gazes at the sky. "Stop. I have to find Polaris."

"The North Star?" I ask.

"How do you know about stars?"

"I read about them in books. Living underground all my life, I have no practical knowledge."

"I lived outside and learned how to hunt, fish and play sports. I'd die underground. Look, see the seven stars that form the Big Dipper?"

I follow his pointing finger. "A handle hooked onto an open square?"

"That's it. Follow the last star on the square and go about five lengths of the handle. That bright star is Polaris. Turn the khorbock in the opposite direction for south."

I do as he says, patting the creature. "What is it like in your world?"

"Too crazy to explain. You'd have to see it."

"Then tell me about your family."

He is silent for so long that I do not think he is going to speak.

"I took them for granted, always expecting them to be there for me."

His grief is equal to mine when I think of Taroc and Bryntar.

"My dad is the greatest guy." His voice chokes up. "I still can't believe he's gone."

"I am sorry."

"He is-was an engineer who specialized in building bridges. He designed our ship. Everyone pitched in to build it since we were all going on the trip. We had a blast."

The sky lightens with the fading night, but the darkness does not leave Daniel.

"You told me your mother and sister stayed behind," I say.

"Yeah. Annie got sick. Mom decided to take her home. I felt bad they couldn't go, but excited to have just us guys, too." He swallows hard. "I'm glad they couldn't come."

I feel his anguish. "What was your brother like?"

"He'd just finished his second year at Harvard Law. He would have been a great lawyer, even if he bossed me around because I was younger." His voice cracks.

"You make me wish I had someone to grow up with."

"I don't envy your childhood," he says.

"It was different."

"You were loved. Maybe that's all that matters."

I feel the ache in his heart.

We ride in silence until dawn glitters over a great forest covered in frozen snow. Soft patches of tundra push up through the thinning ice.

My khorbock snorts and perks up his ears.

I stop as hooves thunder in my chest.

"What is it?" Daniel asks.

"Khorbocks. A lot of them."

We search the vast ice plain and see nothing.

"Can you feel if they have riders?"

"They are too far away," I say.

"We can't take any chances. Let's move."

I think of running and the khorbock bolts across the ice so fast that I slip and bang into a horn. "Help."

"Steady there." Daniel pulls me upright.

I lean over and grab a hunk of khorbock mane. Muscles move underneath us in long strides, hooves kicking up ice and ground. Wind whips my hair and I breathe in gulps of light. I laugh, not caring that we are running for our lives. Racing on the khorbock is the most thrilling thing I have ever done.

"I'm afraid we have company," Daniel says.

I look around, relieved the khorbocks are still far enough away that we can hide.

"Ride for those trees," Daniel whispers in my ear. "We're going to have to get off."

"We cannot run away on foot."

"We'll hide. You have to send the khorbock away."

We race to the trees and jump off. Daniel removes the saddle and bridle and throws them on his shoulders.

I close my eyes and send my feelings to the creature: appreciation for his loyalty, thanks for his help, the need to run far, and lead away those that chase us. The one feeling that surprises me the most is the love I feel for him. And the love he returns when he leans over and nuzzles my neck. I pat him. "Goodbye, my great khorbock." He stares into my face with those huge eyes, spins away, and is gone.

"Climb!" Daniel pushes me to the low limbs of a tree.

The branches are thick. "This is impossible."

"That's the idea. If our pursuers come this way, they won't think of looking here. Even if they look up, they won't see us. Move it. I need to cover our boot prints."

I step on the lowest branch close to the tree trunk.

Daniel shakes a branch. Snow falls off to cover our tracks and he climbs up behind me.

"This isn't going to be easy. Protect your face as much as possible. No matter what, don't make a sound."

The only sounds I hear are hooves smashing through the ice and coming closer.

I wiggle up, weaving over and under and through branches thick with sharp needles. It must be much harder for Daniel to squeeze through because of his size. Especially when he carries the saddle and bridle.

Glad for the protection of my fur clothes, I somehow manage to keep moving higher, grabbing a branch, stepping to the next higher one, squishing between the jabbing needles. My muscles ache with the strain. The tight spaces threaten to suffocate me. Branches turn to smaller limbs and fear of breaking one makes me stop. I look up and down, unable to see anything but tree. Even though Daniel gasps for breath, he is not visible.

Khorbocks snort below us, hooves stomping and thumping in impatience.

I hold my breath and cringe when Jyrr's voice booms through the morning air.

Thirty-Six: The Hiding

"Follow those tracks! They will not escape!"

The khorbocks thunder away.

I shiver, cold as ice.

Oh, Bryntar. Please be safe and on the way to join us.

I gasp in light.

"I need help," Daniel whispers.

"Are you all right?"

"Yeah. The bridle is caught and I can't move."

"I am coming." It is much harder to back down the tree. Even twisting my head, it is impossible to see where to put my feet. I test a step, slip on the snow and straddle a branch. "Ow."

"You okay?"

"Remind me not to climb another tree like this."

He chuckles. "It did save us from being caught."

I wiggle, squirm and succeed in banging knees and slipping on more slick needles by the time I see him. He sits on the saddle over a branch.

I grin. "Going for a ride?"

"Funny. Get me out of this."

The bridle wraps around his neck and the reins are caught in the needles of three branches. I squirm down and step on his hand.

He groans.

"I am sorry."

Trying to find another place to put my foot, I kick him in the head.

"Ow!"

Afraid to put a foot anywhere, I reach over and unhook the bridle. My other foot slips on an icy branch. My knee hits him in the stomach.

"Ooofff. Don't let me climb any more trees with you." He laughs.

I grin and we help each other down.

While I brush off wet snow, he drapes the saddle and bridle over the branches of the tree. The jewels sparkle in the sunlight.

"Are you leaving those here?"

"Yep. Don't want anything that belongs to that jerk."

"Are we close to the first landmark?" I ask.

"We'll have to climb that knoll to see."

We sneak through the trees to reach the top. Below is a deep canyon. Monuments of black stone stretch through low-lying clouds and into the sky. The seven pointed tops are covered with patches of thick moss that look like hair.

"Is that it?"

"Yeah. Bryntar calls the stones, 'The Old Ones'. Says they may be the beginning of life here. It's also a place of silent pilgrimage, so we can't talk."

"Where are we supposed to meet Bryntar?"

"The other end of the canyon."

Glacial ice gives way to dark soil as we sneak down the canyon sides. I am grateful for the gradual incline and easy walk, but lack of sleep and the fear of meeting anyone make the journey difficult. I grow hotter as we leave the ice behind and stumble onto a winding track of pebbles.

We weave between the five-sided stones. Small plants grow on the rough surfaces in beautiful patterns of muted green, orange and brown. I strain to feel anything that might put us in danger. I think I feel something and then it is gone—probably a small animal. Daniel pulls me off the path into the undergrowth to rest.

I gaze up at the giant, silent sentinels. Reaching out to touch the nearest one, I experience a profound tranquility, as if the stone has a serene intelligence. Yet there is a strange foreign quality I do not understand.

A thought flickers in my mind, of Aru destroying this special place. I am again reminded there is no other way but to accept that I will face the beast. I do not want to know where or when.

We continue across the canyon, ever alert to our surroundings. Berry bushes satisfy our hunger. There is no one here this early and I am relieved to feel at peace for once.

Turning a corner and leaving the last stone behind, I jump at the sudden thunder of water that breaks the silence. It is as if the stones can stop sound.

A wide veil of water pours over smooth rock and splashes into the rushing river below.

Daniel grabs my hand. "C'mon. We're almost there." He pulls me straight to the water.

"Wet again?"

He laughs, leads me upriver, and points to stepping-stones jutting from the water. "There's a cave behind the waterfall. We cross here."

"The rocks are barely sticking out of the water!"

"Yeah, that's the tricky part. Bryntar warned that the river is high this time of year."

"The current will wash us away. There must be another place to cross."

"There isn't. I'll go first."

"Do you expect me to rescue you if you fall in?"

He smiles. "Only if you want to."

I hold my breath as he leaps from one rock to another. He makes it look as natural as breathing and lands on the other bank.

"C'mon. It's easy, like jumping croc heads, except the rocks don't move."

"You jumped on crocodile heads?"

"It was fun."

Jumping on the heads of live reptiles is fun? Maybe we are too different.

I shake my head and stride to the river's edge. The first rock is close, but a thin layer of water glides over it. I step on the flat surface and balance with both feet. Water sprays over my boots. The second rock has a top with two points and a flat space between them. I stretch to reach it with one foot, wobble, and almost fall in before my hands grab one of the points. Water brushes my nose.

Daniel laughs. "Good save. Keep going."

"Would you not talk to me?"

"Just cheering you on."

"Stop it." I step on the third rock, closer and higher out of the water. It is the next rock that sends shivers up my spine. One small point protrudes from the river and can only be used to reach the final rock. Two quick jumps. Taking a deep breath and focusing on reaching the tip of the rock, I leap. One boot touches it and I use the forward movement to leap to the other. I slip on moss and plunge toward the river, surprised to land in Daniel's arms.

Water rises to his waist, but he keeps me out of the water.

"Knew that one was too slippery." He sloshes out of the river.

I do not want to wiggle out of his arms, but I do and follow him over plants and boulders to reach the falls.

Daniel stops and points to a slim ledge.

"You expect me to walk on that? My foot is wider."

"I'll go first." He presses against the wall, sidesteps carefully along the ledge and vanishes.

Jumpy, I wait impatiently.

He reappears and grabs my hand. We press our backs against the rock wall and slide along the slippery edge.

I gasp when freezing water hits me in the face and the sheer weight of the falls smashes me against the rock wall. Daniel's arm tightens. Moments feel like forever. Until he pushes me under an overhanging slab and we stumble into the cave.

Sunlight glimmers through the water and ripples inside a deep cavern. I panic. "Where is Bryntar?"

"Calm down. She has farther to go."

"How long are we supposed to wait here?"

"Two days."

My stomach churns. "What if she does not come?"

"Don't worry." He pulls me away from the spray of the waterfall.

Fearful to think of life without Bryntar, I start to shake. "If something happens to her, I will take off my protective shirt and hope Aru finds me."

"Trust her. She'll come." Daniel rubs his hands to keep warm. "There's no way to get dry wood in here to get warm."

"Then we have to get out of these wet clothes." I remove my soggy gloves, coat and fur pants.

Daniel says, "I'm not going to be caught with my pants off when Bryntar gets here."

"She will understand."

"You don't know much about mothers."

"What do I need to know?"

"That's what I mean."

"I do not understand," I say.

"You'll have to ask her."

I shiver in the dampness and collapse against the back wall.

"We'll stay warmer together," Daniel says. He encloses me in his arms. His steady heartbeat thumps next to mine.

I snuggle closer and shut my eyes. It is delicious to feel safe. My mind wanders to all the times Daniel has protected me. All the times he has put me above himself. I know he does not do this so I will save him someday. It is because he is willing to sacrifice his life for mine and for a greater cause. Like my uncle and Bryntar. Am I willing to do the same?

I remember gazing into my mother's eyes the first moments of my life and the impressions she gave me about love. Now I think I understand. The kind of love Daniel has for me is true and pure. It does not matter who I am, what my faults are, or my uncertain destiny. It does not even matter that he hides it from himself. What matters is that my love for Daniel is different. Desire for him will always burn inside me. Heat begins to radiate around us.

"How do you do that?" he asks.

I cannot ever tell him. "We should rest while we can." I have never felt more awake and totally aware of him.

"Elandra?"

I lift my head and am lost in the desire in his eyes.

"I've been an idiot. I can't hide how I feel." He lowers his head and his mouth consumes my trembling lips. Not with softness, but with a passion that leaves me breathless. Desperate, he pulls me closer and strokes my back. I thrill to his touch.

His kiss deepens. Our bodies throb and soar to a place where there is no breath, no thought, only feeling. He pulls away and I moan, wanting to be one with him. He gazes into my eyes. "I've never felt like this before. With any girl."

I pull him closer and devour him with kisses as our hearts race together.

He groans and pulls away. "We can't do this."

"Why?"

"We don't know each other well enough."

"I do know you. You put others before yourself. You are brave. You are kind. You care about the important things in life."

"Stop." He pushes me farther away. "Look. If we were in Florida, we could date."

"What is date?"

"We'd go out and do something fun together."

I frown. "Like jumping on croc heads? How can that make us know each other better?"

He chuckles. "This isn't the right time for a relationship. Okay? It's not safe."

My finger traces his mouth. "We may never be safe."

"You're hard to resist. I wanted to kill Jyrr when you were feeding him."

His words sing through me.

"Don't underestimate him. I know what he'll do to you if we're caught."

I sigh. "I shall be put to death. And so will you."

He shudders. "Who knows what he might do before that happens?"

"We must not be caught." I move in closer. My arms tighten around him. My head whirls with a possibility I never imagined could come true. Could

Daniel and I have a life together?

"Get some sleep," he says.

I lie my head on his chest, confused, but content for this time together. His steady breathing calms me and I fall asleep in his sheltering arms.

...

The damp rocky floor grinds into my cheek. My muscles protest with stiffness when I jump up. Dim light filters into the cave making it difficult to see.

"Daniel? Where are you?" I search the cave quickly. He is gone. Panic streams to every part of my body and I feel sick.

A shadow moves under the overhang. "Good morning." He drops berries and roots at my feet with a grin.

Speechless, I stare at him, the panic draining away and another emotion taking its place.

"Are you all right?" he asks.

I throw the roots at him. "You left me. You could have been seen. Or captured. Or worse."

"I'm starved. Had to get food before it gets too light. Besides, I thought I could get back before you woke up."

"How would you feel if I was the one who left?"

"I'm sorry. It won't happen again." He kisses me.

I pull away from him. "You are all wet."

"We can remedy the problem."

"You think it is easy to create heat?"

He winks. "For you."

"Be careful you do not take me for granted."

His smile fades. "Since I've been shipwrecked, I never take anything for granted. Let's eat."

Soon after we are finished, Bryntar steps through the waterfall.

Relief washes over me as I run into her arms. Her embrace feels strange in her new form. I bury regret that my special moments with Daniel are over.

She holds me tight. "I worried that my decision to take Jyrr away might have been the wrong choice."

"Where'd you leave him?" Daniel asks.

"He kept trying to convince me to let him go. I dared not untie him, which made it necessary to take him to the foothills surrounding the palace."

"You could have been captured!" I say.

"He wasn't worth risking your life," Daniel says. "I hope our khorbock gave him a merry chase."

"He mounted a search that fast? He is more powerful than I thought. How did you avoid capture?" She sways and clutches the wall.

"When did you last eat?" I asked.

"I do not remember."

"You won't believe what happened," Daniel says.

Bryntar listens to our story while she eats.

It is easy to create heat now that I know how and she sits next to me to dry her clothes.

"You are changed," she says, considering my face.

"I accept what I am and what I have to do."

"It is more than that." She looks at Daniel and bristles. "I see."

He shrugs. "Nothing happened." He squeezes my hand. "I told you about mothers."

Bryntar scowls. "We will talk about this, Elandra."

"Tomorrow," I say. "You need to sleep."

She sighs. "It will be a relief to feel safe, at least for a little while. Now that we are known to the Ice Lords, we must take more care not to be seen."

Thirty-Seven: The Persevering

Darkness still fills the cave when a noise awakens me. Bryntar paces up and down the floor. Daniel is gone again.

She stops before me. "You love him."

"Yes."

"He has loved you since the first moment he saw you."

"He does not say so."

"It is in his eyes. Even Taroc knew. I never imagined you could have this kind of love, never dared to hope there would be someone worthy of you here. I was right about Daniel."

"I will not change my mind."

"You misunderstand. Daniel came from another world to find you. I am thankful that you know what it is like to love and be loved. Even if he will not admit it yet." Her eyes meet mine. "I hope you have not completed the union. Until you save the island, this is not the time to worry about a child."

"What do you mean?"

"It is a natural occurrence with having a mate." She hesitates.

"Although there has never been an opportunity for a child to be born to one of your kind."

A child? "Nothing happened between us."

She sighs in relief.

"I am glad you are not angry with me."

She puts her arms around me. "When have I ever been angry with you, dear Elandra?"

I hug her. "Not often. I think you left that to Taroc."

Pain flickers across her face. "You are right. I could not bear to reprimand you."

"He was so happy and grateful to know you transformed."

"You really did see him?"

"As clearly as I see you."

She sighs. "I wonder what we would have done if we had known that I could change back?"

"Do you think you will age?"

"Perhaps. I do not know."

I refuse to think that she can ever die. "What are we going to do now?"

She resumes her pacing. "The Ice Lords are searching for us. There is no safer place than home until we decide on a plan. I never expected. . ." She looks at her body and shakes her head. "I cannot give you and Daniel the kind of protection you need."

"You do not have to."

"Did I hear my name?" Daniel asks. He strides in bearing fruit. "I hope you know where we're going, Bryntar."

"South," she says. "I am concerned about what Jyrr might do. We need to take refuge in a small village of Keprys if we can reach it before the sun is high."

"You hate Kepyrs," I say.

"This tribe does not worship as Kepyr. Their vows of silence can protect us until we return home."

"We need to leave while it's dark," Daniel says.

We eat everything, not knowing where or when we will have another meal.

"Follow me," Bryntar says. She disappears under the ledge.

Daniel looks around the cave, then at me. "I won't forget this place." He kisses me gently and takes my hand.

The icy water pounds me against the wall. I slide after Daniel, glad of his strong hand. When we emerge, Bryntar waits across the river. My eyes adjust to the darkness, but it is difficult to see the rocks.

"Just go fast, but be accurate," Daniel says. He squeezes my hand.

"If you fall in, I'll catch you."

I stare at the rocks and leap. One, two, three, oops, slippery. Four, five, the bank. Made it.

I whirl around, feeling something is watching us. It is too dark to see and the noise of the waterfall interferes.

Daniel jumps across the river and hugs me. "You did it."

"We must hurry," Bryntar says. "We have little time."

We follow the river away from the canyon of The Old Ones, weaving through moss-covered boulders and grasses that reach our knees. There is little talk with the pace that she sets.

The river veers to the east and she stops. "Drink. Soon we cross an open plain."

The boulders disappear, leaving only a few odd-shaped rocks to rise above the flat landscape. Grass becomes sparse and gives way to spindly plants sticking up through irregular squares of cracked ground.

I stop when the sun rises in glory and turns everything pink and orange—a beauty that makes me realize for the first time that I do not want Aru to destroy the island. "Is it much farther?"

Bryntar points to a cluster of white rocks in the distance. "The village is there."

"How do you know they will help us?" I ask.

"They worship the 'One' of all things instead of Aru. If we can get inside their walls, they provide sanctuary for those in need."

"What is the 'One?'" I ask.

"They believe we are all connected and come from the same source," she says.

"Let's hurry," Daniel says. "I don't like being out here in the open."

We start across the barren land.

Drums batter the air. Their sound is such a shock that I cannot move.

Daniel grabs my hand. "Run."

I try to shut out the drums, but they get louder and louder along with the whoops and shouts of the Kepyr warriors behind us.

Bryntar yells. "Do not look back. Keep running."

We race faster. The flat, cracked ground changes into plants with prickly thorns and bright colored flowers that are hard to avoid. The white rocks become low buildings the closer we get.

Ice Lords riding khorbocks race from the sanctuary toward us in a cloud of dust. Kepyr warriors surround us.

Jyrr rides my spotted-nosed khorbock and pushes through the Kepyrs and other mounted Ice Lords. "Did you think you would escape from me, my Enchantress?"

Thirty-Eight: The Capturing

Blood drains down my spine, leaving me lightheaded. If I could save us without causing harm to Daniel or Bryntar I would, for my fear is only for them. With so many against us, the danger is too great. I sway, overwhelmed. Interest, fear, and hatred surge through my body from both Kepyr and Ice Lord. Daniel tightens his hand to steady me.

A tall Kepyr warrior stalks up beside Jyrr, but he must look up to the mounted Ice Lord. "These prisoners belong to us. We watch and track for two days."

Jyrr raises his eyebrows. "Why wait to capture them?"

"Safer than in the canyon."

Jyrr sneers. "Safer for you, a mighty leader?"

The Kepyr leader tightens in anger. "For my warriors. We know the powers of the Enchantress."

"By order of my father, the Ice Lord King, these are my prisoners," Jyrr says.

"As you wish, my Lord," the leader says.

I know that he would rather kill Jyrr than submit to his order.

Jyrr says, "Their trials will take place at Council before all the people of the island. I expect they will be found guilty. Their executions shall be tomorrow. Sound your drums."

Spasms slither through me. I struggle to stand straight. Light bursts in a halo around my head. Snorts and shouts abound as khorbocks and warriors leap away.

"Cover her head!" Jyrr shouts.

Daniel tries to protect me. A spear strikes him on the head and he crashes to the ground.

"Daniel!" A knife to my throat stops me from going to him. I want to cry, to scream, to do something.

Bryntar touches my arm and whispers, "A better time will come to fight."

Someone throws a blanket over my head while I am jerked up to sit on the back of my khorbock. "I will enjoy this ride," Jyrr whispers in my ear.

Sick dread envelops me as he puts his arms around my waist and clasps me tight against his chest. The only thing that saves me from screaming is the feeling of warm love radiating from the khorbock.

"Throw the male prisoner over that khorbock. Let the deformed woman ride with one of you. Keep your weapon on her neck at all times."

Bryntar sends me feelings of love and hope.

I control the rage that starts to burn through me. Controlling my emotions will be my greatest strength now. Tuning into Daniel, I feel his steady breath even though he is unconscious. It calms me. I cannot blame Jyrr for his treatment of us when he was once our prisoner. Yet I have never detested anything in my life until now.

The khorbock tenses his muscles. Jyrr kicks its flanks and all the Ice Lords thunder away, their hooves pounding along with the beating of the drums. Soon, we leave the drums far behind, but they batter my heart and remind me of my mother's death. Will I soon join her?

"Promise not to use your powers and I will remove the covering," Jyrr says.

"Why would you believe the promise of an Enchantress?"

"Because I will kill your Daniel and enjoy it."

My body tightens. "I will not fight you."

He laughs and removes the covering.

I blink in the glare of the overhead sun. From the corner of my eye, I see Bryntar is safe. Daniel hangs over the khorbock on his stomach, still unconscious.

"Where you have been hiding all these years?" Jyrr asks.

I say nothing.

He moves his hands higher than my waist and I cringe with the movement of his fingers. I cannot control the sparks of light that shock him.

He yanks his hands away. "Witch."

"I am sorry, my Lord. Only recently have I acquired my powers. They are not always controllable." I speak in the meekest voice I can, hoping to appease him.

"I do not believe you."

"Because you do not know me."

"Remedied soon."

I die a little inside with the feelings that soar through him.

He kicks my khorbock harder and races toward the Ice Mountains.

I am left with my own thoughts. It is a place I do not want to be. If I had never left my home, we would not be prisoners.

How will I be able to save anyone now?

The khorbocks have great stamina and cover much ground. I am surprised at how soon we reach the Ice Mountains. The sun is much lower on the horizon when I see the tips of great black towers rising into the sky.

"Announce my arrival to the King," Jyrr says to his riding companions.

The Ice Lords race ahead, except for those with the prisoners.

We pass many houses built with square chunks of gray, white and black stone, far advanced from the huts of the Kepyrs. I do not know why anyone would want to live in such cold, desolate places for there are no gardens and nothing that grows with life. Maybe that is why they put such effort into the intricate carvings on their doorways and the unique designs made by the colors of stone. Handsome men, women and children emerge and watch us as we ride by. They all have black hair, black eyes, and icy purple skin.

They gather and follow us.

Bryntar looks straight ahead, but I feel her nervousness.

Before we reach the Palace, Jyrr pulls to a stop and jumps from my khorbock, taking a coil of rope off the creature. He yanks Daniel to the ground. "Stand up."

Daniel staggers up with blood caked on his face.

Heat flares in my every nerve. I want to scream. As if separating into two of me, I force my mind to stand apart, watching my angry self. I look weak. Small. Useless. This mind part of me feels powerful, yet observes without judgment. I can choose not to feel anything that does not serve me. The anger instantly disappears and I am one again. I have control.

Jyrr ties Daniel with his arms behind his back, rope wrapped around his body. I am surprised that he does not tie his feet.

"Time to walk," Jyrr says. He leaps behind me, hanging onto the rope and kicks the khorbock.

Daniel is ready and starts running.

Murmurs from the crowd behind us fill with surprise, then distaste.

Jyrr presses the creature harder. Daniel runs fast enough to keep up. I feel Jyrr's fury. He shoves Daniel with his boot and he falls, to be dragged down the icy path to the Palace.

"Please, stop!"

He laughs and yanks on the reins. "For a kiss." He grabs my chin roughly and presses his cold lips hard against mine.

I cringe with his desire and tremble with growing fury. Until I dispassionately observe myself from afar and choose not to react.

Jyrr releases my lips and smiles. "I am satisfied that you tremble with my kiss."

I smile inside, for at last, I have learned the key to mastering myself.

Someone helps Daniel up.

I breathe, relieved to see his eyes radiate defiance, even though his skin bleeds through torn clothes.

The stark beauty of the Palace soars before us.

"Behold the might of the Ice Lords," Jyrr says. "Are you afraid, now?"

I laugh. "I could destroy everything with one finger."

He grins. "I do not believe you."

I ignore him and concentrate instead on the giant pillars of polished black rock and white crystal that form the Palace walls. Their energy vibrates through me. Is the building alive? The huge structure is carved into the mountain, one level after another, after another, in perfect symmetry. Arches abound, etched with unreadable writing, geometric equations, and patterns of star constellations. The setting sun paints everything red.

Jyrr stops in the middle of the large courtyard filled with the khorbock riders and many other Ice Lords. They move toward us in interest. Everyone is exceptionally tall and beautiful. They wear fur and leather made into vests, jackets, pants, and dresses. Encrusted jewels flash in their clothes. Each adult has a different emblem and fang hanging from one ear.

Carved stone statues decorate the fountains with the births and deaths of former Ice Lord leaders. I long to be warm and bathe in their steaming waters.

Bryntar whispers, "It cannot be." She lowers her head, hair falling over her face.

We pass a beautiful statue of Bryntar made of white stone flecked with gold.

Jyrr dismounts and lifts me from the khorbock, holding me tight.

Bryntar's rider does the same, his knife still at her throat. She stands taller than he, her eyes rebellious. The crowd gasps when she brushes long hair with her claw to reveal the tiny row of iridescent scales on the side of her icy purple face. They do not seem to recognize her from the statue.

A man strides from the Palace, his eyes cold and commanding. Leather breeches and a sleeveless fur vest mold to his muscular body. Hanging from his ear is a large fang and an iridescent three-star emblem. Wide gold bands encircle his upper arms. Jewels ring his fingers. "Welcome, Ice Lords," the man says. His voice is as icy as his demeanor.

They lower their heads in respect. Moving up beside the man is a beautiful woman in a long gown of bearran fur. Her hair is braided and coiled on top of her head, the ring in her ear matching the man's.

Jyrr says quietly. "Father, Mother." He raises his head, his voice loud enough for all to hear. "Mighty Ryz-IL and Lady-Ryz-IL, I bring you the prisoners I promised."

Ryz-IL looks at Daniel and glares at Jyrr. "Do you fear this stranger to treat him in such a manner?"

The crowd whispers and fury rages through Jyrr. He raises his chin. "I was treated to the same."

"That makes you equal to him, not superior."

"Jyrr is just a boy," the Lady says.

Ryz-IL's eyes flare. "That is the problem."

Embarrassment flushes through Jyrr, and something else; a burning dislike for his father. "Ryz-IL, I have brought you the Enchantress and the woman who raised her against the laws of our land."

Lady-IL narrows her eyes in calculation as she stares at me, then at Bryntar.

Ryz-IL circles Bryntar. "What are you?"

"I invoke the law of silent respect," she says.

He frowns. "Obviously, you were once an Ice Lord. It will be entertaining to hear your story."

"That shall never happen," Bryntar says.

Surprise filters through him. "You would defy your Lord?"

"You shall never be my Lord."

Her opposition irritates him, but he hides it well. "We shall see." He turns to me with cold disinterest. "So this is the Enchantress we have so recently heard about. How old are you?"

"I have sixteen seasons."

Although there is nothing in his eyes or his manner, his shock vibrates through me.

"What are you called?"

"Elandra."

His emotions become a jumble of contradiction: astonishment, denial, fear, hope, love. Not once does it show in his face.

There is no doubt that I am standing before my father.

Thirty-Nine: The Imprisoning

I shiver and stare in defiance at him without flinching.

"Take them to the dungeons," Ryz-IL orders.

"I told the Kepyrs the execution is tomorrow," Jyrr says.

"You overstep your authority, Son. I am not dead yet." Ryz-IL disappears into the Palace.

My stomach churns. Is Jyrr my brother?

The Lady pulls Jyrr aside. "Go with care. While I have great influence over my husband, he is not compelled to relinquish his position when the bloodline is not direct." She sweeps into the building.

I release the breath I did not know I was holding. He is not my brother.

Jyrr nods to four of his riders. "Lock them up. Separately. Secure the woman's wrist. Make sure the boy's feet are chained together." He strides after his mother.

One rider leads, another holds his knife to Bryntar's neck, and the others walk behind us. We march through corridor after corridor, past great dining halls set with ornate plates and glasses, meeting halls with stone chairs of embedded jewels, chambers with strange words on closed doors.

I move to Bryntar's side and whisper in her ear, "Ryz-IL is my father."

She is surprised, but shrugs. "He will do nothing."

"But—"

"Unless he has more influence than I think, he will not stand against the law."

"Is there a way to escape the Palace?"

"No. It is built into the mountain and there are no underground tunnels."

I do not want to have to kill anyone.

Daniel limps beside me.

I know how he feels, but ask anyway. "Do you hurt much?"

"Only when I breathe."

"You were very brave."

"Easy when your life depends on it."

Without the riders seeing, I take his hand and touch my fingertips to the center of his palm. Icy power spreads throughout his body, greater than ever as I concentrate on my love and my desire to heal him. His head wound and abrasions disappear. His relief becomes mine.

"Thanks."

"Do not look at me that way," I say.

"Can't help it. You're hard to believe."

"Try harder."

He grins. "Stick around. I don't think Jyrr is through with me yet."

We descend floor after floor and eventually reach the end of a long hall. A rider opens the narrow doors revealing a long winding staircase leading down. The beauty displayed on the upper floors disappears. Strange torches light dull gray stone as we go deeper and deeper into the core of the mountain.

"What magic is that light?" I ask.

"Electricity. Kind of like lightning, only harnessed by people. Wonder where they got the technology?"

Heavy iron doors fold to reveal a long corridor. The rider opens another metal door and points to Daniel. "Get in."

"Can't we be together?" he asks.

The rider lowers his eyes. "I am sorry."

Daniel turns to me. He touches my cheek. "Remember. It's not over while we're breathing." When he disappears into the dark cell my heart goes with him. Chains clink around his ankles and the door slams shut.

Breath stops. I feel the hall go sideways.

Bryntar grabs my arm and whispers, "Control." She enters the next cell. Her wrist is locked to the wall and a spike slides into the stone closing her away.

I gag, struggling to hold my screams inside.

Another iron door clangs behind me. Doomed the moment I was born, I face death once again. Pain throbs up my arm as Bryntar fights the lock confining her wrist. Daniel suffers with chilling fear for me, rather than himself.

I block out all their pain, too much to bear now. For this is my fault. I am responsible for Taroc's death and my uncle's. To face Bryntar's and Daniel's deaths is more than I can bear. I do not care to observe myself or control anything. I sink to the cold stone floor and let dampness slither into my soul. Tears slide silently and then flood down my face. I cannot control the sobs that wrack my body.

I cry until there are no tears left to shed, and am left with a strange peace and acceptance. If I do not find a way to save my friends before their executions, I will go mad. Before the Beast can devour me.

The clang of iron startles me and I stand up quickly.

Jyrr glides inside with a torch. "I bring gifts." He wears tight leather clothing that molds to his muscles. I wonder why Ice Lords do not seem to mind the cold. I cringe when he pulls the door closed.

Wary of his good mood, I move to the back wall and say nothing.

He connects the light to the wall and unrolls a thick carpet of fur. Inside is a container of hot food. "Please eat."

"Why should I eat when you have condemned me to death?"

"Our discussion might change your predicament." He takes the lid off to reveal steaming meat.

"I do not eat dead animals."

Irritation flits through him, but he manages to smile. He opens the door and talks to someone outside. "I need a plate of fruit." He turns back. "I can be accommodating."

"What about my companions?"

"That depends on you. I want to get to know you better. How did you survive all these years?"

"Why does it matter?"

"My position as heir can be helpful."

I glare at him. "You ordered my execution."

He settles onto the rug and indicates that I sit next to him. "I can still save your life. Many wish to see me on the throne."

"No one stands against the law," I say.

"Laws can be changed."

I laugh. "Not in a day."

His black eyes bore into me. "You are wrong. Ice Lords respect power. Tell me of your gift." He moves closer to me and I cringe with his desire. "If your power is strong enough, we can rule this island. Not even the law can stand against us."

I shiver with repulsion as he takes my hand.

"I am most desired by women."

A knock interrupts him. He stomps to the door and returns with a polished stone bowl filled with fruit. My body recoils when his leg touches mine as he sits.

"Eat, Elandra."

I hate the sound of my name coming from his mouth. "Please feed my companions."

He pats my arm. "The boy is a stranger and the woman, deformed."

It is all I can do not to kill him instantly. "I thought power was yours to control."

"Not until I become the true leader. Become my mate."

"You are charming. It is easy to see how you gained power."

He smiles. "See, we are already getting along." He removes his vest, sleek muscles glowing in the light. "Sit closer to me."

"Daniel says you think you can have whatever girl you want."

His eyes turn cold. "Daniel is a coward."

"You were his prisoner."

"A mistake. Let us not talk about him. Many women would love to be my mate."

"I am not one of them. I would rather die."

Jyrr leaps on me and crushes my body into the fur rug. "No one refuses me. Ever."

He is so strong I cannot move.

"Get off," I warn.

"You will learn what it is to be loved by an Ice Lord."

I try to push him away. "This is not love."

His lips devour mine and I cannot escape his probing tongue. I arch against him, trying to escape.

"Yes." He rips my jacket off.

As long as there is a chance to save Daniel and Bryntar, I force myself to maintain complete, cold control. His hands roam. I am thankful for the protective vest.

His mouth moves to my neck. "Your skin is like the softest fur."

My head aches with anger.

He starts to remove my protective shirt with eager, fumbling hands.

"Let me go or you will regret it."

His unbridled passion is so great he does not hear.

The light burns inside and I slowly let it rise to my finger. I touch his chest.

He flies backward with a scream. Jumps off the floor, eyes gleaming. "We will be unstoppable." He takes a step forward.

"Touch me again and your pain will be greater."

He smiles and steps closer to me. "Surely we can come to an agreement? I can free your friends."

Hate throbs inside me. "Free all of us."

"Impossible. An heir to the throne cannot lose face. You stay with me, I free the others." He casually walks around me.

I can feel his lie as he moves closer. It will be difficult not to kill him.

He grabs my arm and twists it behind my back.

I cry out. Light shoots from my entire body.

He shrieks and crashes into the wall.

The door slams open.

Ryz-IL stomps inside. "What is going on?"

Jyrr staggers up, shock on his face. "She tried to kill me."

I sneer. "Yet you live."

"You do not have permission to be here," Ryz-IL says. "Overstep my authority once more and I will disown you."

Jyrr swaggers out of the room without a backward glance.

I know he is even more dangerous now.

My father throws Jyrr's vest out the door.

I pull my jacket back on.

"Are you hurt?" he asks.

"He is lucky I did not kill him."

Ryz-IL laughs. "So like your mother."

Confusion clouds my thoughts.

"You are surprised to hear the truth? Your amazing mother could not love someone who is cold and callous." He realizes the door is ajar and closes it. "I hardly dared hope when the Kepyrs told of an Enchantress on the island. It seemed impossible." Stepping toward me with joy on his face, he stops when he sees my expression.

"How could you leave my mother alone?"

"We had plans to hide her before you were born. We never expected an early birth."

I can only stare at him. "She needed you."

"We wanted a life together. She insisted we stay apart and convinced me it was necessary. I needed to become the Ice Lord ruler and try to effect change."

"Did you change the laws?"

He shakes his head in heavy sorrow. "No. I have been unable to affect the laws that reinforce inequality. Thousands of seasons cannot be changed in a lifetime."

My hidden fear, hope, need and pain burst in the need to hurt him. "I felt the arrow tear into her heart."

A burning pain shoots through his body. He clutches the wall for support.

Hurting him does not give me the satisfaction I thought it would.

His voice cracks. "You experienced it?"

"One of my, gifts."

Guilt shudders through him. "I should have been there. I cannot expect your forgiveness. When word came that you were both dead, I wanted to die."

I feel the truth. "We might all have died. There would be no one to save the island."

My father paces. "I never expected this day would come. That I would meet you only to face losing you again. If I had known you survived, nothing would have stopped me from finding you."

His love seeps into me. "It was hard not knowing if you were alive. Maybe destiny has a better plan for us. How would you have raised me?"

"With difficulty. I wish it were possible to change the past."

"I am concerned that I have no future. Nor will you if your Council executes me."

"I am their King. I will find a way to change their minds."

I shake my head. "You know I cannot escape my ultimate destiny."

"It is one thing to try and save an island. Quite another when faced with the daughter your mother and I created for the purpose. I am truly sorry, Elandra."

"I have accepted it."

His face darkens. "I never expected to see Jyrr. Was he only here only to, to. . .?"

"He wanted me to become his mate and rule the island."

My father shakes his head. "His zeal exceeds his capacity for sound reasoning. Although I wonder where the idea came from. You did not explain your power to him?"

I smile. "Only the effects of it."

My father's eyes twinkle. "That is good. The less he knows, the less trouble he will make."

"What will happen tomorrow?" I ask.

He heaves a deep sigh. "You and your friends will be dressed for execution. Your hands will be tied behind your back and your head will be covered. If I cannot sway their decision and you are condemned, they will cut off your hair."

I shiver uncontrollably, remembering the pain when Taroc snipped only a tiny end of hair. "They will torture and kill me in front of everyone?"

He nods grimly. "The only time you will be able to use your power is when your head is uncovered. Tell me your gifts, for I am determined to help you escape if the vote goes against you. I would rather die than see you executed." He lowers his head to stare at the floor. "Your mother and I had such plans. Not a day goes by that I do not miss her."

"Yet you took another mate."

"I would not have done so. My lady's husband forced me into a battle for the throne. When I killed him, it was my duty to take her as my wife and raise her son. It was unfair that I could never love her."

I take his hand. "Tell me about my mother."

Memories replace his desolation. "She had a wonderful laugh. The gentlest person I have ever known. Smart with an iron will. She had complete trust in me. I failed her."

"It is the lives of my companions that concern me now. Can you give them food and water? Promise you will not fail me. No matter what happens tomorrow, save Daniel and Bryntar, even at risk to your own life. I would not be alive without them."

"You have my word, Elandra."

Forty: The Betraying

"I must go," Father says." It will look suspicious if I stay too long."

I choke up. There is so much more I want to say to him. "When is my execution?"

He clasps me in his arms. "My dear child."

I blink and swallow hard.

"Sunrise," he says. "Eat and rest. Soon you will be given clean garments to wear. I will be sure Daniel gets a knife so he can free himself and Bryntar, in case. I will cut your bonds at the same time I remove the covering from your head. When your light blinds the crowd, we will escape to the khorbock stables. The creatures will be saddled and ready to ride. We will leave together, disappear into your underground home, and decide how to proceed." He hugs me. "Until tomorrow, my dear."

The cell is empty without his presence. I eat and lie down to rest.

. . .

The door clanks open once more. I am surprised to see the Lady Ryz-IL, a wicked knife in her hand. Her eyes rake over me. Although I should fear her, I do not.

"Do not try to escape or I will use this knife."

I smile inside.

"I suppose you have a certain beauty. Undoubtedly, it is the power you yield that makes Jyrr desire you."

"Power attracts the weak," I say in defiance.

She slaps my face and I reel from the strength in her hand. "You should have accepted my son's proposal."

"You would mate with a man who forces himself on you?"

She quickly controls the surprise in her eyes. "He is young and needs guidance."

"He is spoiled and arrogant."

She starts to strike me again.

I point a finger at her. "Do not touch me again."

She stares at the light glowing in my finger and pulls away. Fear, then calculation flashes in her eyes. "You could own this island. No one would dare stand against you and Jyrr. Anything you want would be yours."

"I want my freedom."

"That can happen with my son as the king."

"You do not have enough power as the Lady of Ryz-IL?"

She laughs and it is not a pleasant sound. "Women have no power. However, many young Ice Lords and council members favor Jyrr as ruler. It shall happen soon."

"His father is in good health. Does Jyrr intend to kill him?"

"I have a better plan than that."

Sudden fear grinds through me at her complete confidence.

"You want the throne."

She smiles. "I will control it through my son. Why not?" She spits out words with bitterness. "I deserve to rule after living with a man who does not love me." She sneers. "At least now I know he mated with a lowly Kepyr."

I control my bitterness and the urge to strangle her. "Why did Jyrr's father lay claim to the throne?"

Her guilty eyes betray her. "It was his decision to fight Ryz-IL."

"I think not," I say.

She glares at me. "I loved him. I thought he could win."

"What will you do when Jyrr decides he does not need you?"

Her eyes become slits of contempt. "You are more intelligent than I thought. It will not save you from execution. Come with me. You must bathe to be worthy of a trial before the Council."

I burst out laughing. "I have to be clean to die?"

"You must honor the great Council of Ice Lords."

"What honor is there in executing those who threaten their power?"

She lifts her hand to strike me again and stops. "What a shame that you do not value your potential. Go ahead of me."

I think about my potential as I climb staircase after staircase. Perhaps she is right. Without Aru, I could rule the island. But only because of fear.

We reach a huge room filled with sculptures of trees, every leaf cut in detail. Pillars of pink and green crystal rise around steaming baths carved out of pink stone with tiny, black veins. My heart lurches when I see Daniel in one bath being scrubbed by a Kepyr servant. Our eyes meet in relief. Bryntar undergoes the same thing across the room in another bath. Her eyes question mine, but she smiles when she sees I am not afraid.

The Lady leads me to a private bath encircled with long white drapes. "Strip and hand me your clothes. I must be sure you have no hidden weapons."

As much as I despise doing so, I remove my clothes in front of her and hand her everything except my protective shirt.

"I said all of your clothes," she says, pointing to the shirt.

"It protects me from Aru."

She smirks. "I thought you above the superstition of uneducated Kepyrs."

"Aru exists. I have encountered the beast."

She bursts out laughing. "You do not expect me to believe you. The shirt is some kind of weapon and I shall have it." She rips it off and gives it to a servant.

I watch the old female Kepyr disappear with my only protection against Aru. "You do not believe the beast is a creation of the evil on this island?"

"That is absurd," the Lady says. "Bathe and put on these clothes. I will return when your trial is ready to begin."

I submerge completely in the hot, perfumed bath and avoid the young Kepyr servant standing ready to help me. I close my eyes and enjoy the peace of seeing, hearing, and feeling nothing but steaming heat. It is impossible to stop thinking. I try not to worry about my father's plan of escape should it be necessary. If all goes well, I can protect Daniel and Bryntar and reach home and safety. If not, I know my father will keep his word and save them.

The worry in the young servant hovering above me wavers through the water. I glide up and submit to a thorough scrub, glad to feel clean for once.

She places a gown over my head of soft white material laced with silver thread and places silver slippers on my feet. "You are beautiful. I am sorry for you."

"May I have some time alone?"

She bows and leaves.

I peek through the curtains, but Daniel and Bryntar are gone. It is getting harder to take a deep breath without light, so I rest on a bench.

"Psst."

I look around quickly and see a shadow behind the gauze curtain. Casually,

I slip behind it and blink in complete shock.

"Uncle!"

"Ssshh."

I throw my arms around him and hold on, never wanting to let go. "I thought you were dead."

He grins. "It takes more than a few rocks to kill me."

"What happened?"

"I was knocked into the tunnel by flying rock. When I awoke, rubble blocked the entrance. It took a long time to free myself."

"How did you find me?"

"The drums."

"How did you get in?"

"I know many Kepyr servants," he says.

"You may be in danger here."

"When do I avoid danger? I came to rescue all of you."

I hug him again. "Thank you for coming," I whisper. "My father is Ryz-IL. He has a plan to free us."

His eyes widen in surprise. "Do you trust him?"

"With my life."

"Tell me what I must do."

"Stay as close as you can. Join us when the cover comes off my head. You must not worry about me. If necessary, help Daniel and Bryntar escape with my father."

"It shall be done." He smiles and is gone.

I sink to the bench with hope.

The Lady returns a short time later. "Put your hands behind your back." She lashes my wrists together with leather straps and leads me away.

We climb a myriad of stairs and I gasp for breath. She covers my head with a cloth before we walk out of the Palace. I feel the warmth of sunrise.

Yells and shrieks blast into my ears. Fear and hate from hundreds of people hit me with such force that I stagger. Someone lifts me to a platform and pushes me into a chair.

"Elandra?"

"I am here, Daniel."

"Tell me why I have a knife hidden in my sleeve," he whispers.

"To cut Bryntar free and follow my father."

"Who?"

"He is the Ice Lord King," Bryntar says.

"I'm sorry you can't see anything," he says.

"It is enough to know you are here. Explain what you see."

"Here goes," he says. "We are on a raised platform in front of the Palace. I imagine the King will sit on the fancy throne to our right, three platforms up. His Lady and the jerk sit on the next level down. Five men and two women in robes sit on the level right above us."

"The Council," I say.

He hesitates and his voice quavers. "There are two stakes and a bunch of dry wood in the courtyard. Hundreds of Ice Lords are here: guards, Kepyr warriors and families, maybe the whole island. They don't all fit inside. A lot of them stand on the road outside the Palace."

"Can you find Uncle?"

He pauses. "Did they drug you? He's dead."

"He is alive, Daniel." I feel his doubt. "Please look in the crowd. He will be as close to us as he can be."

"Oh my God, I see him," he whispers.

Bryntar says nothing, but I feel her relief and, what? Joy?

I shiver when a warm hand touches my arm. "Last chance to join me," Jyrr says.

"Get your hands off her, you scumbag."

Jyrr snarls, "I would rather kill you with my bare hands, foreigner. An execution is more spectacular."

"I will not mate with you, Jyrr," I say.

"How I will enjoy your death," he snarls.

The crowd applauds.

"Wow," Daniel says. "Your father looks like a rock star."

A rock star?

"His crown is gold. The three-star emblem on it sparkles like a diamond. His cape is white jaguarat fur and covered in jewels. His vest and pants are gold bearran fur."

My father's voice carries across the Palace grounds. "Ice Lords and Kepyrs."

The crowd hushes.

"You are invited here as a courtesy for the trial of this girl and her two companions. If she is found to be an Enchantress with intent to harm us, she will be executed with the others."

Screams and yells drown the courtyard.

I feel my father step down the platform and stand next to me.

"QUIET," he booms.

The crowd shifts uneasily.

"Anyone who does not remain respectful during this trial shall be escorted out of the courtyard or into the dungeons by my guards. Is that clear?"

Murmurs of agreement fill the air.

"The Council shall listen to proof before assigning judgment," Father says. "Who will speak first?"

"I will."

"It's the witch," Daniel says.

I would know her voice anywhere. My heart skips a beat. I force memories away.

"State your name for all to hear," Ryz-IL says.

"Laruna, Priestess of Kepyr."

"You have proof against the accused?"

"I birthed her. Did not know she was Enchantress until she breathed light. See this?"

The crowd murmurs in unease.

I shiver as her hatred strikes me like a snake.

Daniel whispers. "Is that a lock of your hair?"

"We thought mother and baby dead. Along with my son, the mighty warrior sent to destroy them. I see Enchantress in dream. Vow revenge. Demand the right to cut off her hair."

Cheers erupt from the crowd.

Daniel's horror shoots through me. "She's kidding, right?"

Bryntar whispers, "Savages."

"Does anyone else want to speak?" Father asks.

"I speak for the warriors who track the Enchantress. She kills with light from her hands."

I recognize the voice of the Kepyr warrior who helped capture us.

Shouts and agreements rise from the Kepyrs.

"Will anyone speak on behalf of the accused?" my father asks.

The courtyard is silent.

"Then I should like to speak as representative for the girl. We have no knowledge of her intent to harm the island or its inhabitants." He gently pulls me to my feet.

"First, I have valuable information."

Chills streak down my spine like icy knives when I recognize Jyrr's voice. He stomps down the platform.

There is surprise in my father's voice. "What do you know?"

"She has violet eyes, the result of an Ice Lord and Kepyr mating. She does not breathe air. I, myself, have seen her submerged in water for longer than any can hold their breath."

Sick horror shudders through me, realizing he watched while I bathed. It is the sense of superiority and hatred coming from him that frightens me the most.

"I know one other thing," Jyrr says. "It causes me great sorrow and pain to expose a traitor among us."

Blood slithers to my toes. I sway and would fall but for my father's steadying hand. Chills of dread course through me, striking into my very soul.

"My people," Jyrr says. "Our great leader Ryz-IL, broke the law of the land and mated with a Kepyr. He is the father of this Enchantress. Seize him!"

Forty-One: The Judging

The uproar of men shouting, women screaming, and children crying engulfs the air.

"Jeez, we're dead meat."

"You must believe in the Enchantress, Daniel," Bryntar says.

It is almost impossible to think or breathe with the din around me. I am thankful for the covering on my head. The darkness helps me concentrate and repel the hatred.

Laruna shrieks, "Kill. Kill. Kill."

The crowd takes up the chant. "Kill, kill, kill."

"Silence, my people," Jyrr yells over the noise.

They quiet almost instantly and I quiver in fear. His mother is right. He does have support for his succession to the throne. I focus on the leather straps around my wrists as I carefully burn through them.

"Let Ryz-IL condemn himself if he honors the truth," Jyrr says.

"Jyrr speaks the truth," my father says.

A howl of voices sweeps over me like a vicious wind.

"Let him speak," Jyrr yells. "They will be his last words."

Shouts change to murmurs.

"Most of you know I have always tried to change the law," my father says.

"To save yourself!"

"Death to the traitor!"

"Kill him!"

"I had a vision," my father says.

Nervous whispers flitter through the crowd.

He continues. "The most disturbing vision showed this island being destroyed. The power, greed and selfishness of the people created Aru. That is why I broke the law. To give the island an Enchantress to save us."

Jeers and cries of fear sweep through the crowd.

"Do you ever wonder why there is a law that forbids the creating of an Enchantress?" my father asks.

Mutters of disbelief filter through the crowd.

"No previous king wanted anyone to live who could threaten his rule. To keep our races separate, it was necessary to create fear and doubt."

"Liar!" Laruna shouts.

My father shouts above the dissention. "I have deciphered the ancient records."

"Impossible!" shouts one of the Council members.

"No!" my father yells. "Not for someone who cares enough about the fate of this island. In the ancient records, our Ice Lord ancestors knew we would need an Enchantress or Enchanter every thousand years to erase the influences of the evil inherent in our natures."

Jyrr screams above the rage of the crowd. "This man disrespects our heritage. Members of the Council, do you agree our mighty ruler is a traitor?"

Daniel cannot keep his voice from shaking. "They agree with him."

"Be ready with your knife," I whisper, "and do not wait for me. Promise."

"Done."

Jyrr's satisfaction sickens me. "Tie his hands."

A cheer rings in the courtyard.

My mind shifts to holding the severed leather ties around my wrists.

"Since I am heir to the throne," Jyrr says, "I will officiate over the executions if that is the will of the Council and the people."

An uproar saturates the courtyard. "Jyrr! Jyrr! Jyrr!"

I can almost feel his smile. "By unanimous vote, let the executions begin."

His body brushes against mine as he moves forward. "This boy is a stranger to our island. He will be burned first, then the woman who raised the Enchantress. Tie them to the stakes."

I whisper to Daniel. "Do not worry."

Bryntar warns, "Do not take too long."

I want to scream, but have little breath left.

Jyrr resumes speaking. "Normally, a former ruler would be granted leniency and be pierced through the heart for an instant death. Ryz-IL has broken the greatest law of the land. He should suffer and be burned at the stake with the others. Is the decision unanimous?"

The crowd shouts, "Burn, burn, burn. Destroy the traitor!"

"I am sorry, Elandra," my father says.

I feel many footsteps dragging him away. The only thing keeping me from screaming is that Daniel and Father have knives to cut themselves free. I calm down and concentrate on complete control.

Jyrr removes the cover from my head.

I blink in the brightness. My heart lurches to see my family tied to the stake. I breathe in volumes of light and my hair shimmers.

"Oooh."

"Aahh."

"She is only a child."

I gaze at the woman who spoke and say loudly, "I was a few hours old when your tribe tried to kill me."

She lowers her eyes in shame and for the first time I understand that not all Kepyrs agree with their laws.

"The Enchantress shall watch our enemies die," Jyrr says.

"Light the fire."

The crowd cheers.

Jyrr whispers in my ear. "You should have accepted my offer."

"Arrogance will be your downfall."

He laughs. "I admire your resolve. It will not save you."

One guard lights a torch and touches it to the fire. Anger burns inside me, but I control it as the flames burst over the dry wood. I am relieved to see Uncle sneak toward the fire.

Laruna hobbles toward me with a knife. "I kill Enchantress."

"No, old woman," Jyrr says. "It is my right."

They stare at each other and her eyes lower first. Hatred vibrates through her, but she steps aside.

Jyrr pulls out a curved knife and yanks on a chunk of my hair. He whispers in my ear. "With each stroke, remember you could have been my queen."

I smile at him as leather slides from my wrists. "You shall be lucky to live."

He raises his knife.

I trail a finger down his arm. He screeches. I touch his chest lightly and a thin streak of light throws him against a column of rock.

The crowd gasps.

One woman shies away. "She has the power of light."

"You tried to kill my son!"

I whirl to see the Lady Ryz-IL hurl a spear at me. I disintegrate it in a flash. She screeches and runs toward me with a dagger. I knock her out with one jolt.

I twist around when I feel the heat of the fire. Relief surges through me when Uncle leaps through the flames to cut Bryntar and my father free. Daniel frees himself and jumps after them.

Kepyr warriors and guards rush them, weapons drawn.

I flash bolt after bolt of lightning at their feet. "Stop!"

They halt, fear shimmering in their eyes.

I stalk toward the Council who are rushing into the Palace. I strike the stone floor next to their feet with a stream of light.

"Resume your seats."

They raise their chins and stride back to their chairs.

A tremor abruptly shakes the Palace and grounds.

I knew this day would come. Aru has found me.

Forty-Two: The Reckoning

Thousands of people scream as the ground ripples, tossing them like so many leaves. Terrified, they scramble up and trample each other to get free.

"Stop! You will hurt each other!" my father yells.

His voice is lost as huge cracks split the ground outside the Palace walls. Council members stare in disbelief and scatter.

Daniel grabs my hand. "Let's get out of here." He shelters me in his arms and shoves through people swarming up the steps to find safety inside the Palace. A crystal pillar topples in front of the entrance almost crushing Jyrr and his mother.

Kepyrs kneel in supplication, chanting, crying, or stone-faced in shock. Children scream in terror.

With a deafening grinding, hissing, and rumbling of rock, the gap outside the walls widens and swallows hundreds of shrieking natives.

I tremble with the pain, horror, and confusion, trying to withstand the terrible loss. I drop Daniel's hand and press forward, having no idea how I can master my own destiny and win this battle.

Daniel snatches my arm and yells over the screaming. "What are you doing?"

"What I was born to do."

"You can't."

"We will all die if I do not try to defeat Aru."

His green eyes stare into my soul. He yanks me into his arms and kisses me with such fierceness that our hearts beat as one once again.

"I love you, Daniel." I tear away and it almost breaks my heart.

"Kill the friggin' monster!"

Cracks and crevices expand outside the Palace walls, crawling after the natives like hungry vines, consuming those too slow to leap away in time. The wide hole imprisons those caught inside the courtyard.

I shove through the crowd.

Bryntar pulls me into her arms, enfolding me with love. Tears slide down her face and into my heart. "You can do this, Elandra. Believe in yourself."

Barely able to speak, I pull away and choke out the words, "Goodbye, Mother."

The ground rumbles and I fall to my knees. Smoke hisses from the rifts. I jump away from fountains of fire that burst into the sky with belching rolls of angry, black clouds.

The crowd screams and pushes me toward the gates.

A huge mass of thick, rock and molten lava writhes in the center of the clouds, as wide as it is tall. Red sparks flash like piercing eyes. Aru twists and bellows in fury, spitting stones that burn anything they hit. Shrieks and wails pierce the air.

I struggle through the panicking throng and stumble over a crying Kepyr who crawls on the ground with a screaming child covered in burns. I kneel, to caress the child with my fingertips. The screaming stops.

Tears streak down her face. "I am grateful."

Uncle lifts me up from the ground and hugs me. "I never thought I would see anyone braver than your mother, until now."

"My death will devastate Bryntar. She will blame herself. Please take care of her."

He nods solemnly. "My life is hers."

Great clouds of yellow gas foul the air. Kepyr and Ice Lord screech and run, trying to find places for their families to hide or escape.

I ignore the churning emotions and search for my father in the turmoil, but cannot find him. Goodbye, Father. Do not blame yourself.

Explosions rip through the clouds, hurling fireballs through the sky. An uproar of terror fills the air.

I stride forward to battle with a furious, hovering Aru. Lava expands into a bigger molten cloud, hissing, thrashing, howling. Suffering.

I stagger to the palace gates. Laruna jumps in front of me with a knife, her eyes crazed with madness.

"Die, Enchantress!"

I leap aside, but not before she slices off a tip of my hair. She yells and drops the knife when the light burns her skin.

I gasp with the stabbing pain. Grab the severed ends with my fingertips and close the wound.

Laruna screams, "Grant me my revenge, Mighty Aru!"

A streak of hot lava reaches out and twists around her. She shrieks before disintegrating into ash.

I shake uncontrollably. Will I die as easily?

Slipping around the gaping hole in the ground, I try to gain control of my feelings.

Aru bellows and expands to blacken the entire sky.

I do not need the sun. I think of my mother, Taroc and Bryntar, Daniel, Uncle, and Father. Love throbs with an inner light so bright it cannot be contained. It flashes around me in a huge, bright circle. Even so, I cannot ignore the pounding of my heart. I inhale. Shining silver hair swirls around my face.

I can do this. I have to do this.

I step forward. A gaping maw of smoke sucks me into twisting chaos, snatching away breath and thought. Giant flames, flying rocks and deafening yowls batter me from every direction. I cover my ears, close my eyes and hold onto the light.

I do not waiver. Nothing can stop my determination to save my family and this beautiful island.

The whirling stops. Intense pressure squeezes, trying to crack through my barrier. Explosions of lava cover my protection of light like a burning blanket. Screams and tormented pain claw into my mind. And grief. So much grief and pain and revulsion. I reel, not knowing how long I can hold on.

Do not panic. Do not give in.

Doubt creeps like a worm into my mind, twisting, burrowing deeper into hope.

I fight to ignore it by thinking about my love for Daniel: his arms, his kisses, his promise of unspoken words. Light thickens and draws closer to my body.

I scream at Aru. "What do you want?"

A sea of red, sticky muck surrounds me. Contorted, murky shapes rise around me. They snatch at the light. Scream when it erodes their bodies. Anger, despair, agony, and hatred attack the very center of my soul. I sob uncontrollably in the face of the atrocities and weaken.

"Oh, Taroc, I do not know what to do."

His words filter through my suffering and sorrow. *You have everything you need within your heart.*

I strain against the suffocation of evil. Suddenly I know there is only one way to survive. To let go of everything. To accept who I am. To surrender to the light within. I merge with the power. Become one with it. Blinding light streaks out through my hair, eyes, hands, all parts of my body. Thunder shakes the red muck.

Aru shrieks.

Love steadies my thumping heart.

The melody so long quiet in my heart awakens, warm and pure and beautiful. At last I understand what must be done to save the island. I know Aru.

I begin to sing. In my mind, I hear many voices blending with mine, Enchanters and Enchantresses who have gone before. Their melodies weave through mine. Taroc appears, smiles, and vanishes.

Aru moans.

And still I sing, radiating the pureness of light. I add words to the melody and glow brighter. "Release your pain. Remember the beginning."

Aru wails, writhes. The sea of murk thins to choppy waves. Black tears of misery rain onto the surface and disappear.

"I am sorry. Please forgive them. Forgive me."

I open my heart to enclose the dead and tortured, the unclean sea, the cruelty, the whole of the beast.

Aru stills.

"I love you," I say to Aru.

A melody apart from my own arises, halting. . .growing. . . sounds of wind ruffling rivers, surging seas, grasses and leaves. Racing hooves and songs of birds. Painted skies, purrs and infant cries. All that is the island. Gradually, the red water turns crystal clear.

We sing to each other, each in our own way. I close my eyes to a vision of lava turning into peaceful mountains, acrid clouds fading to blue. Aru dissolves into what it was in the beginning. Before absorbing the negativity of the people to save itself. Before the anger and the anguish, before needing what only I would give.

In a brilliant flash of radiant white light, Aru transforms into the shimmering spirit of the island.

Forty-Three: The Reuniting

I blink in the fading glow, glowing with energy. The rift in the ground is healed, as if it had never swallowed hundreds of people. I breathe in the light, elated and so grateful to be alive.

Thank you, Island.

Thunderous cheers ring through the air. The islanders shout and surge toward me.

"Stand back," my father shouts. "Make room for the Enchantress."

They part and bow as I walk down their pathway. I squirm inside.

Daniel races through the courtyard ahead of my family. He gazes into my eyes and wraps me in his arms. There is no need for words.

Bryntar rushes forward, wiping tears from her face. She enfolds us. "I never doubted you."

"You are our savior," Uncle says, bowing.

"Do not start that again, Uncle."

He laughs and hugs me.

My father turns from the crowd and gets down on one knee in front of me. "When you disappeared, I wanted to die."

Daniel pulls my father up. "Better stand, Sir. She doesn't like that worship stuff. Except from me."

"What are you talking about?" I ask.

Daniel winks.

My father looks at both of us, eyebrows raised. "We must talk, young man."

"Uh, oh. Time to learn about fathers, too."

A low chant begins from the crowd, growing in volume as we walk toward the Palace. Ice Lord and Kepyr kneel as I pass.

"Enchantress! Enchantress! Enchantress!"

Some murmur, some touch the skirt of my ragged gown. Others thank me with their eyes and their hearts. I try not to squirm.

"Help the survivors and repair the damages," my father orders.

Ice Lord and Kepyr warriors scurry to obey.

"I want to heal the wounded, Father."

"You need to rest," Bryntar says.

"I need to heal them."

The Council members gather, grim expressions on their faces.

My father stalks over to them. "Since you chose to execute me, perhaps you should decide who rules before the people choose their own leader."

Jyrr stands defiant next to his mother.

"Get out of my sight," Father says, "and out of the Palace." Your greed for power almost annihilated this entire island." He does not even look at the Lady as he strides past her.

I gaze into her face. She stands tall, but cannot hide her anger or her fear.

As I pass the Council members, I say, "Be careful of your choice." Fear flickers in their eyes. I cannot decide which is greater: their fear of me or their fear of losing power. I shut out their critical feelings.

A few young Ice Lords struggle to remove the pillar that blocks the entrance into the Palace.

"Jyrr, come on. You are the strongest," one says.

Jyrr scowls, but joins his friends.

When they finish, the Lady grabs his arm and hustles him away.

My father watches them leave and stalks inside. He leads us into a small room. "I shall see to food and a room for healing."

"Do not trust anyone," I say.

"May I go with you?" Uncle asks my father.

"Who are you?"

"I am Kydaka."

The color drains in my father's face. "I was told you were dead." He clasps Uncle's shoulders. "We have much to talk about."

They leave and I collapse into soft cushions. Daniel sits next to me, never releasing my hand.

"I'm not sure I know what happened, or that I want to," Daniel says.

"Where is Aru?" Bryntar asks.

"The negativity is gone, for now."

"I'm just glad you're safe," Daniel says.

"There is no real safety for us on this island."

Bryntar takes my hands in hers. "Ice Lords and Kepyrs will be slow to change their ways."

There is a loud knock on the door.

A Kepyr servant slips inside and sets a tray down with an array of fruit, nuts, and strips of meat.

"Now you're talking." Daniel helps himself.

"Please show me to the wounded," I say.

The servant bows. I grab a piece of fruit and follow her.

"You need rest," Bryntar says, following me.

"I am fine."

They insist on going with me. When I enter the room, the silence is deafening. Many of the people with minor burns and abrasions have been treated. I heal those who remain, even though they are suspicious until my fingertips touch them.

I am almost asleep when Daniel sweeps me off my feet. "You're going to rest."

My father and Uncle stride into the room. "The Council has requested your presence, Elandra."

"She's not going right now," Daniel says.

My father scowls at him.

"Are you still the head of the Council, Ryz-IL?" Bryntar asks.

"Technically, yes."

"Are you not the father of the Enchantress who saved their lives?" Kydaka asks.

Father smiles.

I do not want the responsibility of leading these people. "I understand the importance of maintaining your position for the changes that must come, Father. Tell the Council they will attend me at my convenience. Tomorrow."

Daniel grins. "Don't let me get on the wrong side of you."

"Is that possible?" I ask.

"Not a chance." He kisses me and I melt in his arms.

Forty-Four: The Challenging

The Palace is quiet as we hurry along the empty corridors to the Council meeting in the morning.

"We will have a strategic position by arriving before the Council members do," Father says.

He pushes open the huge, ornate chamber doors. Grandeur surrounds us—from the heavy tapestries depicting past warriors to the carved wooden chairs inlaid with gold and silver. Jewels encrust goblets that sit on a circular table with seven chairs and a throne.

"Sit on the throne, Elandra."

"No, Father. I will not rule this island. You must, or there will be no change."

He hesitates.

"If not for you, there would be no island," Uncle says to him.

"The island needs you," Bryntar adds. "You know the laws and the people."

"Obviously not as much as I should," Father says.

"The members are coming," I say in warning.

Father sits on the throne. I take the seat next to him. Bryntar, Daniel, and Uncle sit on benches along the wall.

One Council member bursts through the doors. "Ryz-Il, you cannot sit on the throne!"

"Will you be the one to tell the people I cannot rule, Jaxtyl? The one who was responsible for saving their lives?"

"It was the Enchantress," Jaxtyl says.

"I am responsible for her birth. I suggest you get another chair for the table and sit down."

Six Council members hurry inside, their faces grave.

Jaxtyl spots my family and frowns. "No one is allowed in Council sessions."

"These brave people are responsible for saving the Enchantress. She wishes them to stay," Father says.

Jaxtyl sneers. "Can she not speak for herself?"

"I will have no trouble ending your life if necessary," I say quietly.

Jaxtyl's face pales, but I feel his pulsating hatred.

The Council members hurry to their chairs. Jaxtyl refuses to add a chair and stands, his face turning a dark purple.

"I do not expect sweeping change to happen overnight," Father says. "However, the island needs a ruler. I intend to remain in that position until an election can be held by all the people of the island."

"Blasphemy!" Jaxtyl bangs his hands on the table. "Ice Lords rule this island. It has been so for generations. You have no right to change anything."

"Do the other members agree?" Father asks.

I sense a change in the Council and know that two women and three men agree with my father. I lean over and whisper in his ear.

"Call for their decision now."

"How many of you vote to retain me as temporary ruler?" my father asks.

Five members tap the table and the sixth one joins in.

Furious, Jaxtyl yells. "I resign and will fight your efforts."

"I look forward to it. Your influence will be greatly reduced if you are not on the Council. Please reconsider your decision."

Jaxtyl stomps out of the meeting.

Father looks at each member. "Thank you for your support. There is much to be done. I would like to supervise the repairs and must release those healed by the Enchantress. Are there any other decisions we need to consider today?"

An older woman rises to speak. "Is the Enchantress going to sit on the Council?"

"I am not staying on the island," I say.

I shut out the feelings that bombard me, surprised at how easy it is now. "It is up to the people to save themselves. For if you do not change your laws and treat everyone on this island as equals, with love and respect, Aru will grow again. I will not be here to save you the next time."

The Council members gasp and murmur among themselves.

This time I do open myself to know what they feel. There is relief, regret, and resistance, along with a new sense of purpose. I do not look at my family, for I know they are shocked. My bright spot of hope is Daniel.

"I ask one thing for myself. I need to use your expert craftsmen to build a ship." I stride toward the doors. "The island is in your hands, Father."

Forty-Five: The Building

Daniel, Bryntar, and Uncle hurry after me. I am relieved the future of the island rests with my father. I have no doubt he will remain their leader. Uncle closes the doors behind us.

"How can you leave your home?" Bryntar asks.

"Home was with you and Taroc. This island will never be my home. I will not be seen as anything but an Enchantress to fear."

The turmoil of her feelings crosses her face. "They will come to know you."

I take her hands in mine. "You know they will not accept me."

She nods her head and shudders. "This island is my home." She flees down the hall.

I stare after her. How can I leave Bryntar behind?

"She will change her mind," Uncle says.

"Can you build a ship and craft the instruments you need?" I ask Daniel.

He cannot hide his excitement. "The basics that I'll need. With lots of help."

"I know many skilled Kepyrs," Uncle says. "Make your ship large enough for four."

"It will take months to build," Daniel says. "Stocking supplies, training. The ocean is dangerous, even for experienced seamen."

"Life offers no guarantee, only opportunity for growth," Uncle says. "When can we start?"

"I am going to find Bryntar," I say.

They continue their enthusiastic conversation.

It does not take long to realize she has left the Palace. I look for suitable clothes for traveling home. It takes a while to find anyone to help in the aftermath of Aru. I finally secure fur pants, boots, and a jacket given to me by a Kepyr servant.

As I stride down the hall, I meet my father.

"There you are. The meeting went better than I expected. Tomorrow will be the first time Kepyr leaders and the Ice Lord Council meet. I would like you to attend."

I am torn between wanting to please him and wanting to find Bryntar. "Is it necessary?"

"I am worried about the stability of the island. I need you."

Once again, my destiny seems out of my hands. Not for long.

...

I do not sleep well and wake up feeling empty and lost. I should be happy that the beast is gone and my family is safe. After so long, fear is a hard habit to break. All I can think about is Bryntar and my uncertain future. I dress and eat quickly to meet my father.

He greets everyone who enters the Council chambers. The Council, Ice Lord representatives and Kepyr leaders stand, nervous and uncomfortable. Especially when they look at me.

I shut out their feelings. "I do not want to be here, Father," I whisper in his ear.

"I know. Right now, I believe it is the only way to accomplish an immediate change."

He takes my hand, sits me on the throne and stands behind me. "Thank you for coming. Please be seated. Since I am still your ruler until the people choose differently, I would like to propose that seven members from the Kepyr tribes be appointed to join the present Council members. Today."

Murmurs of dissent as well as cheers echo throughout the room.

I stand up and the room becomes silent. "I have warned you of the consequences if you do not change. You would be wise to listen to Ryz-IL."

One Kepyr warrior rises. "I know of a worthy Kepyr to sit on the Council."

I escape as soon as the discussions begin in earnest and search for Daniel. He and Uncle are in a small library.

Daniel draws pictures of ships. "I won't have all the modern conveniences. We can make a ship to sail us out of here. I am concerned about the invisible barrier that protects the island."

"I will speak to my father about that."

"There is much to do to prepare besides building the ship," my uncle says. "Clothes, provisions, deciding when and where to launch. I have never felt so alive."

"I need to go home to talk with Bryntar."

"Good idea. Do you want me to go with you?" Daniel asks.

I smile, knowing how he feels. "Build your ship."

"I want to stay at your uncle's village and recruit help."

"I will find you, Daniel. Take care of him, Uncle."

"With my life."

I hug Uncle gratefully. "Then I have no concern."

Daniel kisses my cheek. "Be careful."

I feel a loss, but do not let it affect my smile. Our futures are complicated now. I search for my father. When he learns of my intentions to leave the city, he insists on accompanying me. "You are needed here, Father."

"I will feel better if we ride khorbocks to the edge of the Ice Mountains. I do not trust some of the Ice Lords, especially since Jyrr and his mother have disappeared. Wait for me outside the Palace gates."

"I am more concerned for your safety, Father."

I promise to be careful."

On a hill outside the gates, I gaze across the island toward the Western Seas. Father leads two khorbocks around the wall. One runs away from him and rushes toward me, stopping to nuzzle my neck. My heart swells to be reunited with my faithful khorbock.

"You know this animal?" Father asks.

"He saved our lives. I thought he was wild."

Pain etches his face. "Your mother trained him, but set him free. When Jyrr caught him, I could say nothing."

I cannot speak and instead rub the animal's spotted nose.

We mount and leave the Palace. I am relieved to stop shutting out feelings that are not my own.

The mountains glisten in sunlight and I inhale deeply. I ride across the tundra at one with my khorbock. Pounding hooves stop conversation and freedom rushes into me. I want to ride forever. When the green forests stretch across the horizon, my throat constricts with memories of home.

"I do not want you to leave the island," Father says when we dismount.

"I will always be different, feared."

"If you leave, I will never see you again. Will never know if you survive."

"I feel the same, but what kind of life can I have here?"

He sighs. "You love the boy."

"With everything that I am."

"Those of our blood love only once. I cannot say that about your Daniel. You are both young. It will be very different in the outer world."

"I have to take that chance."

He smiles and takes the reins from my hands. "Go with care. We will have time to talk before you leave the island."

"Will you free the khorbock?"

"Of course." He removes the saddle and bridle.

The khorbock snuffles in my face. I stroke his spotted nose. His great brown eyes stare into mine. "Go and be free."

He snorts and bounds away.

I hug my father and run toward the trees, impatient to be home.

The forest seems bigger in my haste. The rays of sunset turn the trees to gold by the time I reach the vine-covered rock. I stop to sense if anyone follows me. Only the sounds of the forest greet me: the breezes, the animals scratching through leaves, the chirping birds. I sneak through shadows and push open the stone entrance.

I stagger with the feelings that overwhelm me and realize they are only memories. Hammering draws me forward until I find Bryntar mending a metal wall. She struggles to hold it.

"This is much harder now that I am not a monster," she says. "I need to finish the repairs to keep out the cold."

"And to keep out everything else. Together, we will put it back the way it was."

She chokes and resumes her pounding. "It will never be the way it was."

Knowing she is not ready to talk, I hold the metal wall and try not to think of life without her.

Forty-Six: The Finishing

I spend many hours devouring the books of Taroc's life and committing them to memory. The books in his study are unlike those in the library. Some of their titles refer to necromancy, mysticism and the occult arts. I read them and discover two books I want to take with me on the ship: one documenting the Enchanters and Enchantresses that have come before me, and one in a language I cannot decipher. Yet.

Will Bryntar write about me if she stays behind?

Rebuilding the walls and floors takes most of our time.

Bryntar talks little as the days pass and I finally confront her.

"When are you going to talk about him?"

She swallows hard. "What is there to say? He is gone."

"I cannot imagine the loss you must feel. I live with the guilt that my birth caused his death. You lived with him hundreds of lifetimes."

Tears well in her eyes. "I thought I would be the one to die first." She collapses in a heap on the floor. "It is all too much: his death, my transformation. I cannot stop thinking about what kind of life we would have had if I had entered the lagoon again."

"You cannot change what has come before. If you insist on thinking about possibilities, what would have happened if you died and were unable to save me? Aru would have destroyed the island and everyone on it. You are the true hero, Bryntar."

She wipes her eyes and pats my face. "Let us continue the repairs."

Much time passes while we finish the caverns. When we are done, they are close to being the way they used to be, but will never be the same without Taroc. I am thrilled when we restore the warmth, never wanting to be cold again. I long to see Daniel, but worry about leaving Bryntar alone.

I water the new plants in the underground gardens. "I need to check on the ship-building."

"You need to see Daniel."

"I do."

She chuckles, the first time I have seen a smile on her face in a long time.

"Help me pack some food for the trip," I say. "Come with me."

"This is where I belong."

"You cannot hide here for the rest of your life. You made me face my destiny. What about yours?"

She starts shaking. "I do not know how to live any other way."

"Is that why you are not coming with me?"

"I do not know if I can change."

"You had to change your whole life when you transformed. All you have to do is want to change."

I stuff extra food in a bag. "What kind of life will you have here alone? You do not like the Kepyrs. I doubt the Ice Lords will accept you."

"I will take you to the village," she says.

We climb the stairs to the outside world once again. I remember the first time I saw the forest after so many years underground. It is more beautiful now that I do not have to worry about losing my life. We enjoy two peaceful days and nights before reaching the Kepyr village.

Bustling activity covers the filled-in pit. Daniel and my uncle are in the middle of it. I am surprised to see several Ice Lords working next to Kepyr warriors.

I wave. "Daniel!"

He looks up and runs toward me.

I laugh as he grabs me and swings me around.

"I missed you," he says. He kisses me and I tingle all the way to my toes. "It's great to see you, too, Bryntar," he says when he releases me.

She smiles, but her eyes are on my uncle as he hurries up and takes her hands. "I am so glad you are here," he says to Bryntar.

She blushes, which brings a beautiful deep purple to the scales that shimmer on her face.

Daniel pulls me over to the workers. "Come and see. You have perfect timing. We're ready to move everything to build the ship by the Western Seas. All the different Kepyr villages sent help. We've cut and cured enough lumber. I made the basic instruments for navigation. No motor, but sails and oars are being made."

"Are they helping you just to get rid of me?" I ask.

"I think they're excited to build their own ships someday. I've even taught some of them how to swim."

"You have been gone a long time, Elandra," Uncle says. "Your father was reelected King in your absence."

Surprise fills Bryntar's face. "By all the people?"

"Yes. And seven Keprys sit on the Council."

"I hope you are one of the members," Bryntar says. "They need someone of your intelligence."

He beams. "I was asked and refused. I am going with Elandra and Daniel to the outer world."

Shock shudders through her. "This is your home."

"Home is a place in your heart," he says. "That is why you have to come with us. We are building the ship to hold four people."

Thrilled, I hug Uncle and seize her hand. "I cannot imagine leaving you behind, dear Bryntar."

"I will consider it," she says.

"We need to talk." Daniel leads me out of the village toward the river.

I stare at the water. It seems like a lifetime ago, when Daniel and I escaped in its frigid depths. "How do the Kepyrs feel about the deaths we caused?"

"Actually, we each killed only one man. The others survived. They are grateful you saved the island."

"I will be glad when we leave," I say.

"That's what I want to talk about."

Uneasy, I stop walking and turn to him.

"Are you sure you want to go?" he asks.

I swallow hard as my heart sinks like a stone. "You do not want me to come?"

"I want nothing else. My world is not like this one." He takes me in his arms. "I can't promise a safe voyage, either. People die at sea."

"Wherever we are or however long we have, I want to be with you."

"That time is shorter than you know, Enchantress." Jyrr swaggers through bushes with a spear in his hand.

Several of his friends stand behind him with spears and knives.

"Not you again," Daniel says.

I tighten and move in front of him.

Jyrr jeers. "Are you afraid and need protection from your little Enchantress?"

Daniel clenches his jaw and moves me aside. "Don't interfere. This is my fight."

I do not understand the aggressiveness, pride, even joy they share.

"If you lose," Jyrr says, "what is to stop her from killing me?"

Daniel looks at me. "Promise not to hurt him."

Have you lost your mind? "You expect me to watch you get killed and do nothing?"

"Have a little faith in me," Daniel says.

His confidence shoots through me. I glare at Jyrr. "Agreed. What if Daniel wins? Can he kill you?"

The Ice Lords laugh.

Jyrr smiles. "Do not expect me to lose."

"That does not answer my question."

"Agreed," Jyrr says. "I never lose." He raises his spear.

"You need a weapon?" Daniel asks.

Jyrr sneers and drops his spear. As he does, he leans forward and hits Daniel in the chest with his head, wraps his arms around him, and throws him to the dusty ground.

I hold back a scream.

The Ice Lords cheer.

Daniel wipes the dirt from his eyes and scrambles up in a crouch. "Good move. Didn't see that one coming."

Jyrr tries the same move again. This time Daniel pushes Jyrr's head away and steps to the side. Jyrr sprawls to the ground.

"Mix it up, Ice Lord," Daniel says. "Can't expect your opponent to be stupid."

Jyrr yells and leaps up, spitting dirt. Wary, he circles.

Daniel grins. "That your fighting technique? Getting me dizzy?"

Furious, Jyrr charges.

Daniel bends down, comes up under Jyrr and throws him over his head.

Jyrr slams to the ground on his back.

The Ice Lords yell in surprise.

The noise of the fight attracts the villagers. They leave their work and surround the fighters. Uncle and Bryntar stand aside.

I move to Uncle's side. "Why is Daniel having fun?"

Uncle smiles in satisfaction. "He is a warrior."

"And worthy of my Elandra," Bryntar says.

My muscles knot.

Daniel starts bouncing around, just out of Jyrr's reach.

Kepyrs cheer.

"Stand still," Jyrr growls. He runs toward Daniel, swinging his long arms.

One connects with Daniel's jaw. He staggers backward.

Ice Lords chant. "Jyrr, Jyrr, Jyrr."

"Quite a punch," Daniel says wiping blood from his mouth. "A little more strength and you might have knocked me out."

"You dare to insult me?"

"Let's finish this." Daniel leaps and twists into the air like a jaguarat, kicking out a leg. His foot smashes Jyrr in the head.

Jyrr yells and crashes to the ground.

"I have never seen fighting like this," Uncle says.

Jyrr stumbles up and snatches his spear off the ground.

Daniel smiles. "I always knew you were a coward."

The Ice Lords shift uneasily.

The crowd jeers.

Daniel leaps for the spear before Jyrr can throw it and grasps the shaft. Each fighter strains for control, muscles bulging. Both are equal in strength.

My heart tries to crawl out of my chest.

Jyrr screams and wrenches the spear from Daniel's hands.

Daniel leaps up and kicks Jyrr in the stomach with both legs.

Jyrr flies backward and hits hard, gasping for breath.

"Excellent," Uncle says.

Daniel jumps up and wrenches the spear from Jyrr's hand. He points it at his chest.

The crowd yells for his death.

Jyrr's face pales. He lifts his chin in defiance. "Finish it."

Daniel turns to the crowd. "No life should be wasted." He turns back to Jyrr. "I win." He breaks the spear in half and throws it away.

The crowd cheers and many young warriors lift Daniel to their shoulders and carry him to the village.

Jyrr drags himself off the ground and turns to his friends. "You saw him cheat. His way of fighting is unfair."

One young Ice Lord reaches over and removes the bearran tooth and jewel from Jyrr's ear. "You are dead to us." He tosses it into the river. The young Ice Lords turn their backs on Jyrr and stalk off.

I shut out the absolute horror and loss that shudders through Jyrr.

He stares at me with absolute hatred. "This is your fault." He races away into the trees.

Forty-Seven: The Leaving

Daniel oversees the building on the coast of the Western Seas. He teaches us the parts of the ship and how to sail it. To his embarrassment, we start calling him Captain. Provisions and clothing are stored.

I show my father the hidden cavern in case he ever has use for it, although we have little time together before the day arrives when the ship is ready to sail.

The morning sun breaks over the Ice Mountains in the distance behind us, a golden sphere shining in a sapphire sky. The ice reflects red, violet and pink.

Our ship rests in a deep hole in the sand, supported by a giant wooden structure that juts into the horizon. The Western Seas churn, held back by a dam of stone and wood.

Craftsmen run out of the deep depression when the ship is ready to launch. One disappears around the side to finish the last preparations.

Daniel's ship is sleek and beautiful, but looks tiny compared to the vast sea. Colorful sails blow in the breeze with Kepyr and Ice Lord designs sewed on them.

Hundreds of islanders watch us from the hillside.

Memories wash through me and I close them away.

My father strides to my side. "I hoped to spend more time with you."

"I wish you were coming with us, Father."

"Under any other circumstances I would. I am needed here."

Daniel strides up, unable to contain his enthusiasm. "Time to board."

My father shakes his hand. "Take care of my Enchantress."

"Yes, sir. Take care of your island."

Father hugs me and does not want to let go. "Thank you for showing me your underground home. No one will know of its existence except me. Have a safe voyage, Elandra. I hope we do not have to wait another sixteen seasons to see each other. I trust your Daniel to know our location and return someday."

I kiss his cheek. "Will I be able to take the ship through the invisible shield?"

"The shield is made of light. If you stand in front and enclose the ship in your light, I have no doubt you will be able to blend together and pass through safely."

I cling to him. "I do not wish to say goodbye, Father."

"Until we meet another time."

I impress his smile upon my mind.

"I almost forgot," he says. "I want you to have these." He takes the three-star jewel from the ring in his ear and connects it to a ring he slips from his little finger. "Your mother made this."

My hand shakes as he places it in my palm. The jewel sparkles against the three hearts entwined in the beautifully carved wood. I slip the ring on my finger, holding in tears. "Thank you, Father."

"Remember us, my dear."

"Always." I kiss him quickly and turn away, unable to say more.

My uncle shouts. "We are ready to sail!"

I run to the ship. My hands slide up the cold, metal ladder. I remember when this special metal warmed bare feet in my underground home, the countless hours in the library when life was new and safe.

I continue my climb and touch the last, bright letter of the ship's name. Daniel insisted that all ships have girl names, but he gave in to my choice, The Taroc.

Uncle takes my hand when I reach the deck, a grin on his face. "Welcome aboard, mate!"

I smile, recalling the stories Daniel told us about pirates.

Someone breaks into song on the hillside and the melody drifts through the air as other voices join in.

Bryntar is still on the ground, her back to the ship. Struggling with the memories and emotions of a thousand years, she turns and climbs up the ladder, her face pale.

I take her in my arms. "You do not have to come with us."

"You are my family. I worry about the outer world. Who will have scales and claws there?"

"When the time comes, we will know what to do," I say.

Daniel places his hands on my shoulders and gazes into my eyes. "No second thoughts?"

"Never."

He signals to the men on the stone dam.

One shouts, "Are all workers off the ship, Captain?"

"I will check," Uncle says and disappears below.

"Are you sure we can sail this ship?" I ask.

"You'll get the hang of it," Daniel says.

"We may know how, but that is not the same as practical knowledge," Bryntar warns.

Uncle returns from below deck. "Shipshape, Captain."

My heart thumps fast while Ice Lord and Kepyr muscles strain to pound open the wooden gate in the middle of the dam. Water bursts toward us like a racing jaguarat, smashing away the supports and slowly lifting the ship.

A thousand voices gasp and cheer.

I grab Daniel as the ship moves under me, breathing with life.

He laughs. "You'll get your sea legs."

Bryntar grabs onto Uncle and his face lights up.

Colorful sails flap in the breeze and the ship glides over the sea.

The island melody resumes, swells, and floats across the water.

I look back at the only home I have known. Standing on a lone hill with his mane flowing in the breeze is my khorbock. I send my love to him. He rears and races away. I swallow the lump in my throat, memories filling my mind. I did not think it would be this hard to leave.

A dazzling spirit of light flashes over the island in farewell. I send it my love and turn to another destiny.

The End

Enchantress Sabotage

One: The Sailing

The breeze whips through the sails taking me away from the only home I know. My mysterious island grows smaller in the morning light. The sudden tightness in my chest is unexpected—regret or dread? I saved the island and its people, but I cannot stay to be feared or revered as an Enchantress.

Bryntar stands resolute beside me, her legs apart and unyielding to the movement of the ship below our feet—hiding her fear of the water. Her long black hair whips across her light, purple-tinted face. Azure eyes brim with tears when the island she has lived on for a thousand seasons shimmers like a golden sun and disappears under the horizon.

"Thank you for coming with me," I say. "We will find a safe new life. I promise."

She swats at her tears. "Be careful of promises you cannot keep. If we survive this voyage, what do you think Daniel's world will think of you? Of us?"

She turns away. Her one, clawed hand grips the railing. It is difficult to believe that she was once the monster who saved my life and raised me as her own. Though her transformation back to Ice Lord also left a shimmering row of scales on one cheek, she is still beautiful.

Large white birds caw overhead and fly to faraway destinations. I breathe in light that flows into my hair. "I want to leave my life as an Enchantress behind."

"It is who you are."

It is always the same argument with Bryntar. I have accepted my burden: to breathe light instead of air, use its energy, sense every emotion around me, and to control myself. I do not like being different.

I close out her terror of the unknown and wobble across the richly-grained wooden deck toward Daniel. Our boat is small in the surrounding sea—twenty-seven feet with one mast, a jib, rudder, and four benches for rowing with extra-long oars.

Daniel's handsome face is pure rapture as he guides the rudder, leaping back and forth to avoid the boom as he tacks into the wind. His blonde hair flies, his muscles lean and strong. He wears jeans, the only part of his clothing from his life before he shipwrecked on my island. Except for those, his clothes match the rest of us; a shirt of soft animal skin and a thick vest of white jaguarat fur.

My heart swells with yearning for Daniel. My kind commits to only one love in our long lives. I am not sure if it is a gift or a curse.

A glimmer of fear darkens his green eyes and I stagger toward him. He does not try to hide his feelings from me as he once did. I have better control over my ability to read emotions and try not to intrude, but I always want to know how Daniel feels.

"How long until we reach the barrier that hides the island?" he asks.

"There is no way of knowing. My father believes the barrier protects the island and has the capacity to expand and contract."

"That's impossible. No one in the world can do that or hide an entire island."

Not in his world.

I remember the faint glimmerings of strangeness that we encountered on the island in the Sunken City and the silent pillars of The Old Ones. "Someone created it."

Daniel tries to hide his worry. Even a year later, his grief is still raw from losing his father and older brother when their ship crashed into the island's invisible barrier. It split in half, engulfed by a giant whirlpool. I do not think he has forgiven himself for surviving and washing ashore on the island.

"Dad never saw the barrier until our ship hit it. How can we avoid the same fate?"

"My father knows I can sense it."

"I'm sorry your father didn't come with us."

I push away thoughts about the father I am leaving behind. A father I barely know and will never see again. "The island needs a strong leader who can bring Ice Lord and Kepyr together."

I twist the wooden ring on my finger. Before my birth, my mother carved the three blending hearts as a present for him. His three-star crystal joins the band, a parting gift to remember the parents who could not raise me. It is the only decoration I own.

I sway, scared of the ship's surging.

Daniel laughs. "You'll get your sea legs, Elandra."

The movement is so different from the sixteen seasons I spent in underground caverns. There native drums of death haunted my memories.

The ship's motion is unceasing, like riding on fluid, breathing muscle. The breeze fills my nose with the salty tang of ocean.

I join my uncle, Kydaka, at the bow. He stands tall and strong. His scarred, dark-skinned back is bare in the warm sun. I try not to stare at his missing finger, for it is my fault he lost it.

He turns and grins at me, his dark eyes dancing. "A new beginning is not without fear, Elandra. Yet, excitement rushes through my blood."

A never-ending expanse of water spreads before me. A shiver slides down my back. I have chosen my destiny. Unbridled. Uncharted. Undiscovered.

"We are so small, Uncle."

He smiles. "Our hearts are not."

"Nothing will ever be the same."

He hugs me and I cherish his warmth. "Change is growth. Your life is with Daniel. He will not be content until he returns home to his mother and sister."

I sigh. "What if he cannot find the place called Florida?"

"We must trust him. Without his knowledge, we would not be on this voyage. Leave your fear. Enjoy freedom."

"In this confined space?"

Uncle laughs. "Freedom in not a place you can see."

He leaves me and strides to Bryntar. She blushes when he greets her. Their growing attraction fills me with happiness.

A sudden gust tips the sails. I slip into the rail and hang over, clutching it. Waves slam against the boat a few feet from my face. My stomach lurches.

"Wahoo!" Daniel yells as he steadies the ship.

Uncle shouts in glee.

Bryntar holds herself in fierce control, azure eyes dark. It is getting harder to remember her tall, strong body as the huge dragon-beast with horn, white fur, and purple scales on her face.

Rougher wind skims across the water and licks the white tips of the waves. The ocean heaves great breaths, rising and dropping in huge swells. I swallow hard against sudden queasiness and look up. Storm clouds fight to win an unending race, covering the once-peaceful sky.

I weave back toward Daniel, clutching everything I can to stay upright.

Large drops of rain slap the deck.

"Better help your uncle reef the sails," Daniel says. "We're in for a storm."

I try to ignore a creeping uneasiness, a worry that knots my stomach.

Soon the rain freezes, battering the deck and stinging like icy knives. I lose my balance and bang my knees on a bench, hanging onto the nearest rigging. Bryntar drags me up and together with Uncle we slip, slide, and fight against the raging wind to secure the jib and then the mainsail.

Lightning bolts crack through the clouds and stab the sea in deafening explosions. The wind screeches at the thunder.

My whole body lights up with sizzling energy.

"She's attracting the lightning!" Daniel shouts.

Uncle sweeps me off my feet and rushes me below deck.

Bryntar hurries behind.

We sit on the floor to avoid being thrown off the bunks. The wood creaks and groans around us like a wounded monster. I swallow hot bile.

Bryntar throws a blanket over me when I start to glow. She fights the tension threatening to overtake her.

Comforted by the darkness, I cannot help but touch Daniel's feelings. His confidence conflicts with his anxiety over the burden of keeping us afloat.

The ship leaps and twists, throwing us against each other.

I peer from the blanket. "Daniel cannot face the storm alone. What if he is washed overboard?"

Uncle pulls on a shirt, fur coat, and lurches up the steps. "I will secure his safety."

"Hope we do not hit the barrier," Bryntar says.

The ship rises. Falls. Slams us to the floor. It tips dangerously one way and immediately the other.

Please, do not let me die this night unless it is in Daniel's arms.

The storm continues, on and on and on. My frustration increases at my inability to do anything except protect myself from the bumps and bruises of being thrown against the bunks.

As suddenly as the storm appeared, it dissolves. The sea is content once again.

Daniel and Uncle stumble down the stairs, shivering and soaking wet.

Bryntar jumps up and rummages for dry shirts and fur pants in the drawers under the bunks.

I want to throw myself into Daniel's arms, but his exhaustion stops me. Instead I hand blankets to him and Uncle.

Daniel sinks onto a bunk. "It's a miracle we survived."

"Only with your skills," Uncle says.

"Couldn't have done it without your help."

I sit beside Daniel and warm his strong hands in mine.

Abruptly, great pain streaks through my body. And fear, but not from anyone in the room.

"Someone else is on this ship," I say.

Bryntar bristles, eyes flaring. "Impossible."

Uncle shakes his head. "I checked the ship before we sailed."

Daniel jumps off the bunk. "There is no place to hide in here."

His eyes scour the bunks, the many crates of water, fresh fruit, and dried meat that fill most of the space. He crawls over the top of the supplies to the bow and yanks open the door to the anchor locker.

"YOU!"

Daniel's anger strikes through me. He drags a squirming, muscular body out of the space.

Cold dread sucks at me when I see close-cropped black hair. Jyrr. Our hated enemy has stowed away.

The Ice Lord tumbles to the floor and grabs his stomach, his light purple face drawn in agony. He tries for stubborn dignity, but cannot keep the contents of his stomach.

I gag with the acrid odor.

Bryntar tosses Jyrr a rag. "Clean it up."

Jyrr glares at her with cold black eyes, but complies.

Daniel grabs Jyrr by the front of his golden vest and raises his fist. "I should kill you right now for what you've done."

Uncle takes Daniel's arm gently. "His sickness is enough punishment."

Daniel pushes Jyrr away. "It isn't. We survived this storm, but I don't know what our chances are now. He threw away the anchor to hide, like the scum he is."

"Can we sail without an anchor?" Uncle asks.

Daniel glares at Jyrr and pulls rope from a drawer. "Sure, if we don't worry about colliding with another ship. Or grounding on a hidden reef. Or mooring to add to our food supply." He roughly ties Jyrr's hands behind his back.

Though pale, Jyrr's eyes shine with malice. The muscles of his bare arms tighten.

Bryntar frowns at Jyrr. "Why did you come?"

The Ice Lord glares at us with raw hatred. "You destroyed my life."

Daniel resists the urge to throw himself at Jyrr. "You're responsible for every bad choice you made. This is your last one. The first land I see, you're off this ship."

Jyrr lifts his chin in defiance. "It cannot be too soon."

Daniel laughs. "Think a pampered prince can survive stranded and alone?"

Jyrr rises and looks down at me. Superiority, disdain, and bitterness ooze from his face. He does not know I can feel his fear.

Jyrr's desire and determination for revenge sizzle through me and I immediately lock them out. My own emotions are enough to handle: the sick remembrance of how he tried to force himself on me, how he almost succeeded in executing us in front of the people of the island.

I do not try to tune out the jagged sensations of my family: Bryntar's contempt, Uncle's sympathy for what it means to be outcast, Daniel's fury at the danger Jyrr has brought upon us.

Daniel stomps up the steps. "Guard the jerk, Bryntar."

Uncle and I hurry up after him.

Daniel heaves debris—seaweed, feathers, and shells into the sea to relieve some of his anger.

Uncle grabs a bucket to remove the water running across the deck. "You built a worthy ship, Captain."

Daniel takes a deep breath. "I've never been in a storm like that. I'm glad The Taroc held fast."

Taroc. I push away the heartbreaking memories of the man I named the ship after, the one who mentored and raised me.

Daniel says. "I'm not waiting for wind. We need to row." He turns to me. "Which way?"

I slowly turn in a circle and stop when a surge of energy tickles my neck. "That direction."

Daniel checks the compass on the leather bracelet his sister gave him. "You sure?"

"It is unlike anything I have felt. Like a pulsing of enormous light."

Daniel unhooks the four oars and secures them to the rowlocks. "West, it is."

Bryntar drags Jyrr on deck, eyes like blue fire. "He is untrustworthy. Throw him overboard."

"Let go!" Jyrr jerks away from her and falls to his knees.

Bryntar leaps to haul him up, but Uncle restrains her. "We can be rid of him without his death," Uncle says.

She pulls away. Hisses through her teeth and grabs her mouth in shock. I feel her embarrassment at the reminder of her life as a monster.

Jyrr glares. Silent, hostile.

"You're just in time, Bryntar," Daniel says. He drags Jyrr up and sits him roughly on the starboard bench. "Time to earn your keep."

Uncle grasps an oar across from Jyrr on the left.

I sit behind Jyrr and take another long oar, facing the stern of the boat.

Jyrr glares. "You expect help when my hands are tied?"

Daniel unties the rope and starts to retie Jyrr's wrists in front of him.

"The ropes will rub," I say.

Daniel clenches his jaw and ties Jyrr's ankles together instead. "Try anything and I will throw you overboard. Slack off and you won't eat. Got it?"

Jyrr sneers. "Aye, aye, Captain."

Daniel stomps off and sits by the rudder facing us. "Row."

Bryntar takes an oar. After a few uneven tries, we synchronize our rhythm and the ship plows across the ocean.

No one speaks with the effort of rowing over the force of the tides. Daniel strains to stay awake at the helm. Time stretches between rest, food, and more rowing. My muscles shake in weariness and scream for an end to the constant pain.

When the ocean changes to black and the sun sinks in a blinding red orb, my body responds to a throbbing power of invisible light. My hair expands in every direction, shining silver. I lurch to my feet, prying my stiff and blistered hands from the oar. "Stop rowing or we will crash into the barrier."

Daniel rushes to my side. "Can you see it?"

"I can feel it. Everyone needs to get to the bow of the ship. Now."

Uncle unties Jyrr's feet and propels him forward.

The strength of the invisible barrier almost knocks me off my feet. I have not called upon the light since saving the island and brace myself against the magnitude of energy. I scream at the white-hot searing pain that burns through me at my resistance.

The song that lives in my heart begins its enthralling melody. It is joined by the words of enchanters and enchantresses who did not survive the Beast.

Surrender. Surrender. Remember who you are and that your gift is the most precious of all.

I relax and let go, loving the heat that transforms to sparkling bubbles of tingling warmth. I close my eyes and concentrate on the energy within. Light shoots from my body and slowly expands to enclose my companions and the ship, matching the intensity of the invisible barrier.

My focus is deep and intense.

A roar pierces the air. I scream as an immense whirlpool rips through my light. The ferocious vortex swamps the back of the ship and sucks it into twisting, shrieking darkness.

About the Author

Denice Hughes Lewis has loved books since she was a child. It wasn't until she had children of her own that she decided to take a writing course from the Institute of Children's Literature. She never looked back.

She is an award-winning author for her teen book, *Dragon Cloud.* Other book titles include *Hye-Jynx: Quest One, Hye-Jynx: Quest Two* and *My Fairy Godmonster.*

Denice also has a series of non-fiction journals. The first title is *A Labrador Retriever's Journal* for pet lovers to have fun expressing what their pets think. These are breed specific with books for cats and mixed breeds.

Feel free to leave reviews!

Denice loves to hear from her readers.
Get a free story about Ice Lord history at
http://www.denicehugheslewis.com/

www.ingramcontent.com/pod-product-compliance
Lightning Source LLC
Chambersburg PA
CBHW061034120726
47910CB00006B/2247